CHRISTMAS
FOR
JOSHUA

Also by Avraham Azrieli

Fiction:

The Masada Complex – A Novel

The Jerusalem Inception – A Novel

The Jerusalem Assassin – A Novel

Non-Fiction:

Your Lawyer on a Short Leash

One Step Ahead – A Mother of Seven Escaping Hitler

Author's website:

www.AzrieliBooks.com

CHRISTMAS FOR JOSHUA

A NOVEL

By Avraham Azrieli

Printed in the United States by CreateSpace, Charleston, SC

ISBN: 146360288X
ISBN-13: 9781463602888
Library of Congress Control Number: 2011910593
CreateSpace, North Charleston, SC

For Steve Wall, who always delivers a perfect balance of critique, praise, and inspiration.

Part One
Thursday, September 24
Rosh Hashanah Eve

Do You Hear What I Hear?

The dashboard gauge climbed to 96 degrees as I accelerated down the Squaw Peak Parkway in my convertible Volvo. The valley rolled out before me like a carpet with a pattern of streets and avenues in tidy little squares, except for the concrete-and-glass cluster of downtown Phoenix, which floated on a cloud of morning smog.

The phone rang and a monotone voice said, "Incoming call from," pause, "Rebecca."

I hit the Bluetooth button. "Why do you always," I yelled over the wind noise, "*always* assume that I'll forget?"

"Experience," she said.

"Skype conference at two p.m. sharp. See?"

"Debra just texted me again," Rebecca said, referring to our daughter, a senior at Columbia University. "Apparently she has important news to share."

"News?" I took my foot off the gas, and the car slowed down. "I thought she was just calling to wish us a Happy Rosh Hashanah. What's the news?"

"That's the point. She wants to tell both of us together. Will you make it on time, or should I come up with an excuse for you?"

"No excuse. I'm not cutting anyone today. Paperwork until noon, lunch conference with some researchers from D.C., and I'll be heading home."

"On time?"

"You can count on it," I said.

"Famous last words."

"Love you too."

Rebecca laughed and hung up. My workdays were long, often stretching into the night due to chronic understaffing at the hospital. She had reheated countless dinners for me over the years, but we had been together long enough to trust each other and nudge only when necessary. And Debra's tip-off of important news definitely qualified for necessary nudging. Now in her last year of pre-med, Debra had to narrow down her list of possible medical schools and begin the application process. I hoped she would stay on at Columbia, as I had done, but Rebecca had been talking up the University of Arizona in Tucson, whose medical school was rising in national rankings.

We had no doubt that Debra would be admitted wherever she applied—her grades and skills placed her at the top of her class. I wondered if she had made a choice and was going to break the news to us this afternoon, disappointing either me or Rebecca. But as I considered the prospect of Debra's returning to Arizona and living an hour away, rather than staying for another four years in New York, I was willing to give up my dream of seeing her graduate from my medical alma mater.

I turned up the volume on the radio. NPR's Diane Rehm introduced her guest, the Reverend Alfred Dulton and his new book: *Jesus and I – Close Encounters of the True Kind.* The reverend thanked his host and said, "Two millennia ago, on this very day, our Savior was preparing to celebrate the Jewish New Year, which begins tonight. But when Christ died for our sins, he liberated us from the strictures of Old Testament rituals—"

I switched to Bluetooth and, for the first time in years of listening to the program, called in. After two rings, a recording told me to hold, and music came on. It was Handel's *Messiah*, I could tell, but it took me a little while to discern the words and recognized *For Unto Us a Child is Born*, an early part of the work. The participation of flutes and clarinets revealed that it was Mozart's arrangement they were playing, and my fingers tapped the steering wheel with the notes. Back in our church, during my teens, I had played *Messiah* on the rickety organ, though the only part that truly excited the parishioners was *Hallelujah*, which I had to play repeatedly while everyone was gathering for the Midnight Mass on Christmas Eve.

I lowered the volume and rehearsed my question, which was directed not at the guest, but at Diane Rehm herself: "Why did you choose to interview a Christian clergyman on the eve of the Jewish people's high holidays? Would you have a Muslim imam as your guest on Easter Friday? Or a rabbi on Christmas Eve?"

At the exit ramp on Indian School Road, police cruisers with rolling lights created a bottleneck that directed all vehicles through a checkpoint, where officers inspected each vehicle. As I was waved through, I noticed Hispanic men and women lined up on the curb, guarded by deputies from the sheriff's department.

Fifteen minutes later, still on hold, I drove into the hospital underground parking garage. Wireless reception was lost, and the music disappeared. I could call again from my office upstairs, but by now the beauty of Handel's composition had cooled my indignation. In all fairness, how many Americans celebrated Rosh Hashanah? One or two percent of the population? Wouldn't it be sheer chutzpah to force the other ninety-eight percent to listen to a rabbi just because it's our holiday?

At the elevator door, I waved my ID card in front of the sensor. My name appeared on the LED display: *Rusty Dinwall, M.D.* I clipped the card to my breast pocket. It was time for a new card with a current photo. My rust-colored hair had turned dirty silver, and it had been a decade since I shaved off that corny mustache à la Tom Selleck.

My assigned operating room was out of commission with a faulty air-handler, which had left us soaked with sweat last night as we finished sewing up the last patient. With today's surgeries postponed, I settled in front of my computer to approve prescription requests, sign off on charts of discharged patients, and respond to Happy Rosh Hashanah e-mails from colleagues. Next, I started on the performance reports for our residents, which tested the limits of my creativity. When it came to med-school graduates, training at a VA hospital didn't attract the sharpest scalpels in the tray, who usually preferred to train at private hospitals, where moneymaking was an honorable part of the job. But those who came here got plenty of hands-on experience, and I made sure to be generous with my praise.

"But he's as pale as a sheet," a woman's voice rang in the hallway. I saw her through my open office door, standing at the nurses' station, her silver hair collected in a rubber band, her summer dress flowery and shapeless. "Something is wrong with him."

"Nothing's wrong," said Nina, the Cardiothoracic ICU nurse-in-charge. "Your husband is recovering just fine."

"He's not the complaining type," the woman said, "but I can tell he's not feeling well."

"No one feels well a day after triple bypass." Nina must have done the midnight-to-eight shift and wasn't feeling so peppy herself. "Dr. Brutsky saw him during morning rounds and was pleased with his progress."

"But—"

"He'll get his color back in no time."

I returned to typing the report when the woman said, "He already got his color back. This morning, when he woke up, he looked great. But now he's pale again."

Nina mumbled something and walked away.

The woman sighed and went back into the patient's room—not my patient, not my case, and not my responsibility. Aaron Brutsky was an excellent surgeon. He would have noticed if there was a problem.

I tried to keep typing, but my mind was already racing down a diagnostic track. Bypass surgery left patients weak and anemic. They were pale, and their color returned gradually. But this patient's wife was telling of an initial recovery followed by an onslaught of paleness, and I had noticed a trace of dread in her voice. Was I imagining it? Nina had obviously heard nothing alarming, and it was her decision whether to alert the surgeon on the case or not.

I added another sentence to the performance report, but paused upon remembering Rabbi Rachel's sermon last Sabbath morning at the synagogue. She had discussed the story of Moses sacrificing his pharaohic lifestyle when he struck down an Egyptian guard to save a Hebrew slave. This moral duty to aid a stranger in peril later inspired a Talmudic decree that a traveler who failed to stop and help a man fallen by the roadside was considered by God to have committed murder.

With the half-filled performance report still on the computer screen, I grabbed my white coat and stethoscope and left my office.

The patient in the bed wasn't pallid. He wasn't ruddy either. Rather, he was dark skinned, either from years in the sun or from having Hispanic or Native American genetics. It was hard to tell, especially because there was a grayness to his brown skin, as if he had spent too much time indoors—or had been losing blood. I didn't know his baseline color and could make no informed judgment by what I saw. His wife knew him best, yet her impression could be tainted by stress.

"Good morning." I draped the stethoscope around my neck. "I'm Dr. Dinwall. How are you feeling?"

"Like a flyer…who's been hit by flak." His voice was scratchy, the common result of having had a breathing tube in his throat for hours. "Been injured before," he added. "Feels the same."

The wife crossed herself. "Jesus be merciful."

"Amen." I chuckled. It wasn't the first time I heard a veteran compare bypass surgery to a battle injury, a tragic misfortune that's out of one's control and must be accepted with a fatalistic resignation, as if heavy smoking and a fat-laden diet had nothing to do with it.

"Are you my new doc?"

"Dr. Brutsky and I are the two CT surgeons on staff here. We cover for each other."

"Like co-pilots?"

"Basically, yes." I looked at his chart. Xavier Gonzales. Air force mechanic. One tour in Vietnam. Injured during the 1968 Tet offensive. Multiple shrapnel wounds. Eighteen months' recovery, but no permanent functional disability. Stayed in the service for another twenty-two years, last station at Luke Air Force

Base. After honorable discharge, he spent another twenty years as a jet-engine specialist for Southwest Airlines, finally retiring a month ago. Smoked for forty-six years, been married for forty-one. Admitted the day before yesterday with severe chest pains. Catheterization revealed 95 percent blockage of the left main coronary artery and lesser blockages in two others. Triple bypass surgery. No complications. Weaned off the ventilator without a hitch. All good—except for the wife's complaint of worsening paleness, which could hint of internal bleeding. For my peace of mind, I had to rule it out.

"So," I said, "looks like smooth flying so far."

"Engine's sputtering," he said. "Feels like…sludge in the fuel line."

"You got new fuel lines yesterday. Shouldn't be sputtering now." I browsed the heart-monitor printout and the nurses' notes. No meaningful fluctuations, but I noticed a subtle downward trend in blood pressure and a slight increase in heart rate—both very minor, but consistent with an early internal bleed.

What else?

Nina entered the room and gave the wife an angry look. "I believe Dr. Brutsky has already rounded here."

"Rounded, yes," I said, "but has he squared yet?"

My joke fell flat. She jingled her keys.

"This is just a courtesy visit," I said, faking deafness to her displeasure, "to make sure Mr. Gonzales will put the highest marks on our customer satisfaction survey."

The patient laughed. "Do you know what VA stands for?"

We waited for him to tell us.

"Vietcong Accomplices."

"Didn't Kissinger make peace with them?" I smiled and took his hand, which was meaty, coarse, and a bit cool considering the room temperature. "May I examine you, sir?"

He had used a military decoration to fasten his hospital gown. The blue and golden-orange ribbon stood out against the greenish cloth. I detached it and looked at the bronze medal hanging from the ribbon. It portrayed an eagle, charging downward with two lightning rods in its talons. It was a United States Air Medal. I handed it to his wife and exposed his chest.

The cracked sternum was held together with steel staples, and the skin was reattached with tiny stitches that ran down the long incision like a black zipper. The wound seemed perfectly normal, and the transparent tubes showed nothing more than the usual murky drainage. There was no unpleasant smell or excess bruising. The yellow paste of iodine should have been cleaned up after yesterday's surgery. I scrubbed it off with a wet wipe, which I held out for Nina. She took it with pursed lips.

Pressing his abdomen in different places, I poked through layers of fat that told of eating habits common to men who end up here. I detected none of the hardness associated with internal hemorrhage. Turning him on the side, I was taken aback by the abundance of old scars that covered his back, dozens of little craters, each about the size of a thumbnail. Otherwise, I saw no discoloration signs of ecchymoses on his back. The bleeding, if any, might be contained in the chest cavity until it was too late.

With the tip of my finger, I pressed down on one of the scars. When my finger lifted, the scar was white, but within five seconds it returned to its former redness. I tried another one. Same result. His circulation was slow, but not abnormal.

"Disgusting," Mr. Gonzales said, "isn't it?"

"Extensive scarring." I helped him return to lying on his back. "You must have been close when it went off."

He pointed at himself. "Cannon fodder."

I placed the stethoscope cup against his ribs, moved it down, listened to his abdomen. Gas movement, but nothing suspicious.

"Did you serve, Doc?"

His wife stepped forward. "Xavier, please."

On the left side, higher up, my ears caught a swish of fluid that didn't sound right. I stayed there, waiting for a repeat performance. But the sound failed to revisit my stethoscope, and I started moving it again.

"You're too young for the draft." He thumbed the button that made the bed rise toward a sitting position. "But a real patriot could volunteer."

"Sorry." I moved the stethoscope, continuing my search. "Never wore the uniform." My exam hadn't yet solved my dilemma, but it seemed to have emboldened the patient. Or was his mood change another ominous indication? I added, "Never been injured either."

"Feeling lucky?"

"Don't you?"

"*Ha!*" His loud exhalation sent an odd rumble through his airways, which were otherwise clear—no blood in his lungs. "Some luck," he said. "Haven't allowed anyone to see me without a shirt since nineteen sixty-eight!"

I adjusted the hospital gown back over his chest and fastened it with his Air Medal. "You came back alive, didn't you?"

He knuckled the side of his head. "No one came back from 'Nam. Not really."

His wife caressed his thinning hair. "We've had a good life," she said. "The doctor is right."

"A civilian." He looked away. "What does he know?"

"I know my dad only from photos," I said. "He *really* didn't come back."

The wife sucked in air and turned to the window with a hand over her mouth. But Mr. Gonzales was an old soldier who wouldn't shy from meeting my gaze. "Sorry," he said. "I was out of line. Should've kept my damn spigot shut."

"No sweat." I took a deep breath, resolving to keep my own spigot shut, and drew blood from the arterial line at his wrist. "Let's check the numbers." I ran a stat blood count on the machine and compared it with the last few numbers in his chart. Minor decrease, but still within post-op anemic range. "No bad news here either," I declared with a light tone of optimism that I didn't feel.

"As expected." Nina turned to leave. She obviously hadn't grasped that this was no longer a matter of pacifying a pesky wife, but a question of life and death that must be answered promptly despite inconclusive data. "Should I tell Dr. Brutsky to come by when he's done in the O.R.?"

"Sure," I said. "And kindly get mine ready too. Engineering should set up a portable air cooler. It's still morning, so we'll be okay for a while, you agree?"

Her eyes widened, but she said nothing more and left the room to prepare my operating room for Mr. Gonzales.

My mind wasn't made up yet, though. I pretended to study the heart monitor again while reviewing the facts in my head: The changes in blood pressure and heart rate were mild, and he wasn't demonstrating discomfort. Blood count and physical exam weren't helpful either. The only unambiguous fact was the wife's impression of recent paleness. Such subjective complaints could be dismissed, as Nina obviously thought, for the common neurotic harassment of the medical staff by overly protective spouses. But this couple had been married for twice as long as Rebecca and I, and my gut told me to take her seriously. The easiest path was to prescribe a CT scan and leave it to Aaron Brutsky's handling, based on the results. But a delay was risky. If there was a bleed, it could rupture and kill him. Still, how could I reopen this man's chest based on little more than a gut feeling?

The electric motor buzzed as Mr. Gonzales made the head of his bed descend. The sound filled my ears. It could be a benign move, the patient merely making himself more comfortable, but to me it sounded like an alarm, triggered by his need to lie flat in order to counter the declining blood flow to his brain.

My decision made, I adjusted his IV to get morphine flowing. "Luke Air Force Base," I said. "We used to take our daughter to see the air show. It was a lot of fun."

"I maintained them." He cleared his throat. "The Thunderbirds. Great machines."

"We also took our son every year," Mrs. Gonzales said, eager to reciprocate my friendly tone. "How old is your daughter?"

"Debra is all grown up now." I didn't mention that she'd be expecting me and Rebecca on Skype at 2 p.m., an appointment I might not be able to make, depending on what transpired with this patient. I watched him get sleepy. Any sudden excitement could shoot up his blood pressure and turn a small bleed into a terminal gushing before we could reach it. "She's a senior in college," I added.

"Very nice," she said. "And your other children?"

I held his wrist, feeling the steady pulse. "My wife couldn't bear more children, so now we're early empty nesters."

"There's good in every bad," Mrs. Gonzales said sympathetically. "In my experience, grandkids are much more fun. They bring joy and light into your life without the hardship of childrearing. You'll see."

"We're in no hurry. Debra plans to attend medical school and finish training before starting a family." I glanced at the heart monitor. All well. "How many grandkids do you have?"

"Three precious ones from our son. He's an electrician in Prescott." She looked at her husband, whose eyelids fluttered and closed. "Xavier?"

He didn't respond.

She shook his shoulder. "*Xavier!*"

I put a finger to my lips.

"What's wrong with him?"

Leading her out of the room, I said, "He's asleep, that's all."

Despite my complete honesty about how little evidence I had for this drastic step, Mrs. Gonzales consented, and we rolled him to the operating room.

Scrubbed and ready, I murmured a quiet prayer behind my mask, reciting the Hebrew words that had become my private good luck charm: "*Blessed be Adonai, Master of the Universe, healer of the sick and infirm.*"

Minutes later, peering through his parted ribcage with a mix of satisfaction and concern, I watched the nurse suction out the blood that was pooling around his beating heart until the source was exposed—a fissure in the artery, less than a centimeter up from a bypass stitch.

It was the peculiar nature of my profession that making a correct diagnosis meant bad news for the patient. But more often than not, I was able to do something about it. I hoped this was one of those cases. I flexed my fingers and held out my hand. "A suture, please."

When I left Mrs. Gonzales, she was clasping her sedated husband's hand while thanking Jesus for saving him, which was fine with me—I didn't mind sharing credit for success. The repair had been delicate, but I managed without reattaching him to the heart-lung machine, which saved a lot of time and risk.

Peeling off the sweaty scrubs, I took a cold shower, put my clothes back on, and headed downstairs to the first-floor conference room. A cardboard sign had been propped on an easel:

VA MEDICAL STAFF – CONTINUING MEDICAL EDUCATION
PRESENTATION BY THE
EFFICIENCY RESEARCH SECTION OF
THE U.S. DEPARTMENT OF VETERANS AFFAIRS

The word *oxymoron* came to my mind, but as the session would count toward our CME requirements, most of my colleagues were in attendance, munching on their brownbag lunches.

Rebecca had made me tuna on wheat, accompanied by a New York pickle and a tall can of Arizona Green Tea. I ate while listening to the speaker. She was a bespectacled statistician with a Ph.D. and a nasal voice, who flipped through a drab Power Point presentation, reading aloud the text on the slides verbatim as if we were illiterate.

Their research aimed to show that VA hospitals could save money by discharging post-op patients as soon as they were off the ventilator. Over the past two years, they had managed to convince over six hundred patients nationwide to participate in this experiment in exchange for modest remuneration and a free instructional booklet titled: THE VIRTUES OF HOME-BASED RECOVERY. They calculated the average cost of keeping a patient in the hospital each day and multiplied that number by the total number of days their subjects would have stayed for in-hospital recovery, which resulted in a large dollar amount of theoretical savings.

Aaron Brutsky came in, still wearing his scrubs, the soft mask hanging under his double chin. He was a short man with short arms and short fingers that defied their stubby appearance with a delicate touch and a meticulous exactness that I could only aspire to match. He must have heard how I had plucked his patient from the Grim Reaper's clutches, because he mouthed "Thank You" from the opposite side of the room and held both thumbs up. I grinned and patted my own shoulder. Technically

Mr. Gonzales's bleed wasn't a surgical failure per se, but a patient's death within twenty-four hours always reflected negatively on the surgeon, and I was happy to save one for Aaron.

The last slide was filled with numbers. The elaborate calculation was in fact a simple process of extrapolation of the research results to the whole VA hospital system, reaching a grand total of potential budget savings that could cover the costs of invading a small country.

Visibly proud, the speaker turned off the projector and invited questions. Everyone glanced at their watches and finished their cold drinks.

I raised my hand. "What was the consequent increase in patients' mortalities, compared with the control group?"

"There was no control group," she said.

"Budgetary constraints?"

She nodded, relieved that I understood.

"How about using available statistics?"

Ph.D. and all, she clearly hadn't considered the holes in her thesis. "Which statistics?"

"The department tracks mortalities of VA hospital patients, classified by the type of illness, procedure, treatment stage, and so on. We use such statistics all the time to advise patients on risks. You could pull data by specific parameters; for example, the survival rates for post-op patients who stayed in the hospital for recovery, and compare them with the survival rates of your early-release research subjects."

She removed her reading glasses. "We didn't track our subjects' survival rates."

The room went dead silent.

"Let me understand," I said. "You convinced hundreds of veterans to go home right after a major surgery for so-called *home recovery*, but didn't check if they actually recovered?"

She blinked behind her glasses a few times. "Treatment results were outside the scope of our research."

I bit my pickle in half. It was crunchy. I took my time chewing, swallowed, and asked the obvious: "Isn't patients' survival the very purpose of post-op care? Or better yet, the whole reason for existence of the VA hospital system?"

Her face reddened. "We concentrated on measuring financial results—how much could be saved by shifting to home-based recovery."

I should have left it at that, having exposed their research to be a farce. But all the chickens in the room looked to me for the deliverance of the coup de grâce. I pointed the remaining half of my pickle at her and asked, "Have you measured how much could be saved if the federal government stopped funding pointless research?"

My colleagues laughed, but our medical director, Larry Emanuel, shook his finger at me and said, "Rusty is fortunate that tonight is the Jewish Rosh Hashanah, so he can atone for a year's worth of poor jokes."

———

Jingle Bells

I made it home by 2 p.m. and found Rebecca in front of the computer in the study, biting her lower lip as she pressed the keys to sign in to Skype. I had no doubt that Debra would be on time for our video conference. Our daughter was a perfectionist, which also meant that she studied hard and had no time for cross-country trips home, even for Rosh Hashanah. We missed her, but thanks to the Internet, with a bit of preplanning we could chat face-to-face despite the thousands of miles separating us.

Placing a ten dollar bill on the table, I said, "Want to bet?"

Rebecca glanced at the money. "I think she'll stay in New York."

"Then I'll bet against my wishes. My money's on Tucson."

"Mine's on Columbia, but it's a bet I'll be happy to lose."

"Me too." I kissed her cheek, but Rebecca held my face and planted a kiss on my lips.

Debra's face showed up first, then her voice. "Hi, Mom! Hi, Daddy!"

"Hi, sweetie," we chorused. "How are you?"

Debra laughed, as if the question was rhetoric, which in a way it was. She looked great, her black, shoulder-length hair framing her clear face, and her dark, jewel-like eyes glinting with enthusiasm. From the neck up, Debra was a carbon copy of the young Rebecca I had met in college more than twenty-five years ago. But unlike Rebecca's petite stature, our daughter had taken after my physique—tall and long-limbed.

And so, with Debra's smile lighting up the screen, Rebecca and I settled in for the digital version of a family get-together

But before our empty-nesters' chill had a chance to thaw under our daughter's adorable glow, she said, "I'd like you to meet Mordechai," and a young man joined in, his smooth cheek next to hers in front of the camera. He wished us "Happy New Year" with seriousness befitting an offer of condolences rather than a holiday greeting and promptly asked for Debra's hand in marriage.

I chuckled, certain that he was a new boyfriend making an awkward attempt at humor. But the boy glanced at Debra, his cheeks apple-red, and she looked back at him with an expression that made me realize he wasn't joking. He was really asking for Debra's hand, and he was expecting an answer!

Rebecca yelled, "Oh, my God! I can't believe it!"

Neither could I.

"What a surprise!" Rebecca clapped her hands. "How long have you known each other? Tell us everything!"

Still in shock, I listened as Debra described their initial meeting at a Friday-night service at Hillel, which for Jewish students was like speed-dating with an extra shot. The following week, they had shared a bumpy ride in a yellow cab after a breakfast dinner on the night of Tisha B'Av, a day of mourning for the destruction of the Temple in Jerusalem two millennia ago. They discovered mutual friends and common interests, went to the movies, and visited museums. I calculated in my head—the ninth of the month of Av under the Hebrew calendar was less than two months ago, which apparently was long enough for them to fall in love and commit to a life together—"According to the laws of the Torah," Mordechai chimed in.

Debra nodded, smiling, full of hope, resembling Rebecca at her age. We had also been students at Columbia when I asked for Rebecca Greenbaum's hand—only Skype hadn't existed back then to facilitate proposing from a safe distance. We rode the subway to her parents' Bronx apartment where, upon hearing my tremulous offer of matrimony, my future in-laws burst out crying as if the worst of their fears had come true. Which, in a way, it had. They had each lost a spouse and children in the

Nazi concentration camps and met after the war at the Hebrew Immigrant Aid Society's center in New York, where both had been coming daily to browse lists of survivors. Neither of them had found any lost relatives on the HIAS lists, but the camaraderie of grief brought them together.

Despite physical ailments and mental scars, they managed to bring Rebecca into the world—a strike back at their former Nazi tormentors, a pitch for Jewish continuity. Rebecca had prepared me for their negative reaction to her bringing home a gentile boy who was nothing like the Jewish son-in-law they had dreamt of. She expected disappointment, disapproval, and a few tears, but knew they would accept me because our future children would be Jewish based on the maternal hereditary laws of Judaism.

Yet Rebecca had clearly underestimated her parents' feelings about the matter. Standing in their small living room among the second-hand furniture, shelves of religious books, and charcoal portraits of dead relatives (drawn from memory as no family photos had survived the war), I was stunned by her mother's heart-wrenching sobs and her father's repeated murmurs, "*A shaygetz! A shaygetz!*"

What had I done but expressed my love for their daughter in the most honorable way—a commitment to share the rest of our lives? And even if they found a non-Jewish boy, a shaygetz like me, to be unacceptable, did it justify such an extravagant expression of misery? And to throw it in my face like that? Didn't they know Christians had feelings too? I almost burst out with a borrowed Shakespearean protest: *If you prick us, do we not bleed?* But I held my tongue, as my good Christian mother had taught me to do, and watched them cry while Rebecca grasped my arm in brave-yet-tearful insistence until they calmed down, wiped their eyes, and shook my hand with moist, slack palms.

Later on, as I learned about the painful history of my young bride's people and discovered the pivotal role my Christian church had played in inflicting torture and death on the Jews for two thousand years, I understood better my in-laws' reaction. For them, and for their fellow Holocaust survivors, every flaxen gentile was a dormant Nazi. And who could blame them? For Jews who had experienced the German people's regressive transformation from a cultured, emancipated society to the brown-shirts' nightmare of burning books, reeking cattle trains, and ash-spitting chimneys, even the friendliest shaygetz was a hyena in sheep's clothing, ready to snap back into his beastly self.

And now, long after Rebecca's parents had departed to a better world, free from worries about docile gentiles transforming into Nazis or a shaygetz stealing their daughter's heart, the sting of their early rejection occasionally pestered me like a pang of pain from a long-healed injury. Which was why, when my wife and daughter calmed down, I saw the anxiety in Mordechai's face and said, "Yes, of course, you have our blessing!"

"Thank you, Dr. Dinwall," he said. "I'll take good care of her."

"You better!"

We all laughed, and Debra said, "Mordechai's dad is also a physician."

"Really?" I leaned closer. "What's his specialty?"

"Urology," Mordechai said. "He's at Mount Sinai in Manhattan."

"Please give him my best regards—from one plumber to another." I assumed Debra had told Mordechai that I was a heart surgeon.

"A perfect match," Rebecca declared and launched into a barrage of questions about their brief courting and plans for the wedding, which Debra answered while sending frequent, loving glances at Mordechai. They planned to marry in New York, where his large family resided. I suggested that our rabbi, Rachel Sher, fly to New York to officiate, but Debra explained that they wanted an Orthodox ceremony. She made Mordechai lean his head forward so we could see his yarmulke—a black skullcap that gave me an ominous premonition. Or was I merely experiencing a normal father's apprehension at a young man's claim to his daughter's heart?

"I'll ask Rabbi Rachel," I said, "if she would conduct an Orthodox ceremony."

Mordechai turned to Debra, who said as if on cue, "A woman can't officiate at a wedding. It's against *Halacha.*"

I recognized the Hebrew term for the extensive body of strict Jewish law, which my in-laws had observed. We, on the other hand, belonged to a Reform congregation. The King Solomon Synagogue was like an extended family that practiced progressive Judaism, which respected the ancient letter of Halacha as belonging in ancient times, a wonderful part of our people's history, while current Judaism required adaptation to modern times. In fact, Debra's Bat Mitzvah speech had won applause for contending that the advancement of women among Jewish clergy should be supported as a form of affirmative action. And her valedictorian speech at her high-school graduation was titled *The Prophet Debra – a Role Model for Female Leadership in the Twenty-First Century*. So why was my daughter opting for a wedding ceremony that would exclude a woman rabbi?

Before I had a chance to inquire, Mordechai explained that Rabbi Yakov Mintzberg, the spiritual leader of their Brooklyn community, had officiated at his parents' wedding and at his older siblings' weddings—a tradition they wished to continue.

"And he's old," Debra added, "so we decided to do it soon. December twentieth!"

Mordechai grinned, exposing a set of big, white teeth.

"That's in three months!" In my mind I envisioned the schedule on my office wall. Open-heart surgeries were complex, orchestrated events with lots of moving parts and anxious patients. My vacations usually required long-term advanced planning. "What's the hurry?"

"Winter break." Debra lifted a calendar to show us. "We'll have two weeks off for a honeymoon!"

"But you could have two months," I said, "if you wait until the summer."

Rebecca knuckled my thigh under the desk. "We're delighted," she declared. "It's your wedding, so it's up to you to fix the date and select the rabbi. We're so happy!"

"I agree," I said, "as long as you love each other and feel certain in your choice."

They nodded, and Debra showed the back of her left hand to the camera.

"Look at this!" Rebecca fingered the screen. "It's gorgeous!"

"A ring." I swallowed hard. Why had Debra accepted this symbol of commitment before discussing it with us?

Rebecca must have sensed my impending protest. She turned to me and asked, "Isn't it beautiful?"

"Ah." I exhaled. "Yes. Pretty."

On the screen, Debra and Mordechai looked at each other, and I was grateful to my wife for stopping me before I said something objectionable that could poison the new relationship with my daughter's husband. I gulped at the thought: *My daughter's husband!*

"If your grandma and grandpa could only see it." Rebecca's voice broke. "Our baby's getting married!"

I felt my eyes water and blinked to hide it. "We love New York," I said, "even in December. And you could spend your honeymoon in Arizona, all expenses on us. We'll throw a party, and Rabbi Rachel will bless your marriage—"

"It's settled then!" Rebecca leaned forward until her nose almost touched the computer screen. "Show me the ring again!"

The two women delved into details of invitation lists, color themes, and kosher caterers. I listened, making sure to keep smiling at the tiny camera lens atop the computer screen. With tuition and board at Columbia University approaching the cost of a nice house, I wasn't keen on feeding hundreds of Orthodox guests a menu of kosher gourmet at New York prices. But Debra was getting married, and even if it was a few years earlier than expected, we would do the right thing.

In the end, we wished them "Happy Rosh Hashanah!" and waved as their faces disappeared, replaced by the Skype logo.

I picked up the ten dollar bill and gave it to Rebecca. "I think you won this one."

She laughed and stuffed it in her purse. "I'll use it toward the wedding."

Rebecca phoned several friends to share the news. I typed an e-mail to Rabbi Rachel on my Blackberry:

Debra's engaged. Big surprise. We're still digesting the news. They're planning an Orthodox wedding in NYC, Dec. 20. Let's talk more tonight at services. Rusty.

I sent it and sighed. This wouldn't sit well with the rabbi. She had never married, and the congregation was everything to her—career, family, life's purpose. And as a woman in a traditionally male profession, she was even more sensitive when it came to issues of respect or recognition. Having served as volunteer trustee and board president for over a decade, I had earned her trust with my sincere devotion to the wellbeing of the synagogue as well as my loyalty to her as its spiritual leader. Debra's decision to *de facto* exclude Rabbi Rachel from the wedding ceremony would sting badly, and it was up to me to explain the situation and smooth things out. But how could I do that when my own feelings about the marriage were still so raw?

Driven by an urge to engage in physical activity, I went outside and unfurled the garden hose, pulling it toward the driveway at the front of the house.

A dark color wasn't the best choice for a car in the desert. It absorbed more of the sun's heat and showed even the thinnest layer of dust. But I liked the way my Volvo looked in midnight-blue. It was a handsome car whether the hardtop was up or folded away.

I set the sprayer to medium pressure and watched with satisfaction as the water washed away the dust. With quick, round motions I toweled off the drops before they had a chance to form white stains on the paintwork.

Panting and a bit sweaty, I went back inside, where Rebecca had a glass of iced tea waiting for me on the kitchen counter. She had tied her black hair in a high ponytail and was cutting fruit for a giant platter—our contribution to tonight's holiday dinner at the Brutskys. Her hands moved efficiently, the muscles on her forearms pronounced under her smooth skin. I drank half the glass, watching her.

She smiled. "What? I look like Julia Child?"

"Julia Roberts," I said, "on her best day."

"Yeah, right!" Rebecca lifted a watermelon and set it on the cutting board. "Everyone is very excited. Miriam promised that she and Aaron will make the trip to New York, no matter what. The others weren't sure."

"Late December isn't the best time for a short-notice wedding. And anyway, who would want to travel from Arizona to the northeast in December?"

"I still can't believe it." She used a large knife to break the watermelon in half. "We're marrying off our daughter!"

"I would like to meet the groom beforehand."

"You just did."

"I would have preferred a three-dimensional encounter." I gulped down the rest of the glass and set it down. "And why did she keep the relationship secret?"

"Because she's just like you."

"Me?"

"Keeps everything bottled up inside until you're absolutely certain it's ready to be shared." Rebecca tossed a piece of watermelon skin at me. "But I knew something was up with her. When we spoke last week, I could tell—"

"Is she pregnant?"

"Don't be ridiculous. He's observant, for God's sake!"

"He's a guy. The black yarmulke covers his head, not his—"

"Orthodox men don't sleep with their fiancée before the wedding." She landed the blade too hard, spraying red juice. "It's forbidden!"

"Let's send him a photo of you with this bloody knife, just in case."

Rebecca pointed it in my direction. "Watch it, buster!"

I made like I parried her jab.

She returned to slicing the watermelon. "Don't you think they look happy?"

"For now, yes." I picked a piece off the cutting board. "But what if after the wedding she discovers he's lousy in bed?"

"Good sex is a byproduct of a good relationship, right?"

"Yes, dear. But still, they barely know each other. And she's changed, all this Orthodox stuff. Did you notice how she kept looking at him for approval?"

"She's in love. And who can blame her? He's so handsome. Did you see his eyes?"

"All I saw was teeth. He's like a big bad wolf."

Rebecca laughed. I gave in and joined her. We had raised Debra to make her own decisions. It had paid off during high school, as she fended off peer pressure to engage in unsavory activities. But three years in New York had given Debra independence that was both reassuring and painful.

"So," I said, "the rush to marry isn't about the old rabbi. It's about abstinence. They're dying to jump into bed."

"Kosher sex!" Rebecca gave me a long, wet kiss that cheered me up.

I drew the Blackberry and typed a task with my thumbs: CLEAR SCHEDULE IN LATE DEC., CONTACT PATIENTS, ARRANGE COVERAGE, ETC. "Looks like I'll have to work around the clock from now until the wedding."

"What else is new?"

We put on helmets and gloves and went for a bicycle ride along a path that dissected the City of Scottsdale lengthwise. We stopped at the manmade lake at Chaparral Park, drank a bottle of Gatorade each, and did some stretching before heading back. The heat usually peaked in the afternoon, and if not for the rare layer of patchy clouds, it would have been too hot for me to ride. Rebecca didn't mind the summers, but I had not acclimated despite all the years in Arizona and waited longingly for November, when daytime temperatures finally dipped under 80 degrees.

But it wasn't November yet, and the heat soared with the departing clouds. We rode back on the same path, Rebecca leading the way, pumping the pedals, glancing over her shoulder occasionally to see that I was still there. Her ponytail was threaded through the back strap of the helmet and shifted left and right with the movements of her head.

At the underpass by Indian Bend Road, I tried to get ahead. Her butt immediately came up from the seat as she sped up, yelling, "No, you won't!" I laughed too hard to give it my all, so I fell back and followed the beacon of her ponytail all the way home.

It was a good workout, which helped me clear up the heaviness left by the wedding announcement. As we parked the bikes in the garage, I felt optimistic. Our Debra was smart and perceptive. She had always been more mature than her age, not one to make a hasty choice. Mordechai must be a very special guy, and I would accept him as a son—the son I had always wanted to have, or the son I had always wanted to be for that dashing Marine in the photo by my mother's bedside.

Rebecca pulled me into the shower with her. "What's bothering you?"

I described what had happened earlier with Mr. Gonzales.

"You saved him." She kissed my fingers. "With your magic wands."

"The medical result was good, but I shouldn't have mentioned my father."

"Why not?"

"First of all, it threw me off, emotionally speaking, which shouldn't happen when I'm dealing with a possible emergency, when I need pure concentration."

"You're human, even when you wear that Godly white coat."

"I rarely think about my parents anymore, so it was…jolting."

"He was an ass. Who's going to fault you for being provoked?"

"It's not my job to win arguments with patients, especially not by exhibiting my personal life."

Her hands cradled my face. "Your job is to diagnose and cure, and that's exactly what you did while you also kicked him in the shin to stop his whining about Vietnam and to make him appreciate life."

There was something about New York Jews that turned crude bluntness into refreshing candor. I put my arms around her. "Kicking is something I learned from you."

"Damn right!"

Our lips locked, and we hugged under the running water.

B y the time we were ready to come out, feeble and satisfied, the water was lukewarm. I shut it off, and Rebecca wrapped a towel around us.

"Not bad," I said, "for the elderly parents of the bride."

"*Youthful* parents."

"Okay. Gracefully mature." I sighed. "But isn't she too young?"

"We were about the same age when you proposed."

"Just imagine Debra's reaction if we started bawling like your parents."

She slapped my butt. "They came around to love you."

I paused, thinking, did they love me? Not at first, not during the early years, when we were a young couple living in Manhattan, studying and working and seeing very little of Rebecca's parents. Following my graduation from Columbia Medical School, I had accepted a surgery residency in Phoenix, and we left New York with the intention of moving back a few years later. We joined the King Solomon Synagogue, and Rabbi Rachel Sher, then a fresh graduate of the Hebrew Union College, proved to be a gifted teacher who didn't dodge my questions. As my love for Rebecca expanded to her heritage and faith, I considered a conversion to Judaism.

The main difference, as I saw it, was the question of Jesus. Was Mary a virgin? Was her baby the son of God or of the man she lived with? And had Jesus really died and come back to life? Reflecting on my teenage years, I had always doubted the tall tales of my mother's unquestioning faith. Especially during college and medical school, when my scientific education made it harder to accept the biblical fables as factual, I had come to see Jesus as one of those well-intentioned biblical characters who got himself into trouble with the authorities. And when Rabbi Rachel explained that appreciating Jesus as a charitable, righteous Jew didn't conflict with Judaism, my decision to convert was the next logical step. It took a few years for me to shed all remnants of my gentile underpinnings, but with time, I managed to laugh at Jacky Mason's self-deprecating jokes, which poked fun at Jews' own quirks. And after my mother's sudden death, I lost contact with my relatives—much to their relief, I was sure.

But not all had been sunny for us in Arizona. Rebecca had several miscarriages before conceiving Debra, only to experience a high-risk pregnancy that kept her bedridden for months. As I was still in my training, her parents came and took turns at her side until Debra's harrowing birth. By the time mother and baby were out of danger, Rebecca's parents decided to stay in Arizona, and we did the same. They enjoyed their twilight years in Scottsdale, and our little girl enjoyed the spoils of doting grandparents, a privilege that neither Rebecca nor I had experienced as kids. Debra had spent many of her school vacations with them, wrote class papers based on their stories of Jewish life in pre-war Europe, and didn't seem to mind their insistence on observing kosher dietary laws and no TV during the Sabbath.

A year or two before he died, at a dinner party celebrating my election as president of our synagogue, Rebecca's dad was asked to give a toast. Leaning on his cane, Mel Greenbaum held up his glass of sweet wine. "To my son-in-law," he said, "a good husband, a good father, and also…a good Jew. *Le'haim!*"

"They did love you," Rebecca repeated, more to herself than to me. "And we will love Debra's husband as well."

"I'm not ready for her to have a husband," I said. "What about her professional aspirations? Her independence? I don't see how this Orthodox guy—"

"He has a name."

"Do you think *Mordechai* will join her for services at King Solomon, with a female rabbi and a coed choir?"

"For love he'll do anything." Rebecca rubbed lotion on her legs, which had remained as sculpted as they had been back at Columbia University. "But I think she's more likely to embrace his traditions, and we should be understanding too."

I lathered my face and began shaving. "Does she understand the practical implications of sharing a life with an Orthodox guy?"

"She's been attending an Orthodox synagogue in New York."

"That's a social thing, not a religious choice. Student life is all about hanging out with friends, wherever they go. But in terms of faith, Debra's like us, Reform through and through."

"Did you forget her summers with my parents?" Rebecca placed a long-sleeved blouse against her chest, looking at the mirror. "And he's modern Orthodox, not a Hasid from Borough Park."

"He might as well be a Hasid." I compared my sideburns, making sure they lined up with the middle of my ears. "The cultural gap between them is like the Grand Canyon."

"We managed, didn't we?"

"That's different."

"Why?"

"I converted to Judaism."

"And I gave up keeping kosher and observing the Sabbath, and I stayed home so you could pursue your career as a workaholic life saver."

It was true. Rebecca had given up the Orthodox lifestyle and the tight community of her upbringing, as well as her aspirations for a doctorate in history and a teaching career. She had also supported my choice to continue practicing at the VA hospital, where I earned a fraction of the income I could be making in private practice.

"Remember the Eskimo proverb we learned from the tour guide in Alaska?"

I nodded. It was one of Rebecca's fondest quotes. My hands reached forward to grab imaginary reins as I recited dutifully, "*Compromise is the dog that pulls the marriage sleigh.*"

"That's right. Debra will keep kosher, and he'll support her career. They'll work it out."

"I hope."

Rebecca gestured in dismissal. "Listen, she's better off marrying Mordechai than some Thai guy who bows to Buddha and eats cats."

It's the Most Wonderful Time of the Year

Rebecca and I arrived early at the synagogue and lingered in the foyer to shake hands and hug friends. Other than Yom Kippur, which was ten days away, Rosh Hashanah attracted the highest attendance. It was heartwarming to see everyone gather to celebrate the ancient holiday.

Jose Santoro, our part-time custodian, beckoned me from the service door. We walked outside together, around the back. The AC compressor sat on a concrete pad near the wall. It rattled in an uneven cycle, pitching up and down with a metallic knocking that I recognized from last year.

I groaned. "Not again."

"Sorry, Señor Doctor," Jose said. "Is no good. Is broken."

"We can't afford a new system now." Even if the cost had remained the same as last year's replacement quote, it would wipe out the synagogue's meager financial reserve and require borrowing on top of it. We had managed to keep the AC going another year, but here we were again. "Is Mat Warnick here?"

Jose nodded. "I see truck in parking lot."

"You're a good man."

He smiled, showing a cracked front tooth. We "shared" Jose with a church down the street, paying him cash for half-time while getting more than full-time from him. Other than Jose, the two congregations had little contact.

"I'll call Mat Warnick." Heading back inside, I prepared myself for unpleasantness. A hardworking man didn't come to the synagogue with his wife and kids expecting to be asked to work in the outdoor heat while everyone else celebrated the New Year Eve service.

I found Mat in the prayer hall, wearing a pressed shirt and a tie, seated with his twins, one on each side, reading to them from a children holiday book. I heard his son ask, "And when will the rabbi blow the shofar?" It reminded me how Debra had always been excited at hearing the ram's horn.

"Happy New Year!" I shook Mat's hand.

"And to you." He let go of my hand and buried his eyes in the book. "Don't even ask."

"How did you know?"

He pointed at an air vent overhead. "How do you know when a patient's blood flow is screwy?"

"Take a quick look, that's all. Maybe it's just a loose bolt, or a hose."

"There are three hundred heating-and-cooling guys in the yellow pages. Can't you call one of them?"

I knew Mat couldn't say no, so I just waited.

"Pretend I'm not here."

I couldn't do that, so I asked, "How is your brother doing?"

Mat gave me a look that said: *Not fair!*

Jonathan Warnick, a healthy communications specialist in the U.S. Army, had come back from Afghanistan with multiple internal injuries. Neglectful with his medications, he developed blood clots, and I operated on him in the last minute. But he was back at the hospital a month later with a stomach full of sleeping pills. I spent the night with Mat and their elderly mother until Jonathan's condition turned around and had visited him every day during weeks of psychiatric treatment. A year later, we all danced together at his wedding to a nurse from the psych floor, who made him add an extra marriage vow: *I shall never try to kill myself again.*

"My baby brother is the new king of Silicon Valley," Mat said, getting to his feet. "His company is preparing for an IPO. You should call him up, ask for a donation. A new cooling system maybe?"

Jonathan had started a website while still in the hospital—VetBestMate.com—which had become the largest singles site for veterans and those who want to date them.

Marching up the aisle with clenched fists, Mat said, "I'm doing it for you, Rusty, but it's not fair!"

"You're right, and I really appreciate it." What else could I say? If the AC died now, the prayer hall would quickly heat up to match the oppressive temperature outdoors, when the parched rocks and mass of urban concrete released all the accumulated heat of a long day. Then our celebration of Rosh Hashanah Eve would turn into something resembling the Israelites' escape from Egypt.

"If your home system broke, I'd come to fix it anytime, day or night." He pushed the exit door open, and a wave of heat slapped us. "But this is not your home!"

"This is our spiritual home." I patted his shoulder. "And I'll call Jonathan tomorrow. Promise."

Jose had already removed the metal grate. Mat crouched by the spinning steel fan, peered at the contraption underneath, and shook his head. "I need my toolbox," he said.

Flushed from the outside heat, I came down the middle aisle, pausing briefly to say hello to friends and their relatives, and mounted the three steps to the dais. As president of the congregation, I always sat during services in a tall chair between Rabbi Rachel and Cantor Bentov.

The rabbi, in a white pantsuit and a gold-embroidered prayer shawl, a white skullcap pinned to her curly hair, welcomed me with a big smile and open armed. "Congratulations! I'm so happy for Debra—she's such a special girl!"

"I feel terrible about the Orthodox thing." I embraced her. "Rebecca and I would much prefer that you conduct the ceremony, but the young couple already made their own—"

"Don't be silly. It's a big *simcha*, a cause for happiness."

I could tell she was hurt. Despite countless match-making efforts by the congregation's sisterhood, our rabbi had remained single. Perhaps her scholarly demeanor or ecumenical position had intimidated the men. Now in her late forties, Rabbi Rachel seemed to have accepted her singlehood, even embrace it. She often spoke of the members of the congregation as her family and of the members' children, whom she had taught in Sunday school, as her children.

"We just heard today," I said. "It's a complete shock. We've never even met the boy. Once we can discuss the whole thing with Debra alone, she could still change her mind about the type of ceremony. And the location. What's better than Scottsdale in December? It is, after all, the bride's parents who traditionally throw a wedding party, right?"

"That would be nice, but I advise against pressuring Debra in any way."

"Why?"

"A good marriage must be founded in harmony, not conflict. I completely understand her choice."

"You do?"

"She loves him, and therefore she loves his Orthodox tradition."

"And our tradition?"

"God is our tradition." Gesturing around, Rabbi Rachel explained. "All of us are created in God's image. Our tradition is to be tolerant and inclusive. With time, I'm certain that Debra will share this tradition with her husband."

Relieved, I asked, "But you'll attend the wedding, though?"

"I would have liked to—"

"We'll pay for the flight and hotel, of course."

"Thank you, Rusty. That's very kind." She pressed my hand. "You and Rebecca are always in my heart, and I share in your happiness as if Debra is my daughter too. Nevertheless, I think it's better that I don't attend."

This wasn't the answer I was hoping for. "Why not?"

"My presence at the wedding would put Debra in an awkward position."

"Why?"

Rabbi Rachel smiled. "Perhaps you underestimate how deeply the Orthodox rabbis object to the idea of a female rabbi. Think of it as a bull fight, with me as the red cloth."

It wasn't my place to argue with the rabbi, but I thought she was exaggerating. "You'll attend as our guest. Why should there be any problem with that?"

"You'll have to trust me on this. The officiating rabbi will insist that I stay behind the partition with all the other women, and Debra will feel guilty. Our sages wrote that rejoicing a bride on her wedding day is the most important mitzvah. Nothing should cloud her happiness. In fact, it would be a sin for me to attend."

The rabbi's thoughtfulness had led her to this logical conclusion, but it clearly pained her. There was a forced undertone to her voice. She had been with us through every family event in over two decades, whether it involved joy or mourning. How could we celebrate a wedding without her? "What if I let you walk her down the aisle in my place? Is that a strong enough enticement to attend?"

Rabbi Rachel laughed. "They haven't told you yet, have they?"

"Told me what?"

"In an Orthodox wedding, the two mothers accompany the bride to the chuppah, and the two fathers walk with the groom." She must have seen the disappointment on my face and added, "We'll have a big party when they come to Arizona. It'll be a lot more fun than Brooklyn."

My mind swirled with this hurtful piece of information. How could I not walk my daughter down the aisle? Scanning the prayer hall for Rebecca, I located her in a circle of friends. Would this be news to her? She had grown up Orthodox and probably knew of this custom. And from the few Orthodox weddings we had attended together over the years, I recalled that none of them had the formality of a typical American wedding. They were rambunctious affairs, held in large halls that were partitioned between men and women, and the guests crowded around the chuppah canopy, trying to get a glimpse of the marriage ceremony.

The rabbi stepped down from the dais to shake hands and greet members of the congregation. Rebecca finally caught my eye and waved. I waved back. My wife's response, no doubt, would be to accept reality and make the best of it. And she would be correct. What could we do but go along with Debra's wishes? Twisting her arm, even if we were successful, would only cause resentment and interfere with our harmonious happiness at this once-in-a-lifetime event of our only daughter's wedding. I comforted myself that at least we would be standing next to Debra under the chuppah while everyone else had to push and shove for a good spot.

With a few more minutes to kill, I sat in the president's chair next to the Torah ark. Ours wasn't the usual cabinet-type ark, but rather a hollow space in the east wall, where three Torah scrolls were kept behind a pair of stunning doors made of coarse mesquite logs bound in strips of Arizona palm fronds. The doors had originally been conceived for the grand entrance to a Paradise Valley mansion, but the artist, Judy Levy, had quarreled with her client, who didn't like the three-foot-long door handles that had previously known life as rattlesnakes. They were "scary and unwelcoming," the client had complained, a concern Judy pooh-poohed as "artistic provincialism." After back-and-forth arguments over the effectiveness of plasticating rattlers and defanging venomous critters, the client paid Judy in full and walked away from his doors. She told us the story during a synagogue board meeting, and when the laughter died down, I suggested she donate the doors for the Torah ark. She agreed, and thankfully her creative vision for the Torah ark was less reptilian. She substituted the controversial handles with two halves of a giant Star of David, composed of linked miniature scrolls—meticulously made of epoxy-hardened shreds of actual calf-parchment, the same material used for a Torah scroll. Three months ago, Judy and Jose mounted the doors over the Torah ark, using oversized hinges she had found in an old copper mine near Tucson.

My Blackberry chimed with a reminder. It was 7 p.m., and as president I was about to deliver the annual state of the synagogue address on behalf of the board of trustees, a tradition that signaled the end of the Jewish year.

Rabbi Rachel returned to the dais and signaled Cantor Bentov, who banged on the lectern three times and roared, "The president of the King Solomon Synagogue! All rise!"

No one heeded him. They couldn't rise because they hadn't yet sat down, too busy catching up on a year's worth of gossip.

I approached the podium and waited. The rows of seats formed succeeding crescents, all the way to the back of the Prayer Hall, filled with familiar faces, men and women I had known for many years, with their children and elderly parents. I whistled into the microphone, and the chattering quieted down. Halfway across the hall, Aaron Brutsky, my hospital colleague and vice president of the synagogue, tapped on his watch and said something that made his neighbors laugh.

"Next year," I said, my voice booming from the loudspeakers, "our esteemed vice president will give the annual speech, so remember to bring your pillows."

Aaron buried his face in his hands while people clapped. When quietness returned, all the way to my right Larry Emanuel yelled, "No more jokes until after Yom Kippur!"

"Larry is right." I raised my hands in surrender. "My new year's resolution is to join the local chapter of Humorous Anonymous."

My announcement won cheers.

I took a deep breath and said, "On behalf of the board of trustees of the King Solomon Synagogue, I would like to wish our rabbi, our cantor, and all of you a Happy Rosh Hashanah."

The congregation chorused, "Happy Rosh Hashanah!"

"Tonight we begin the Ten Days of Awe, the culmination of our relationship with God. It's like an annual physical, but rather than seeing your doctor for a medical checkup, you undergo a spiritual checkup. On the upside, this procedure involves no sharp needles or poky fingers."

They uttered a collective groan. In the rear, the door opened and Mat entered. He walked to his seat, giving me a quick thumbs-up.

I sighed in relief. "Winning God's grace," I said, "is the challenge we face. It's written that on Rosh Hashanah God inscribes a preliminary judgment for each one of us, and ten days later, on Yom Kippur, He reaches a final decision and lands

His fateful seal: *Who is innocent, and who is guilty, who shall live, and who shall die.* The question is simple. How can we improve our chances before the divine judge?"

The question got their attention.

"First, the facts. Synagogue membership has grown by a net gain of six families, which brings our community to a total of two hundred and seventeen families."

A few applauses. They must have sensed that the good news ended here.

"However, due to the poor economy and other factors, our income from membership fees and fundraising has dropped for the third year in a row, while expenses increased due to necessary maintenance, insurance costs, and Sunday school staffing. In other words, we are operating at a deficit. As a result, I agreed to take a ten-percent pay cut."

They clapped. Everyone knew it was a voluntary position. Not only wasn't I getting paid as president of the synagogue, but this lay leadership role often kept me awake at night, worrying about the next set of bills.

"Our Sunday school is growing nicely," I continued. "As a matter of policy, we don't turn away Jewish children who seek to attend. It's your dollars that support our educational programs." I paused, seeking words that would communicate the urgent need for donations without sounding desperate or heavy handed. "Our holiday prayers include the following words: *Repentance, prayer, and charity shall reverse a guilty verdict.* I can't help you with repentance and prayer, which are up to you alone, but the third one—"

They laughed.

"That's right," I said. "This is my first pitch of the year. Each one of you must remember that your charity will not only win points with the Almighty, but will also enable our congregation's mission." I paused, looking at a hall full of faces. What I really wanted to say was: *If you don't write some checks, we'll have to cut into the flesh—reduce services and slash our educational programs. And manage without air-conditioning!*

But I couldn't say that. Instead I smiled and asked, "What is our mission? Torah is our mission—to inspire, to teach, and to provide an open and hospitable place of worship. But our mission requires time and money. As the Torah says: *God knows the secrets of the heart.* So please give with an open heart, without conditions or reservations. Between now and Yom Kippur, I will call each one of you, and if you don't pick up the phone, I'll show up at your doorstep with the tool I use at the hospital to touch people's hearts—my electric rotary saw!"

This threat generated a few catcalls and fearful pantomime.

"Seriously," I said, "let's come together and support our communal mission, each to the extent of his or her ability. May God accept our prayers, show us His mercy, and seal our verdict for another year of life, happiness, good health, and pleasure in our children and loved ones. Happy New Year!"

While the Sunday school choir assembled on the steps of the dais, I walked over, sat at the piano, and rested my fingers on the faux ivory keys. Rabbi Rachel approached the podium, and Cantor Bentov signaled the choir, which broke into the Hebrew song that always opened our Rosh Hashanah prayers: "*Hineh mah tov u'mah naim…How good and pleasant, sitting together as brothers…*"

Part Two
Sunday, December 20

Winter Wonderland

The three months since Debra's engagement had gone by quickly. My fundraising efforts during the high holidays had generated enough cash for the synagogue to get through the end of the calendar year, but not much more. Jonathan Warnick had not responded to the message I had left with his assistant at the headquarters of VetBestMate.com in Silicon Valley, California. It was the moment of truth in our synagogue's finances. I prepared a list of drastic austerity measures for the agenda of the annual meeting of the board of trustees, scheduled for the Wednesday after Debra's wedding. The prospect of downsizing vital aspects of our communal life saddened me, but there was no alternative.

Besides my volunteer duties, work had been all consuming. My plan to take off the last ten days of December had required moving up all the surgeries scheduled for that period. In addition, October and November had brought in the usual crop of emergency bypass operations on elderly snowbirds, who came down to Arizona for golf and sunshine only to find their hearts incapable of handling all that fun. Meanwhile Rebecca had handled all the wedding preparations, providing me with daily updates. I trusted her to do everything in a way that would make Debra happy. And judging by the dollar amounts we were spending, happy she would be.

Rebecca had left for New York a week ago to deal with the final arrangements. I continued to work every waking hour and took the red-eye flight on Saturday night, December 19. I was out cold before takeoff and barely managed to rise five hours later as we pulled up to the gate at JFK.

A few minutes of waiting in the taxi line sufficed to freeze up my extremities and cause the rest of me to shiver uncontrollably inside the inadequate windbreaker I was wearing. The years in Arizona must have thinned my blood.

But the cab was overheated, and the ride into Manhattan tossed me around hard enough to clear off any remnants of sleep. The roads were slushy with a mix of melted ice and soaked-up grains of salt, and the sights of urban decay jostling with constant gentrification was familiar, almost heartwarming.

I walked into the lobby of the Muse Hotel in time for the continental breakfast. Rebecca and Debra were sharing a corner sofa, looking more like sisters than mother and daughter. It was warm inside the hotel, but while Rebecca was wearing a short-sleeved blouse, Debra's sleeves reached her wrists and her skirt went down to her ankles. A plain white bow kept her thick, coal-dark locks out of her clear face, giving her a sweet, girlish look.

"Excuse me," I said, "are you ladies free for breakfast?"

"Finally!" Rebecca jumped up and kissed me. "I checked your flight on the Internet—it showed that you landed two hours ago!"

"Sounds about right," I said, turning to my daughter. "Tunnel traffic was light, thank God."

Debra stood, almost a foot taller than her mom, and gave me a big smile. "Now I can get married."

I held her to me tightly and whispered in her ear, "Did Debbie do doodie for Daddy?"

"*Dad!*"

We laughed, sitting down. The phrase came from her terrible twos, when she had engaged in a war of attrition against her stressed-out, inexperienced parents. Her weapon of choice was bowel retention, and we fought back with mineral oil, milk of magnesia, and outright bribery. Every night when I came home, I picked up our dark-haired treasure and posed the same question: "Did Debbie do doodie for Daddy?"

At first she would proudly declare, "No doodie for Daddy!" But gradually our tactics worked, and my question turned into a sort of habitual greeting that made her laugh pretty much through high school—unless she had a friend over, and then she'd push me away before I had a chance to embarrass her.

Rebecca brought me a plate of pastries, scrambled eggs, and a slice of honeydew. For herself she got a bowl of oatmeal, and for Debra an apple on a paper napkin and a plastic knife.

"That's all?" I caressed Debra's cheek. "You ate already?"

She shook her head while cutting a slice off the apple. "I can't eat here. It's not kosher."

"What's not kosher?" I looked down at my plate. "Eggs and fruit?"

"The restaurant isn't kosher. They use the same pots and kitchenware for dairy and meat." She slipped the apple slice into her mouth. "They even serve bacon here," she added as if that fact made the food practically poisonous.

"You don't have to eat the pork," I said. "Anyway, since when have you become so strict?"

"Keeping kosher isn't strict. It's the basic tradition of Jewish life over many centuries. I feel really good about it, like…it's the right thing to do."

"I understand the charm of tradition, but modern life—"

"It's just food," Rebecca said, giving me a sharp look. "Let's talk about the wedding."

I saluted. "Yes, dear."

Debra and I chewed our different fares while Rebecca reported on the final preparations, such as table linen and dinnerware, seat assignments and chuppah pallbearers. Every small detail had been discussed, analyzed, and decided in perfect harmony with Mordechai's mother—an incredibly capable woman, according to Rebecca. Beside setting the stage for this elaborate event, which would give my daughter a *ba'al*—a Hebrew word that meant both "husband" and "owner"—Rebecca had also helped Debra prepare the studio apartment that the couple had rented, stocking it with furniture, knickknacks, and separate sets of dishes for dairy and meat. "It will be a lovely first home," Rebecca said. "And it's only two blocks away from their favorite synagogue."

Favorite synagogue? I glanced at Debra, and she nodded as if this was normal criteria in choosing a place to live. "We love it," she said. "It's a wonderful congregation, mostly Columbia college and grad students and young couples who work in Manhattan. We fit right in!"

"Me too," Rebecca said. "It's a lively group, very religious, but modern and sophisticated. I joined them for Sabbath services yesterday morning, and we were invited for a kiddush lunch at the apartment of a friend of Mordechai. It was so…cozy, familiar, like I was back home."

I understood. *Back home* meant the home in the Bronx, the home of her parents, the home of Orthodox life where the Sabbath was observed strictly, not the home in Arizona and the life we'd built together over the past decades. It was odd to hear Rebecca say it, maybe even painful to see the cloud of longing that passed over her face.

"On your next visit," Debra said, "you'll join us for services. You'll see. It's very New York."

"When in Rome," I said. "Anyway, everyone at King Solomon is looking forward to seeing you and meeting Mordechai. Rabbi Rachel sends her love and best wishes."

Because only few of our Arizona friends were able to make it to tonight's wedding, we had planned a party on Thursday night at the synagogue back in Scottsdale. The newlyweds would be the guests of honor, and Rabbi Rachel would preside over the *Sheva Brachot*, the "Seven Blessings" recited daily over dinner during the week following a Jewish wedding.

"You lost weight." I hadn't seen our daughter since last summer. "All bones."

"Thanks, Dad!"

"It wasn't a compliment. You have to eat well—"

"—to stay well," she ended the sentence for me, laughing in that special way that melted my heart.

I looked around the lobby. "Where is Mordechai?"

"He's forbidden from seeing me. We've been apart for a week!"

"Builds up the tension." Rebecca poured orange juice for the two of us. "I should be the one losing weight."

"Start keeping kosher again," Debra said. "Seriously, it makes you think twice before eating anything. I've been kosher for a year now and I really don't miss any—"

"A year?" I felt Rebecca's knee bang against mine, but ignored it. "I thought you only met Mordechai in July."

Debra looked at me as if my question made no sense.

"I like kosher food," Rebecca said in a discussion-ending tone.

"You also like shrimp." I shifted aside to get away from another knee collision. "And lobster."

"I grew up without shrimp and lobster, and it didn't kill me." She unfolded a sheet of paper. "Here's the plan. The bride and I have a busy day ahead, with a few shopping stops and most of the afternoon at the beauty salon. From there, we'll go straight to the wedding hall in Brooklyn. I need to check on the caterers, table settings, and so on. Debra's friends will be there to keep her company and help her get ready. Then, a half-hour before seven, we'll prepare to receive the guests—Debra in the big chair, and the two of us with Mordechai's parents at the door."

"Anything you want me to do between now and tonight?" When she shook her head, I asked, "Maybe I can meet with Mordechai? He looks fine on Skype, but I'd like to see him in the flesh once before the deed is done, you know?"

"He's in seclusion," Debra said. "Under the rules of Halacha, a groom is required to spend his wedding day fasting and studying Talmud."

"That's too bad." I glanced at my watch. "So what am I going to do for a whole day?"

"Rest." Rebecca kissed me. "You look exhausted. I really wish you came a day or two earlier."

Looking at Debra, I said, "There was no way I could have taken more time off. But starting today, I'm free for ten days. Mom and I will fly home on Tuesday morning to get ready for your arrival on Wednesday. Mordechai has never been to Arizona, right?"

She nodded.

"We'll make sure he loves it. We'll go hiking at Pinnacle Peak on Thursday morning, then the party at the synagogue in the evening. Friday happens to be Christmas Day, so everything will be closed, which makes it perfect for sightseeing. We can drive to Sedona—"

"We'll have to be home early," Debra said. "Sabbath begins at sunset."

"No problem. I could arrange a private tour of the Heard Museum's Native American exhibit on Friday morning, and we'll do Sedona after the Sabbath, maybe on Sunday?"

"I ordered kosher meals," Rebecca said, "for Friday night and Saturday. The deli at Chabad provides the whole meals, soup to nuts, literally, even the plates and utensils. But let's get through the wedding first. I had your tuxedo cleaned and pressed. It's hanging in the room with your shirt. Everything else you need is in the blue suitcase."

"You're the best," I said, meaning it.

Rebecca pierced a piece of cheese with a toothpick and held it out for me. "Tonight will be a late night, and tomorrow night Mordechai's parents are hosting a Sheva Brachot dinner."

"Seven blessings only? Can't they afford more blessings?" I bit the cheese off the toothpick.

Debra made a face, and Rebecca said, "Come on, Rusty."

"What?"

"You'll have to hold back on your jokes. These people are very religious."

"Religious Jews survived for centuries on humor. That's why they invented Yiddish—to tell jokes at the expense of the gentiles without them knowing what's being said. For example, *Nisht geshtoygn un nisht gefloygn,* which literally means, *Didn't climb up and didn't fly.* A non-Jew would think they're talking about a rodent, not about Jesus Christ and his climactic role in the New Testament, that just like he didn't climb up onto the cross, he also didn't fly off to heaven. See my point?"

"*Dad!*"

"Okay. Okay." I raised my hands. "I'll be good. Promise."

Rebecca and I polished off a plate of cheese while Debra told us about the bachelorette party her friends had thrown her and the little gifts Mordechai was sending every day with his mother. Debra was bursting with excitement over the wedding—the hall, the food, the important guests from Brooklyn's rabbinical apex, and the kindness of Mordechai's parents, who had picked up the tab for the klezmer band even though the bride's family customarily paid for everything. I was tempted to point out that almost all of the five hundred guests were from the groom's side, but held my tongue. It wasn't important. Watching her so happy made me feel guilty for thinking of money. I exchanged a glance with Rebecca, and we smiled at each other. Tonight our daughter would become the happy wife of a young man she deeply loved. Nothing could spoil our joy.

The driver came in to help Rebecca and Debra with the clothes hangers and other accessories, including the wedding dress, which I helped him carry to his black Lincoln Town Car. He would take them to each appointment and wait outside—a necessary luxury in New York City.

I went up to the room and lay on the bed. Mordechai's Talmudic seclusion at his parents' house made him unavailable for the man-to-man talk I had always imagined having with Debra's fiancé on the eve of their wedding: *She's a special girl. The best!* After a dramatic pause, I'd proceed to count on my fingers the virtues I expected my daughter's husband to exemplify during their lifetime together: *Kindness. Consideration. Respect. Generosity. Integrity.* "And if you ever cheat on her, I'll make sure you spend the rest of your days living in a cardboard box over a subway vent." The last sentence I spoke out loud, which sounded silly in the empty hotel room. Perhaps I could still manage to whisper my message in Mordechai's ear when we met to sign the ketubah—the traditional marriage agreement—before the ceremony, or while we walked down the aisle to the chuppah. The boy would probably think Debra's father was completely insane.

I tried to take a nap, but the constant hum of the city, the car horns and police sirens, were too exhilarating. Rebecca had bought a real coat, a pair of gloves, and a wool hat for me, all folded neatly over the back of a chair as if she had expected me to go out and about despite the arctic temperature.

The wind, channeled between the skyscrapers, stung my face, but the streets bustled with energy. I joined the flow of purposeful pedestrians, shook my head at offers of discount coupons for various goods and services, and waited at corner crossings as traffic flew by. I walked and walked, enjoying the vibrancy of Manhattan, reminiscent of my student years here.

After a while, the physical exertion calmed me down. I had every reason to be happy: Debra was getting married, I was gaining a son, and soon...*grandkids?* The idea made me chuckle, but I drew no attention from the New Yorkers around me.

At Rockefeller Center, I stopped to admire the enormous Christmas tree. Steps away, onlookers lined the railing over the ice rink. On an impulse, I rented a pair of shoes and went skating. Rather than fall on my ass, as I'd expected, my body found its old groove, my arms and legs adjusting to the rhythm of the steel blades on the sleek surface of the rink. From the loudspeakers, Louis Armstrong sang, *"A beautiful sight..."*

The words came to me, surfacing from deep-seated memories, and I joined him, *"We're happy tonight..."*

A kid bumped into another and knocked him down in front of me. I panicked, bending over, ready to fall, but my legs slid left and right in tandem, the blades whistling in that fresh, slashing sound of a well-executed swerve. I glanced back and saw the kid pull himself up and accelerate after his friends. I clapped, more for myself than for him. It must have been over thirty-five years since the last time I skated, back home in Tarrytown, a short train ride up the Hudson River. My mother had considered ice skating nothing less than an attempt to break your neck. "Christ is watching over us," she had said, "but why make it harder for Him?" Still, she let me go down to the frozen pond with my friends, giving in like she'd done with all my boyish whims as long as they involved no spending of money, of which we had very little. I later understood that she felt responsible for my fatherless childhood, as if it had been her fault, as if she had instituted the draft and sent him on a one-way trip to Vietnam.

Executing another sharp swerve to avoid a man and his son, I glanced up at the spectators above, imagining my mother's worried face, her right hand gripping the stem of the cross that never left her necklace.

Armstrong kept singing, and I remembered playing "Winter Wonderland" on the organ at church in the hours before Midnight Mass, resentful to be there while my friends played outside in the snow, getting *their* noses chilled. But even though my fingers ached from hours on the keys, Christmas had been my favorite holiday, maybe because it was my mother's only vacation day of the year. I had asked her once why she wasn't taking a day off on *my* birthday, to which she responded: "Christmas is the birthday of all of us."

Mom died suddenly a couple of years after Rebecca and I had married. "Massive coronary," the doctor in White Plains told me over the phone. "She had no chance." It was a terrible shock to lose her, not only because she had always been the solid foundation of my life, but also because she had just turned fifty, never smoked, and wasn't short of physical activity. In retrospect, I recalled her pressing a fist to her chest when something upset her or taking a deep breath with her eyes closed, but I had assumed those to be mannerisms, not manifestations of physical pain. I bemoaned not asking her about it. Her sudden death, and my remorse for missing those oblique signs, had contributed to my choice of a medical specialty that put me in the operating room for endless hours, re-plumbing the hearts of other people's mothers and fathers, giving them the chance Mom didn't get. It had been a long time, but I had lived my life as if she watched over me from above, as if she understood the choices I made and continued to love me even though I had joined the Jewish people who rejected her beloved Jesus Christ, the son of God, the Messiah who had died for her very few sins.

Skating one more time around the crowded rink, when Armstrong's voice caressed me, "*We'll frolic and play, the Eskimo way,*" I joined him for the last line, "*Walking in the winter wonderland.*" And as I sat down to pull off the rented shoes, sadness tightened my chest and I sighed. If only my mother was still with us to accompany Debra down the aisle in that beautiful white dress!

———

Silver Bells

Pillars of Joy looked like a Brooklyn version of the White House, only not as white, its marble columns blackened by soot from the heavy traffic on Flushing Avenue. A huge menorah was propped beside the front steps, all eight of its electrical candles lit up, even though Hanukkah had ended almost a month ago. Perhaps they kept it on year-round. Rebecca had told me that Pillars of Joy was the most popular wedding hall for well-to-do observant Jews in New York. Eager to enter and see for myself, I paid the cab driver and stepped onto the sidewalk, the frozen snow crunching under my dress shoes.

Despite the early darkness and freezing wind, the avenue was teeming with people, and I had to wait for a family to pass. The parents—a black couple in professional garb—each lugged a small child while two older kids carried shopping bags, chatting happily in rapid New York vernacular that I could barely follow. One of the boys, maybe twelve or thirteen, noticed me looking at them and called, "Merry Christmas, sir!"

"Thank you," I said, buttoning my coat. "Happy Holidays!"

The steps had been swept clear of snow and lain with nonslip mats. Inside the first set of double doors, an LED sign blinked: *Levinson-Dinwall Wedding.*

The second set of doors led me into a vast foyer. At the other end, Rebecca stood in her ankle-long burgundy dress and matching little hat. The high heels caused her shapely rear to peak out in a way that tempted my hand for a pat, maybe even a squeeze, but she was talking with a bearded man wearing a black coat and a black hat. As I came closer, he put down a bottle of sweet red wine and said, "I must check the crate for the label, just to make sure."

I watched him go. "Make sure of what?"

"He's the *mashgiach*," Rebecca explained. "It's his job to verify that all the food and drinks are kosher."

"Kiddush wine could be non-kosher?"

"Regular kosher isn't enough. It has to be *glatt*-kosher with a special seal from an ultra-Orthodox authority. Rabbi Mintzberg is very strict, and there will be other rabbis as well. Mordechai's family is very prominent here."

"You look beautiful." I gave Rebecca a light peck on the cheek, careful not to crack the crust of makeup that cocooned her face. "They'll mistake you for the bride."

She rolled her eyes. "They're religious, honey, not blind."

I kissed her again, this time on the lips. "We're religious, too. Reform Judaism is much more spiritual—"

"Don't get defensive." Rebecca patted my tuxedoed chest. "They've been perfectly gracious."

"I should wear a T-shirt." I drew imaginary letters. "Reform Is Not Diet Judaism."

"Dr. Dinwall, I presume." A short man in a black tuxedo and a gray goatee marched toward us with his hand outstretched, smiling with familiar big teeth. "Mazal Tov!"

"Mordechai's dad," Rebecca murmured.

"Dr. Levinson!" I shook his hand. "We finally meet. May Hashem bless us with lots of joy in our children."

"Amen." He seemed pleased that I had pronounced God's name as the Orthodox do, "Hashem," which literally meant "The Name," rather than uttering the actual Hebrew name of God, *Adonai*.

Turning to Rebecca, he said, "And thank you, Mrs. Dinwall, for all you've done to prepare for the wedding."

Rebecca curtsied, not offering a hand. "We're family now."

"Almost." He turned to watch his approaching wife, who was panting from the few front steps in a manner that reminded me of my pre-op patients. Her long-sleeved dress was a mosaic of beige and pink octagons, worn loose over a thick trunk. The longish brunette wig contrasted with her weathered face.

The two women hugged.

"Mazal Tov!" I extended my hand, but Rebecca pushed it down.

"Traffic is terrible," Mordechai's mother said. "I was sure we'd be late. This year, the winter is vicious. *Vicious!*"

"In Arizona we wait for winter," I said. "It's the best time of the year—seventy degrees and sunny every day."

"I've been to Scottsdale once," Dr. Levinson said, "for a medical conference. It was August, and the heat was unbearable, straight out of Dante."

"Timing is everything," Rebecca declared, threading her arm in mine. "Debra should be ready any minute."

The four of us proceeded across the foyer, which was lined with flowers in golden vases. A large white cardboard box waited for the wedding gifts, and a metal case with a narrow slit awaited the checks. At the back of the foyer was an armchair adorned with greenery and white roses. The sight of the bride's throne stopped me. "She's only twenty-one," I said.

Mrs. Levinson waved a dismissive, bejeweled hand. "I was eighteen, and not a single regret in twenty-nine years."

"Ah!" Rebecca clapped. "Here comes the bride!"

Debra appeared with Mordechai's two younger sisters, who carried the trail of her dress. Seeing her in white shocked me with the reality of it, as if until now the whole thing could have been a stage set for a play titled *Debra's Make-believe Wedding to Brooklyn Mordechai,* as if we were all going to take off the tuxedos and yarmulkes and have a good laugh.

"Hi, Daddy!" She tilted her head slightly the way she always did.

I blew her a kiss, and she caught it and pressed it to her heart.

We followed Debra to the big chair, where she sat down to greet her wedding guests. I stood next to the decorated throne, held my hands over her head, and recited the prayer that summarized what Jewish fathers wished for their precious children: "*May God bless you and guard you; May God shine His face upon you and judge you kindly; May God watch over you and keep you in peace.*"

"Amen," Debra said, looking up at me with glistening eyes.

Everyone around us repeated, "Amen."

I stepped aside. The foyer opened to the left into a cavernous wedding hall lit with fluorescent chandeliers. The space was divided in half by a lacey partition to keep men and women apart during the celebration. Round tables in cream linen crowded together, set with shining silverware and small plates of lettuce. A path of red carpet crossed the hall to a stage by the opposite wall, where the blue canopy of the chuppah awaited. *My daughter's chuppah!*

I turned to Debra and realized that she'd been watching me while Mordechai's sisters arranged the trail of the dress around her feet. "Are you okay, Daddy?"

"Of course." I swallowed hard. "Couldn't be better."

The guests arrived en masse at 7 p.m., a flood of unfamiliar faces that resembled Mordechai's parents—the men in black, the women in fancy wigs and baggy outfits. The four of us stood at the door to greet them. Dr. Levinson and I shook hands with the men while our wives made small talk with the women. The klezmer band started off with clarinets, a joyous tune that accompanied the guests as they dispersed among the tables— men to the left of the partition, women to the right. They knew the routine as if they attended weddings twice a week, which they probably did.

Finally the small Arizona contingency showed up. Aaron Brutsky jogged toward us with open arms. His wife, Miriam, followed behind with Judy Levy, who carried a large gift-wrapped package, which I hoped wasn't another artistic mummification of a deceased reptile. Cantor Bentov came last, carrying his colorful prayer shawl under his arm. He was due to recite one of the blessings under the chuppah.

Aaron hugged me, and we slapped each other's back. Miriam and Judy told Rebecca about the Broadway show they had seen earlier that afternoon, which apparently featured a muscular star in his birthday suit. Cantor Bentov sang the first line of the theme song, and Rebecca hushed him. I would have liked to see more familiar faces among the guests, but the short notice and the holiday season made it difficult for people to travel across the country.

Debra was talking animatedly with each of the guests who lined up to greet her. I was struck by how mature she seemed, so gracious and confident. What else could I hope for? She was happy, right? The rest was unimportant. I recalled her as a little girl, barely taller than my knee, throwing a ball in the backyard. My eyes blurred.

"Hey, kiddo!" Aaron leaned over to kiss Debra, "You look absolutely smashing—"

She dodged him. "No touching, Uncle Aaron!"

He stepped back. "Why not?"

"You know!" She shook a finger, her face beaming. "I already dipped in the mikvah. Tonight, only my new husband can touch me."

"Ho! Ho! Ho!" Aaron feigned shock. "Did your new husband ever change your diapers? Did he ever bandage your scraped knee? Did he ever beat up your ninth-grade boyfriend?"

"You didn't beat up anyone," Debra protested, laughing.

"I should have!" He took a flower from a nearby arrangement, kissed it, and tossed it in her lap. "We love you, baby. Go get 'em!"

"Hee-hah!" Judy made like whipping. "Here comes Arizona!"

"That's right," Miriam cheered. "Watch out, Brooklyn!"

Cantor Bentov inhaled deeply and boomed a musical scale, "*Da, da, da, da, da, da, daaaaaah!*"

We had a big laugh just as a hush fell over the chattering crowd and the lively band.

"Blessed be He," Dr. Levinson said. "Rabbi Mintzberg is here!" He rushed past us toward the entrance, where an old man with a white beard surveyed the foyer through thick, black-rimmed glasses.

———

Deck the Halls

Aaron agreed to accompany me as a witness for the signing of the ketubah, a traditional Jewish marriage contract scribed in Aramaic and Hebrew. I had also signed a ketubah at my wedding, though ours was written in English by the female Reform rabbi who presided over the ceremony. Rebecca's father kept blowing his nose and groaning pitifully lest we mistook his wet cheeks for tears of joy. But he did sign our ketubah as the bride's father, and Rebecca mounted the framed parchment on our kitchen wall. Sometimes, when we discussed money, she pointed to the yellowing document and declared: "You still owe me a thousand shekels!" And I'd pretend to pull the ancient coins of Judea from my pocket and toss them at her. Watching Debra and the circle of well-wishers, I wondered if she and Mordechai would continue to enjoy each other for as long as Rebecca and I had managed to.

We put on the black-felt yarmulkes, embroidered in gold: DEBRA & MORDECHAI'S WEDDING.

Inside the ketubah room, Mordechai stood up to welcome us. He looked even younger than on Skype, a mere boy in a black tuxedo and a large yarmulke over a fresh haircut that left his ears exposed prominently while a thick lock of hair came down to his eyebrows, trimmed in a straight line. He shook my hand with a sweaty palm and cold fingers. "An honor to meet you, Dr. Dinwall."

"Great to see you in person," I said. "You have a beautiful bride waiting for you out there."

Mordechai glanced at the door with longing that melted away any reservations I still had.

"Meet Dr. Brutsky," I introduced him to Aaron. "We've practiced together since we came out of school."

Aaron took Mordechai's hand in both hands and gave it a vigorous shaking. "I first met Debra at the moment she opened her eyes. You're a lucky man!"

"I know, but I haven't seen her in a week. It's very hard."

"Don't worry, kid." Aaron slapped his shoulder. "You'll see her every day for the rest of your life. Before you know it, you'll be sick and tired of seeing the same—"

I elbowed Aaron.

"What?" He grinned. "I'm just psyching the groom, giving him strength."

Mordechai seemed oblivious to Aaron's humor. He sat down and resumed reading from the prayer book. He must have been obeying some Orthodox rules. Was he required to recite a set number of verses before the marriage could take place?

We stepped aside.

"Nice kid," Aaron whispered. "Has he had his Bar Mitzvah yet?"

"Don't be stupid," I said. "He's a senior in college."

"That means nothing. I've read about a twelve-year-old who graduated from Duke *summa cum libidio.*"

The last words Aaron said loud enough for Mordechai to hear, and we both turned to look at him. Nothing. He was completely focused on murmuring the verses from the book.

"A righteous boy," Aaron said. "Shouldn't we also be praying?"

"Too bad Rabbi Rachel isn't here. She'd know the protocol."

"It's better she stayed in Arizona."

"Why?"

"She would stick out like a bagel on Yom Kippur." Aaron squeezed my arm. "I spoke with her earlier. She sent her love and blessings, but I could tell she was hurting—the president of the synagogue is marrying his daughter, and the rabbi can't attend."

"Are you trying to make me feel worse?"

Aaron grinned. "Don't worry. An e-mail has already gone out to the congregation to remind everyone of the Sheva Brachot dinner on Thursday. Rabbi Rachel thinks we'll have at least a hundred people or even more."

"Better be more. Rebecca ordered enough food for an army."

D r. Levinson came in with Rabbi Mintzberg and his stocky assistant, who took their seats at the table. I sat across from the rabbi, Aaron on my left, Mordechai and his father on my right. The klezmer music filtered through the closed door as if trying to inject jolly into this somber, ancient ritual in which the bride's father transferred ownership of his daughter to the groom, who assumed legal responsibility for her living expenses and wellbeing.

"Rabbi," Dr. Levinson said, "this is the bride's father."

"Mazal Tov." Rabbi Mintzberg's round spectacles focused on Aaron. "God has blessed your daughter with a fine, fine match—"

"That's the father." Aaron pointed at me.

"*Azoi.*" The rabbi turned to me, smoothing his white beard. "Mazal Tov to you, then. Your daughter is blessed in joining such a wonderful family."

"Thank you, Rabbi," I said. "The blessing is mutual. We're grateful to Hashem."

His gnarled, tremulous hands unrolled a large parchment and held it flat on the table before us. The letters resembled the script of a Torah scroll. "You are here today," he said, "representing your daughter in executing this ketubah, by which you agree to transfer her from your possession to her husband's, yes?"

I nodded.

"It is the greatest mitzvah," Rabbi Mintzberg continued, "bringing your daughter under the chuppah." He closed his eyes and chanted, "May God reward you with the joy of grandchildren and great-grandchildren, who will grow up to a life of Torah and good deeds."

We all chorused, "Amen!"

The assistant, swaying as if in prayer, read from the ketubah, starting with Mordechai's ancestry and continuing with Debra: "The bride, the virtuous virgin, Debra, daughter of Rebecca, daughter of Leah and Melvin Greenbaum of Warsaw, Poland, later of the Bronx, New York."

The reason for the long description of Debra's ancestry, I knew, was to satisfy the Jewish hereditary test of a kosher Jew, based on her maternal line.

The assistant switched to Aramaic, except for numbers, which he recited in English, setting forth Mordechai's future monetary obligations to Debra. It went on for ten minutes. Then it was time for signing.

The rabbi's assistant signed as a witness for Mordechai, who then executed the ketubah deliberately, his fingers slightly trembling. In an hour or so, my daughter would bear his last name: *Debra Levinson.*

"And the name of the bride's father's witness?" Rabbi Mintzberg looked at Aaron.

"Aaron, son of Golda and Herschel."

"Last name?"

"Brutsky."

"*Broo-tseh-kee?*" The rabbi creased his eyes. "Let's see now. From Galicia?"

"That's right," Aaron said. "My father came from the Zmigrod Shtetl before the war. My mother is from Bialystok."

I watched the assistant's pen travel slowly, drawing the Hebrew letters on the parchment. He turned the ketubah around, pointing. "Sign here."

Aaron signed, handed me the pen, and winked. "Ready to dance?"

The rabbi cleared his throat. "And where is the *yid* from?"

"I live in Arizona," Aaron said. "But I grew up in Lakewood, New Jersey."

"*Azoi.*" Rabbi Mintzberg nodded. "Which synagogue?"

"Rabbi Ackerman's."

"A Hasidic boy?" Rabbi Mintzberg clicked his tongue. "Well, nobody's perfect, yah?"

Mordechai and his father laughed, and the rabbi's assistant said, "Could be worse!"

"And the father?" The old rabbi looked at me, his eyes large and watery through the thick lenses. "Also from a *Hasidischer* stock?"

"No," I said. "A regular Jew. My Hebrew name is Reuben, son of Abraham and Sarah." This was the way I was called up to the Torah at the synagogue. The parents of every convert to Judaism were Abraham and Sarah, the ancestral parents of the Jewish nation, and Rabbi Rachel had chosen Reuben for me as it shared a first letter with my nickname, Rusty.

The assistant scribbled the Hebrew letters carefully. "Family name?"

"Dinwall," I said, and spelled it out of habit, "D-I-N-W-A-L-L."

"*Deen-Aeh-Oyl?*" Rabbi Mintzberg creased his forehead. "A Littvak name, yah?"

I shook my head.

"Hungarian?" The rabbi's eyes lit up. "A Gurr Hasid?"

"Not really. My father's family originated in Scotland."

"*Say-cott-lund?*" Rabbi Mintzberg pursed his lips. "*Azoi?*"

"I'm not sure where exactly." I held up the pen. "My great-great-grandfather, Patrick Dinwall, sailed across the Atlantic on a whaling ship and worked in the Great Lakes region as a trapper."

"*Trepp-err?*"

"He was known in the fur trade along the Canadian frontier for inventing a paw-trap to catch otters underwater." I winced as Aaron kicked me under the table. "They named a lake after him. You can still find it on the map: Saint Patrick Lake."

Rabbi Mintzberg repeated, "*Pah-tree-kheh?*"

"Back then," Aaron said, "they couldn't pronounce Pinkhas." He laughed, but no one else did.

I signed the ketubah and turned it around.

The stocky assistant tilted his hat back and peered at my signature. "What's this?"

"My legal name," I said. "That's how I sign checks. Do you want me to sign with my Hebrew name?"

The assistant wasn't listening. He moved the ketubah slowly until it was in front of the old rabbi, who bent over it, lifting his glasses, and examined my signature, reading it aloud: "*Keh-rees-tee-anne?*"

"That's right." I pulled the driver license from my wallet. "Christian Dinwall. My full and legal name."

Rabbi Mintzberg uttered a strange squeak and turned to his assistant, who said something in Yiddish, which I didn't understand. But I saw Dr. Levinson's face go white. He whispered urgently in his son's ear, and Mordechai said, "How could I know? She calls him Daddy!"

Aaron sighed. "Dr. Dinwall's first name is Christian, but he's no longer *a* Christian."

"That's right," I said. "I've gone through the whole conversion process twenty-some years ago."

"True," Aaron said. "Our rabbi can confirm it."

The assistant flipped open a mobile phone. "What's the rabbi's name and number?"

"Rachel," I said. "Rabbi Rachel Sher. Area code—"

"*Ray-shayle?*" Rabbi Mintzberg shook his head. "*Oy vey zmeer!*"

"A woman?" The assistant put down his phone. "A woman cannot be a rabbi or perform a valid conversion under Halacha!"

"For God's sake," Aaron protested. "Rusty is the president of our synagogue!"

"President schmesident!" Rabbi Mintzberg's age-spotted hands grasped the edge of the table for support as he slowly stood up. "He's a shaygetz!"

At first the whole thing was too surreal for me to get upset. I remained seated at the table with Aaron and Mordechai while Rabbi Mintzberg, his assistant, and Dr. Levinson huddled in the corner of the room, conversing intensely in Yiddish.

After a few minutes, Levinson came over. He rubbed his goatee and seemed to be searching for the right words. "The rabbi…will not proceed."

Mordechai jumped to his feet and stepped over to the wall, facing it, his back to us. His father watched him for a moment and said quietly, "We must call it off."

"Are you kidding?" I gestured at the closed door and the music that came through it. "Listen to them—it's a wedding, for God's sake."

"I'm sorry." He looked at his son's back. "We have…no choice."

"But why? My daughter is perfectly Jewish!"

Levinson shrugged. "Rabbi Mintzberg isn't sure anymore. He wants to reexamine the whole lineage. He feels deceived." From the tone of his voice I gather that he too was feeling cheated, as if we had been hiding a dark family secret from him.

"This is outrageous!" Aaron pounded the table. "We're in America, not in Galicia!"

The old rabbi beckoned Dr. Levinson, who came over and stood before him like an admonished student before his headmaster. Rabbi Mintzberg murmured something we couldn't hear and leaned on his assistant's arm as they headed for the door.

"It's a *shanda*," Aaron said, "a desecration of God's name!"

The rabbi stopped and turned slowly. He didn't look at me or at Aaron, but at Mordechai, whose forehead was pressed to the wall, a slight tremor in his shoulders the only evidence of his crying. Rabbi Mintzberg adjusted his glasses, shook his head again, and continued to the door.

"Wait!" I was surprised at the loudness of my voice. An image jostled me into action—the vision of this revered old rabbi and his assistant leaving the ketubah room, walking slowly across the foyer in plain view of hundreds of guests, right in front of my daughter in her bridal throne, to the exit. "In the name of God," I said. "Please!"

Dr. Levinson raised his hand to stop me, but I ran to the door and blocked their way.

Rabbi Mintzberg was a small man, but his assistant was massive. Judging by his bulging belly, pinkish skin, and heavy panting, he was a good candidate for bypass surgery or a massive heart attack, whichever came first. But neither would come soon enough to stop him from pushing me out of the way, so I held my open hands forward and said, "These hands might belong to a shaygetz according to strict Halacha, but they operate every day on very sick patients."

The assistant looked at the rabbi like a dog seeking permission to attack. But Rabbi Mintzberg removed his glasses and looked at my hands as if examining an unusual specimen.

"And every day," I continued, "when I cut open my patients' chests, the hearts I find inside look the same, smell the same, and beat the same, no matter if it's a Jew, a Christian, or an atheist."

The rabbi looked down at his own chest. His lips parted, but he didn't interrupt me.

"I've held hundreds of beating hearts in my hands—human hearts that look no different than what's inside this chest!" I pounded on mine. "Or what's inside yours!" I reached forward and touched the rabbi's black coat, which caused him to take a step backward, almost losing his balance.

The assistant's bearded face reddened as he steadied the rabbi. "Let us pass, or else!"

"If you leave, my daughter's heart will break in a way that I can't fix." I reached behind my back for the door handle. "I'm going to step out of this room and let the five of you—righteous, kosher Jews—find a solution in accordance with Halacha."

"Move aside!" The assistant stepped closer to me.

"*Love your friend as you love yourself.*" I focused my gaze on the rabbi. "Isn't that how Rabbi Akivah summarized the whole Torah?"

The old rabbi looked at me, surprised.

"Think of this boy." I pointed at Mordechai. "And of my daughter, who by her mother is also one of you, a kosher Jew, correct?"

Rabbi Mintzberg didn't respond.

"Use the wisdom God gave you," I said, halfway out the door, "and find a solution so that you can marry these kids."

I slipped out and shut the door behind me, grasping the handle, ready for the bully assistant to try and force it open. But he didn't, and despite the klezmer music in the hall, I could hear their voices inside the ketubah room, rising in rapid, angry Yiddish.

Eventually Aaron came out of the room alone. He wiped his forehead on the sleeve of his tuxedo. "Here's the deal," he said. "The old fart agreed to recognize your daughter's Jewishness—"

"Was there a doubt?"

"—after calling some rabbis in the Bronx who knew your in-laws way back when."

I nodded, swallowing my anger. From their Orthodox point of view, the shock of discovering that the bride's father wasn't Jewish had put everything else in question. But they had come around, accepting that Rebecca's family was Jewish beyond blemish, and therefore so was Debra. "That's very good," I said. "So he'll go forward with the ceremony?"

"It depends." Aaron averted his eyes.

"On what?"

"Please don't get upset. It's the best I could negotiate under the circumstances."

"Tell me!"

"Rabbi Mintzberg won't proceed unless you stay out."

"Out?"

"He quoted a bunch of Talmudic rules, something about impurity of gentiles. Clearly it's all because he's pissed that no one had told him beforehand. He thinks it was intentional trickery so that you could sign the ketubah as if you're a Jew."

"That's ridiculous! And where was it written that someone like me may not sign?"

"I don't know enough to argue. It's been decades since I opened a page of Talmud, you know?"

"I'm not angry at you. Fine. I won't sign it."

"Signing isn't even on the table." Aaron paused and looked at me.

"Spell it out already!"

"Rabbi Mintzberg issued a *Psak Halacha*, a religious judgment. He would go forward with the marriage ceremony only if you comply with certain conditions."

"What conditions?"

"First, you may not continue to pretend to be a Jew."

"But I *am* a Jew!"

"Not by his criteria. He wants you to stop misleading *real* Jews."

"Asshole."

"I agree." Aaron sighed. "He demands that you remove the yarmulke and don't participate in reciting blessings or in any singing or play a Jewish tune on any musical instrument."

I felt my face burning. I had been a Jew for so long—not only because I had fallen in love with Rebecca, but because I had fallen in love with Judaism as well and embraced it as my own spiritual identity. I was a Jew when I woke up every day, chanting, "*Adon Olam, Master of the Universe, creator of all,*" and I was a Jew before falling asleep every night, reciting quietly, "*Hear, O Israel, Adonai is our God, He is one.*" And I was a Jew during the day, every day, especially when a patient's condition turned for the worse, and my lips moved as if on their own, "*Heal us, God, and we shall recover, save us, and we shall be saved, because You are the king of healers, compassionate and loving.*" And my little prayers helped to clear my mind and sharpen my eyes and steady my hands as I tightened a loose suture or singed a stubborn bleed. For over two decades I had spoken to God as a Jew, and He had listened to me as a Jew. But now, standing in a corridor at the Pillars of Joy, I was told to pretend that I wasn't a Jew at all, that my embrace of this purest form of worship and my direct and honest relationship with the God of Abraham must be broken off. Rabbi Mintzberg had decided that I was a fake, and if I refused to acquiesce, my daughter's happiest day would turn into her saddest night.

"Here!" I removed the yarmulke from my head. "What choice do I have?"

"There's more." Aaron hesitated.

"Go ahead." I mulled the yarmulke, my thumb rubbing the golden embroidery, DEBRA & MORDECHAI'S WEDDING.

"No physical contact. In other words, you may not shake hands with any relatives or guests unless you first inform them that you are a gentile so they know to wash their hands afterwards."

"Do you have a red Sharpie? Just scribble it on my forehead: BEWARE! FILTHY SHAYGETZ!"

"I'll write something on Mintzberg's forehead!" Aaron blew air through his teeth. "Also, you may not touch food or wine or any tableware, dishes, cups, or containers that might come into contact with food or wine."

"I've lost my appetite already. Tell him I agree."

"It's not all." Aaron glanced up at me—he was a head shorter—and I saw tears in his eyes.

"You kept the worst for last?"

He nodded. "You must remain at least nineteen feet away from the bride and groom. You may not come near the chuppah nor participate in any dancing nor speak with Debra or Mordechai for the duration of the wedding. No exceptions."

I coughed to clear the tennis ball that suddenly materialized in my throat. "Why nineteen?"

"It's the numeric value of the Hebrew letters *Gimal, Vav,* and *Yod.*"

Even I, with my limited Hebrew, knew the word: "Goy."

He nodded.

"It's a good thing he didn't go with SHAYGETZ. I'd be swimming in the East River."

Aaron wasn't fooled by my sarcasm. He could tell I was about to break down. "It's an abomination. You don't have to agree."

"Really?" I pointed down the hallway at the crowded foyer, where a group of young women clustered around Debra. Beyond the foyer, the wedding hall was already full with guests. "There's over five hundred people here!"

"Screw these black hats. If Mordechai really loves her, he could walk out of there right now, fly to Arizona with us tomorrow morning, and get married in our synagogue."

For a moment I was able to imagine it actually happening.

"Let me go back in there," Aaron said, "and have a word with Mordechai!"

The idea was tempting, but at that moment the group around Debra squealed in delight at something she said, and I caught a glimpse of my daughter in her white gown. "He won't go against his father and their rabbi," I said. "He's not the type."

"I can try."

"The cards have been dealt. I have to play with what's in my hand."

"It's not a card game."

"You're right. It's not a card game. It's my daughter's one-and-only wedding, and I'll do anything to avoid spoiling it. Tell Rabbi Mintzberg that I agree to comply with his conditions."

Aaron bowed his head. "This is so wrong."

"Tell him I'll turn myself into mere wall decoration, but on one condition: Debra mustn't know about this."

"How could she not know?"

"You'll stand in for me—down the aisle, under the chuppah, the whole thing. And you'll recite the blessing I was supposed to recite as her father."

"Are you crazy?" He was mortified, shaken more than I had ever seen him during our long friendship, during years in the operating room, when deadly crisis often struck. "I can't!"

"Promise me!"

His face twisted as if he was about to weep.

"Dr. Aaron Brutsky!" I grasped the lapels of his tuxedo and shook him. "Get a grip on yourself!"

"You're asking too much. I'm not her father. You are!"

"Only one thing matters tonight. Debra's happiness. Do you understand?"

He nodded.

"For the rest of her life, tonight's memories will stay with her. It has to be perfect! She mustn't notice a thing!"

"But how would she not notice that you're missing? *How?*"

"Lie to her. Tell her I'm sick with a stomach bug, that I have the runs and asked you to stand in for me. And make the others swear to do the same." I pushed him back toward the ketubah room. "*Go!*"

Mordechai's friends formed a crescent of dancing and singing to welcome him out of the ketubah room. He emerged pale and red-eyed. His father and Aaron held his arms, leading him, neither of them smiling. But the groom's friends were unperturbed, their voices strong, the floor shaking under their feet as they danced before him, advancing toward Debra.

I met the glassy gaze of Rabbi Mintzberg and turned away from him. At the opposite side, I found a chair and got on it to watch over the crowd's heads.

The dancing men surrounded the bride's throne. Debra laughed with joy, clapping with the rhythm of their singing.

Mordechai approached her. She looked up at him. He said something. She nodded and smiled. He lowered the veil back over her face.

I exhaled in relief. She only had eyes for him. And the veil not only hid her face from us, but also hid the world from her. She wouldn't notice my absence for a long while.

The dancing men circled Mordechai, his father, and Aaron as the three of them proceeded down the red carpet to the chuppah. The men sang and danced with complete abandonment, as if in ecstasy. The pounding of their black shoes, the loudness of their soaring voices, the tightness of their interwoven arms electrified the hall with elation that was physical, embracing, penetrating, until even I, despite my shock and pain, could not resist it. I was taken in, my heart filled with joy for my daughter and her groom, who were blessed with such devoted friends. By the time Mordechai, his father, and Aaron reached the chuppah, I had been clapping so hard that my palms burned.

The music changed from joyous to melancholy. Rebecca and Mordechai's mother, holding candles, walked Debra along the lacey partition that corralled the women on the right side of the hall. The procession reached the chuppah, where Debra and the two mothers began to circle Mordechai, who rocked back and forth, eyes shut devoutly as he murmured more verses. The sad song repeated itself, the Hebrew words too garbled for me to comprehend, while my veiled daughter was led blindly around her groom seven times.

By now the chuppah was surrounded with tiers of spectators, leaving me with only the audio part of my daughter's marriage ceremony. Rabbi Mintzberg's voice sounded from the loudspeakers as he made the initial blessing. Mordechai recited his lines, slipped the ring on, and stomped on a glass cup, winning applause as if for an act of great courage. Then a series of dignitaries, starting with Aaron and Cantor Bentov, were honored with the recital of more blessings.

The couple left the chuppah, and the men's singing reignited. They formed several lines, their arms on each other shoulders, facing Debra and Mordechai, and danced before them while moving backwards across the hall, back to the foyer, and down to the ketubah room, where the newlyweds would spend a little time alone with food and drink and, I assume, smooching to make up for a lost week. Soon they would reemerge, and the real party would begin, the men forming tight circles, dancing on the left side of the partition, and the women doing the same on the right.

But I belonged in neither side.

I stepped down from the chair and found myself surrounded by men wearing beards and black yarmulkes or hats, none of them familiar. I could no longer stomach the prospect of watching strangers rejoice at my expense while I was shunned. I felt lightheaded and feeble. It was as if all the air had been sucked out of the crowded hall and I was going to suffocate, me alone among the hundreds of celebrating strangers.

A moment later, I was across the foyer, pushing through the two sets of double doors, stumbling down the marble steps. My fingers unbuttoned the tuxedo and pulled it open to the icy breeze. I inhaled deeply, and again, teetering on the verge of collapse.

The sidewalk was still busy with pedestrians. Behind me, the tall, bright windows of Pillars of Joy muted the sounds of music and singing. A yellow cab swerved out of traffic and screeched to a halt by the curb.

As I was getting in, I heard a yell. "Rusty?"

I turned.

Rebecca stood among the white columns under the lit-up menorah, her arms stretched sideways in a gesture that said, "Where are you going?"

Aaron emerged from behind her and spoke urgently, pointing at me, rubbing his stomach.

I blew a kiss and slammed the door. "Take me to the Muse Hotel. Midtown Manhattan."

The cabby hit the gas.

A moment later, my Blackberry rang. I ignored it.

As we were crossing the Brooklyn Bridge into Manhattan, Bing Crosby sang "Silver Bells" on the radio. When he reached "*Children laughing, people passing, meeting smile after smile,*" I pressed my forehead to the frosted window and, for the first time since my mother had died, burst out crying.

———

Part Three
Monday, December 21

Chestnuts Roasting on an Open Fire

Rebecca returned to the Muse long after midnight. I was in bed, covered up, facing away from the door, feigning sleep. She didn't turn on the lights, but came around the bed to check on me. I felt her hand rest lightly on my forehead, then her lips, barely touching.

I opened my eyes, but she had already turned away, which was just as well. Tonight my wife deserved to be happy, and I didn't trust myself to speak with her casually as if nothing had happened to me at Pillars of Joy but an upset stomach.

She took a long time in the bathroom, humming a klezmer tune. I felt her slip into bed behind me, inching closer, her warm breath on my neck. Her arm threaded between the blanket and my stomach, caressing it gently. Aaron must have lied well about the reason for my departure.

Shortly after sunrise, I tiptoed out of our room. Rebecca hadn't woken up yet, but I knew my Blackberry would ring as soon as she did, so I turned it off.

In the elevator, I quietly chanted *Adon Olam*, my favorite morning prayer: "*Master of the Universe, who ruled before any creature was created. He is one, and there's no second, no one comparable or akin to Him. In His hand I deposit my soul, when asleep and when awake. God protects me, I fear none.*"

The revolving lobby doors propelled me onto Forty-sixth Street. I walked east across town, huddled in my coat and wool cap. Manhattan was waking up, and delivery trucks grunted as they vied for curb space while plodding vehicles with spinning brushes threw off chunks of blackened ice and refuse. The noise and frost didn't bother me. The mental pain had numbed all my senses.

Was this how my patients felt, waking up to find their cracked ribcages stapled back together with stainless steel rings? No. My patients had pain, but they always reported feeling better after the operation, as if a heavy weight had been lifted from their chests when the blocked arteries were replaced with clear ones, allowing oxygen to nourish starved heart muscles. My pain was different. It was a deep, all consuming, the-world-is-coming-to-an-end kind of pain.

I descended the escalators into Grand Central Station and boarded the first Hudson-Line train going north. Sitting by the window on the left, I watched the river flow by, as wide and as blue as it had been during my childhood. We passed under the Tappan Zee Bridge and stopped at the Tarrytown station. I was the only passenger to disembark. The opposite platform was filled with Monday morning commuters waiting for the next train into Manhattan.

Outside the station, a taxi dropped off a passenger, and I got in. The driver, a bearded man wearing a turban, drove slowly up the steep road and turned right on Main Street, joining slow traffic headed south. I paid him and walked the rest of the way.

It had been many years since I last visited my hometown, and most of the ma-and-pa stores were gone, replaced by familiar chains—Kinko's, Great Clips, Subway Sandwich, Allstate Insurance, Pizza Hut—a generic set of signs that made me stop and look around. I was momentarily disoriented. Had I taken the wrong train and reached a different town?

The sight of our church reassured me that I was at the right place. It had not changed much in my long absence. I stood for a moment, gazing at the squat building with the fake bell tower on top, which seemed like a glued-on afterthought. But the interior, I knew, was genuine and homey, filled with warmth every Sunday morning, voices rising in hymns, familiar faces and kind smiles, the hearth glowing with burning wood. In my memories, it had been a cozy and comforting place for a boy growing up at the outer fringe of poverty.

I followed the cracked-concrete path around the chapel. The cemetery in the back was muddy, patches of snow crusted with brownish ice.

Mom was still there, lying under a block of granite. "It'll stay clean, better than concrete," she had told me as part of an impromptu set of interment instructions a year before her death, which had seemed odd considering she wasn't even fifty, younger than my current age. "There will be enough money in my savings account," she had added, ignoring my protests that she was too young to plan a gravesite. "And put both names on it. Your father would appreciate a proper grave."

I pulled off my gloves and touched the line: MaryAnn and Joachim Dinwall

Would my father appreciate this grave, which no one ever visited? I didn't know. He had shipped off when Mom was pregnant and died when I was three months old, buried at sea, sort of, his Swift Boat blown to pieces on an estuary of the Mekong River. According to his mates, my baby photo was in his pocket when the rocket hit his boat.

I put a pebble on the stone as was the Jewish custom. "You were right, Mom," I said. "In the end, it didn't work out so well."

Back then, her response to the news of my engagement to Rebecca had been a long pause followed by one of her off-the-cuff metaphors: "A cat with a cat, a dog with a dog, a duck with a duck. Only a turkey tries to mate with a swan in hopes of flying south for the winter."

Mom's heavily mixed metaphor had not originated in anti-Semitism. She cleaned Jewish homes in Scarsdale as willingly as she labored in the white-shoe mansions of the Protestant bankers in Irvington. But she wasn't deaf to her employers' kitchen table conversations, to their prejudices, bigotries, and clannish attitudes.

"We're not birds," I had responded. "I'm in love with Rebecca, and she's in love with me. Isn't love more important than how or whom we worship?"

Mom's response was practical, as always. "I'll ask Jesus Christ to watch over you and bless your marriage, even though you don't attend His church."

When I later returned to my dorm at Columbia and opened the suitcase of laundered, folded clothing, I found her dog-eared book of hymns lying on top. The dedication, in her block letters, said only: IN CASE YOU EVER NEED IT. LOVE, MOM.

My fingers lost sensation on the cold granite. I pulled the gloves back on. "I'm hurting as hell," I said. "And angry."

I imagined her hand on my cheek, her palm clammy after a day's work.

"What am I going to do?"

There was no answer.

I blew my frosted nose into a tissue and stuffed it in my pocket. Why did I come here? To seek answers from a tombstone? To find a sympathetic ear under six feet of granite and soil? To pour my heart out and feel better? If so, it hadn't worked. There was no noticeable relief in the hollow wound that had been throbbing inside my chest since I had mounted the chair at the Pillars of Joy and watched my daughter's marriage ceremony proceed without me. If anything, I felt even worse now, having realized that my dead mother was the only person with whom I could unreservedly share my hurt.

On my way out, I stopped to put a dollar in the box. Soft music drew my attention. A nativity scene, very basic, almost primitive, except for the loudspeaker under the manger, a thin cord running from it toward the church. Nat King Cole was singing "Chestnuts Roasting on an Open Fire," and I suddenly realized it was the physical equivalent of my mental pain—my nuts roasting on an open fire! This crude image, which came out of nowhere into my mind's eye, knocked me out of my melancholy. I laughed out loud and said, "It's a bloody nightmare!"

I bent my head to enter the makeshift tent. Inside, baby Jesus was a gold-painted doll of indeterminable gender. Mary had black, braided hair and red lips. And Joseph stood over them, looking anxious. The wise men's beards had caught strands of hay, which a recent wind must have picked up.

A movement drew my attention, and I noticed a woolly sheep and a scrawny goat in a fenced enclosure beside the tent. A hand-written sign was attached to the kiddy gate: PLEASE KEEP GATE CLOSED. MERRY CHRISTMAS!

I collected a fistful of hay and held it out, but neither the sheep nor the goat came forward. I shook my hand, making it rustle. "Come on," I said, "have some."

They looked at me blankly, shifting about, staying put.

"What's wrong?" I tossed the hay toward them. "You won't take food from a Jew?"

I took their silence as admission while Cole wondered *"If reindeer really know how to fly…"*

"Then you better cover your ears." I pointed to the loudspeaker under the manger. "Who do you think wrote "Chestnuts roasting?" A couple of New York Jews, that's who!"

The sheep half-turned as if this piece of information offended her, and the goat smacked its wet lips.

"Sorry," I said, backing out of the tent. "It's not you I'm angry with."

As I was leaving, two mothers herded their children down the path from the street, all of them bundled up in coats, scarves, and hats. The boy in the lead, five or six years old, looked up at me with wide eyes. I smiled and said, "Merry Christmas."

Back on the street, I raised my coat collar against the chill. It was a long walk back to the train station, but I needed the physical exertion and the time to think about what had happened last night and what should happen next.

The train heading to New York City was full. Rather than squeeze between two passengers on a bench, I remained standing and watched the river through the large windows. Ten minutes into the ride, I turned on my Blackberry, called the Mount Sinai outpatient center, and asked for Dr. Levinson. He had impressed me as someone who would be back at work on the morning after his son's wedding, and sure enough, a receptionist said he was with a patient. "*Azoi*," I said. "Please tell him Rabbi Mintzberg is holding."

A moment later, Mordechai's dad came on the line. "Hello? Rabbi?"

"Mazal Tov," I said. "It's your shaygetz-in-law."

After a brief silence, he laughed.

I waited.

"I'm so sorry," he finally said. "I hardly slept."

"Guilty conscience?"

He laughed some more. "Master of the Universe! Now I see where Debra got her sense of humor!"

I held on as the train slowed down and a deep voice announced the Greystone Station. "So how did you enjoy the wedding I paid for?"

"Wonderful," he said. "Thank you. It was worth every penny."

Now we laughed together. He must have been under great stress and was relieved that I could joke about what in fact had amounted to a parental disaster.

"Listen," I said, "what happened was unfair and very painful, but I don't want to dwell on it. These kids make a beautiful couple, and we all want them to be happy, even if it means staying out of the way."

"I agree. But you'll come to the Sheva Brachot dinner tonight, yes?"

This was the reason I called him. The traditional dinner, in which the seven blessings would be recited, was to be hosted by the Levinsons at their home. "Debra expects us there," I said, "but if I sit at your table without a yarmulke and warn people to wash their hands after shaking mine, she'll figure out something's up."

He sighed. "Together we could surely find a subtle way to comply with Rabbi Mintzberg's conditions without—"

"Extortionist conditions, you mean?"

Another sigh. "We live by the rules of Halacha. It's not easy for us either."

"I believe Rabbi Akiva would have said that being technically correct yet morally abhorrent is still a sin, even under strict Halacha." I gripped the pole as the train accelerated, pressing the Blackberry to my ear. "For me, the agreement was a one-night stand. I bent over so that the wedding could go forward. That's all. As far as I'm concerned, my conversion by a Reform woman rabbi is as valid as a conversion performed by a rabbi wearing the blackest hat and the longest beard. I'm as good a Jew as Rabbi Mintzberg himself. Perhaps even a better Jew!" I paused, realizing that my voice had risen and the passengers had stopped what they were doing to watch me. I turned away and said more quietly, "I didn't mean to yell at you. Sorry."

"Your anger is understandable. But in matters of faith, one man's cherished truth is another man's kidney stone."

I chuckled at the urological metaphor. He was a smart man, who seemed to understand my frustration. And he was correct—when it came to religious beliefs, even an absolute truth was relative. For them, I was a gentile whose participation in rituals was forbidden. Halacha controlled every facet of their lives from birth to burial—how they dressed, what they ate, whom they married, and when they could make love. How could I expect these people, who pray three times a day, recite a blessing before and after every meal, and wait six hours between eating meat and dairy, to suddenly become flexible and break Halacha rules to avoid hurting my feelings?

"The dinner tonight," I said, "is at your home, and you have every right to insist that whoever enters it must honor Rabbi Mintzberg's conditions. I won't embarrass you in front of your guests, but I cannot abide by these conditions. My wife will attend while I stay at the hotel."

"Let me call the rabbi," Dr. Levinson said. "He'll know what I should do."

I wanted to ask him: Why would an educated and accomplished man like you choose to submit so completely and unquestioningly to a little old rabbi who classified people with the prejudicial criteria of a long-extinct Eastern European shtetl? But instead I only said, "Of course, and please remember to give him my most gentile regards."

As soon as we hung up, my Blackberry rang. The display said: *Muse Hotel.* I pressed the red button, sending Rebecca to voicemail. I wasn't ready to talk to her yet.

Two stops later, Dr. Levinson called back. "I spoke with Rabbi Mintzberg and explained the situation. His response was that he wasn't feeling well and therefore won't be able to attend."

"How's that helping us?"

"Consent through silence. It's a Talmudic way to acquiesce without giving explicit support."

"You mean, passive-aggressive?" I held on as the train doors closed. "Don't you need a rabbi to lead the seven blessings?"

"Not necessarily, but in fact Rabbi Mintzberg suggested that we invite Rabbi Doctor Yosef Schlumacher. He is a graduate of Columbia University, like you, though his doctorate is in psychology."

I was surprised he knew my alma mater. "Is he going to ask me to sit in the corner and write *'I am a shaygetz'* two hundred times?"

Dr. Levinson chuckled. "Nothing of the kind. Schlumacher is a brilliant scholar with much experience in the outside world. I spoke with him briefly. He accepted, of course, and reminded me that his book on *Shalom Bayit, Peace in the Home,* contains a whole chapter on how parents should not challenge the fragility of their kids' young marriage with their own old problems."

"So, no conditions?"

"None." He hesitated. "The only thing that I ask is that you don't hold up an open bottle of wine. You see, it could cause—"

"The wine will become *nesekh,* not kosher for drinking."

"Correct." Dr. Levinson exhaled into the phone. "I really appreciate it, Dr. Dinwall."

"Call me Christian," I said, but the train was already descending underground toward Grand Central, and the line went dead before he indicated whether or not he heard me.

I hoped to find Rebecca alone, but she was having breakfast with Aaron, Miriam, and Judy Levy. The cantor had gone to visit relatives in Yonkers. I tried to sneak in via the lobby, but Rebecca saw me through the glass partition, and I changed direction and entered the restaurant.

"Where have you been?" She hugged me. "I called and called and called!"

"Went to visit my mom's grave."

Her eyes widened. "In Tarrytown?"

I shrugged. "She hasn't moved."

"The jokes are back," Judy said. "He feels better!"

Miriam poured a cup of coffee for me, and I sat down next to Rebecca, who took the cup from my hand. "Not with an upset stomach. You should only drink water until everything clears out."

"Everything is clear," I said, my hands embracing the cup over her hand.

Aaron picked up a menu, his reading glasses at the tip of his nose. "Would you like something to eat, Rusty?"

"Christian." I took a deep breath and exhaled. "From now on, please call me Christian."

Rebecca pulled her hand away, and the coffee cup almost tipped over.

"You too, my love." I turned to her. "Call me Christian. It's my real name, and I want it back."

"Do you have fever?" She put her palm to my forehead. "Maybe it's dysentery."

"I feel fine."

"Rubbish." She took her phone out of her purse. "You need to see a doctor. You're not yourself!"

I took the phone from her hand and put it on the table. "Actually, that's exactly the point. I feel like myself again. Christian Dinwall. That's me. That's my name."

Aaron put down the menu and looked at me over his reading glasses. "What's wrong with Rusty?"

"Rusty has gone down the toilet, flushed away by the old rabbi at Pillars of Joy, remember?"

He whistled. "Here comes trouble."

Standing up, Rebecca took a step back, her chair falling over. "What's going on?"

"Oh, please!" Judy laughed. "He's pulling your leg. Nice try, Rusty!"

"This is not a drill," I said. "Or a joke. You must call me Christian."

Everyone looked at me.

I pointed at Aaron. "Tell them what happened last night."

He started to shake his head, but Miriam glared at him, and he told them in great detail how we sat down to sign the ketubah, how all went well until they saw my name and Rabbi Mintzberg yelled, "President schmesident! He's a shaygetz!" New even to me were the details of Aaron's negotiations with the rabbi and his short-tempered assistant, while Mordechai was praying against the wall and Dr. Levinson was wringing his hands. By the time Aaron reached the part where he stood next to Debra under the chuppah, reciting the lines that I was supposed to recite, Rebecca buried her face in my chest, her tears wetting my shirt. Miriam and Judy used napkins to wipe their eyes, and Aaron finished the story with my departure in the cab and him lying to Rebecca about my supposedly volcanic stomach ailment.

Rebecca looked up at me, her lips quivering. "It's terrible."

I nodded.

"I feel so guilty. You should have told me!"

"And spoil the wedding of the century?"

"I'm your wife!"

"You're also Debra's mom, and last night was her night. Had I told you what was going on, you would have been too upset to hide it from her."

She knew I was right, but still, she looked at Aaron. "How could you?"

He shrugged and pointed at me. "He made me do it."

Miriam gave him a hearty elbow in the ribs.

"What's going on?" Debra was standing at the dining room door, her hair collected under a headdress, Mordechai behind her. She looked from one face to another, finally focusing on me, the only one with dry eyes. "Are you guys having a crying party?"

By her question I deduced that she had just arrived. I stood up. "You didn't hear?"

"Hear what?"

"Terrible news." I held my hands together under my chin. "Elvis Presley is dead."

She rolled her eyes. "You're showing your age, Dad."

"Okay," I said. "It's really about Michael Jackson."

She approached our table. "Mom?"

Before Rebecca could respond, Aaron said, "I was telling them a sad story, some old friend of ours, a family crisis."

"Who?"

"Don't worry about it." I kissed Debra on the forehead and extended my hand to Mordechai. "Not on the morning after your wedding, right?"

Mordechai avoided my eyes. "Good morning, Dr. Dinwall. I hope you're feeling better."

"It'll be a slow recovery." I pulled two chairs from another table. "Regards from your father. We spoke earlier. A most pleasant chat."

He looked at me, uncertain.

"We're all set for tonight," I said. "Rabbi Mintzberg can't make it, so your father invited Schlumper."

"Schlumacher," he corrected me. "Rabbi Doctor Yosef Schlumacher."

"That's the one." I beckoned the waiter. "So how was your first night together?"

"Yeah, tell us!" Aaron rubbed his hands. "We want to know all the details!"

"Leave them alone," Rebecca said.

Having recovered their composure, the three women surrounded the young couple like mother hens, and the conversation turned to last night's extravaganza, how great it was, and who was who among the relatives and friends in attendance.

I stepped aside, Aaron joined me, and we watched them for a few moments.

"You're a good friend," I said.

He patted my shoulder. "*Et tu*, Christian."

Go Tell It On The Mountain

The rewards of private practice, as contrasted with my VA hospital career, were in evidence as soon as we arrived at the Levinsons' front steps. This wasn't the Brooklyn of Mayor Ed Koch, of public housing, rent control, and record-breaking murder rates. It was the Brooklyn version of Westchester County, with grand houses set back from tree-lined streets, expansive lawns accented by designer shrubs, and three-car garages matched with foreign-made SUVs. And an Orthodox synagogue within walking distance.

A maid took our coats and hats, and Mrs. Levinson greeted us with hugs for the women and touch-free greetings for the men. "Please, come in," she said. "My husband and the others are in evening prayer. They'll be back shortly."

While the rest of the group entered, I lingered behind, pretending to inspect the intricate brickwork that formed an arch over the entrance.

"Dr. Dinwall," she said to me, "I hear you're feeling better, thank God."

"It's good to be here." I smiled politely and wondered whether her husband had told her the truth about what had happened. If he had, then she would know that I couldn't be feeling any better, that the wedding expulsion had left me with an injury that felt as real as a broken arm or an infected tooth. And now, back in Brooklyn, standing outside their home, I hesitated. Could this evening end with a repetition of last night, with another humiliation, another stab to the heart? *President schmesident! He's a shaygetz!*

"Mordechai called a few minutes ago." She held the door open, leaving me no choice. "They'll be a little late."

"Kids," I said. "They're still kids."

"May God protect them from the evil eye," she said.

"Amen." Taking a deep breath, I entered the house. Dr. Levinson had made it clear that no conditions were imposed. I had to trust him, if not for me, then for Debra. By showing her an example of my tolerance of the Levinsons' observant lifestyle, of my respect for the Orthodox version of Jewish worship, I would earn the right to expect her and Mordechai to show similar flexibility in Scottsdale. And as Debra's infatuation cooled off and the routine of married life took over, she would recover her Reform ideals of progress and modernity and let go of her temporary adherence to rules meant for the challenges of an ancient world and traditions created by rabbis who had not seen running water, refrigeration, motorized transportation, or a telephone.

The living room was a spacious display of Louis XIV furniture, Persian rugs, and original oils. The opulence was topped by the Bechstein grand piano, occupying its own bay-windowed section, which made my fingers itch with a sudden urge to play. I turned away and passed through a pair of tall wooden doors that led to an even bigger dining room, where a long table reminded me of historic movies depicting the royal feasts of European monarchs. The white tablecloth was laden with soft drinks, wine bottles, and Saran-wrapped dishes of salads and cold appetizers.

Rebecca, Miriam, and Judy marveled at the Rosenthal china, Gorham crystal, and Wallace silverware. Meanwhile, I pulled over Aaron and Cantor Bentov to show them the books lining the built-in shelves, including Hebrew originals, English translations of Talmudic texts, and volumes of philosophy and history. A whole shelf was dedicated to Nachmanides, a thirteenth-century rabbi whose writings covered both Jewish scholarship and medicine.

While browsing Nachmanides, I was assailed by an aroma that nagged me like a voice from the past. It was familiar and pleasurable, yet completely inappropriate. I tried to ignore it, but gave in and approached the wide granite counter that separated the dining room from the kitchen. There, the smell became dominant, threading through my nostrils like a vaporous hook, reeling me in until I leaned on the counter, stuck my head into the kitchen, and sniffed like a dog on a trail of heat.

"What's wrong?" Mrs. Levinson wiped sweat from her forehead and rearranged the bangs of her wig. "You lost something?"

"I know this smell!"

The cook, a voluptuous black woman in a white apron and a chef's hat, was standing over a stovetop, which had ten burners, all of them occupied by pots of various sizes. The pots were colored blood-red, which I guessed was intended to mark them as meat rather than dairy. She pointed a giant red spoon at me. "Is this the Scottish boy?"

"That's him," Mrs. Levinson said. "Dr. Dinwall, please meet Jeanie, our food magician."

"Hi, Jeanie." I licked my lips, swallowed, and went around the counter into the kitchen. "I'm being seduced by an aroma, but it's impossible!"

"Everything is possible." The black cook lifted a cover off a squat pot and revealed its bubbling content. "*Voilà!*"

"I don't believe it!" Bending over the pot, I buried my face in the steam and breathed through my nose until my lungs were filled to capacity. "Oh, Mama!"

Mrs. Levinson clapped, and everyone came in from the dining room, congregating around me.

The plump cook asked, "What do you call this, boy?"

My hand pressed against my heart. "Scottish Pork Apricot à la Crème. But how did you know?"

Rebecca raised her hand. "I told them."

I looked at Mrs. Levinson, and she waved a dismissive hand. "No big deal. We wanted to make something special for you, since you missed most of the fun yesterday. Before we went home last night, your wife told me this was your favorite childhood dish, but you haven't had it since—"

"I became a Jew?"

She nodded. "This is only a token, to show how grateful we are for the wonderful wedding and the beautiful daughter you gave us."

"You're welcome." Again I smelled my fill, shaking my head in amazement. "But how did you make it?" I looked around the kitchen, which was divided in half for dairy and meat, all color coded blue and red. "I don't understand."

"The recipe," Mrs. Levinson said, "was hard to find, even with Google."

Sniffing again, I shook my head. "Incredible!"

"Aha," Jeanie hollered, "I got it right, didn't I?"

"You did." I wiped my lips, afraid I'd start drooling. "But—"

"Don't worry, boy." She stirred the pot with the red spoon. "It's perfectly kosher."

"*Glatt* kosher," Mrs. Levinson declared. "Even Rabbi Mintzberg would eat it."

"No, he wouldn't!" I made like I was protecting the pot. "I'm going to gobble it all up. But still, tell me, how?"

"Goat meat, from this part." Jeanie pounded on her bulging buttocks. "Almost like pork, same texture. I sliced it thin and fried it in schmaltz."

"Ooh!" Judy twisted her face. "You used chicken fat?"

"Beef. Real schmaltz. Thick, lots of flavor, best for frying, much better than oil. I fried the meat with onion, added non-dairy butter, mushrooms, bay leaves, and red wine." The cook leaned closer to me and said conspiratorially, "and chopped-up fake bacon, you know?"

"Here, come see the packaging." Mrs. Levinson led Rebecca, Judy, and Miriam to a huge refrigerator. "They make it from tofu, but it tastes and smells just like bacon."

"Then you let it simmer," I said, remembering my role as my mother's helper, "and when the meat is tender, you add canned apricot, orange peel, and—"

"Double cream!" Mrs. Levinson held up an empty jar.

"They make non-dairy cream?" Rebecca took the jar and looked at it. "I've never thought of trying to make it for him. I mean, it's a pork dish, right?"

"Not anymore," Mrs. Levinson said.

"Here, boy." Jeanie spooned up a bit and reached up to bring it to my mouth. "You be the judge."

My tongue cradled the juicy morsel. The initial tang spread inside my mouth, down my palate, and radiated throughout my whole body. The taste was as genuine as the smell. I leaned down and kissed her shining black cheek. "You really are a magician, Jeanie."

"Oh, Lord," the cook laughed, "boy's in love!"

Unable to resist, I gripped her hand with the spoon and scooped up some more, making sure to catch bits of apricot and onion with the thin strip of pork-like goat. I chewed slowly, savoring it, letting the food linger until the juices soaked my taste buds and saturated my brain's gustatory center.

They all looked at me, but I didn't mind. I closed my eyes and thought of those rare occasions when my mother had splurged on fresh meat and spent the night in the kitchen producing her magical Pork Apricot à la Crème, which we carried in a toweled pot to relatives' homes on Easter, Christmas, or a funeral wake.

Dr. Levinson returned from the synagogue with a small group of men in black suits and black hats. They remained close to each other, talking in hushed voices. None of them brought wives or daughters, and the only female presence beside our little group was Mordechai's mother and his two younger sisters.

At the head of the long dining table, Dr. Levinson knocked on his wineglass with a knife. "I want to welcome everyone to our home, especially the important guests from Arizona." He gestured at us. "First and foremost, my new in-laws, Rebecca and Dr. Dinwall, the best cardio thoracic surgeon in Phoenix."

"That would be him." I pointed at Aaron.

"Okay," Dr. Levinson conceded, "we have the two best heart surgeons in the southwestern United States, Dr. Dinwall and Dr. Brutsky!"

Aaron bowed and his yarmulke fell off.

"Dr. Brutsky's wife," Mordechai's father stumbled, having forgotten her name.

"Miriam," she said while picking up Aaron's yarmulke and pressing it down on his bald head. "I'm his better half."

"More than half," Aaron said, and made like he was dodging a punch.

"And I'm Judy Levy," our forthright friend said, not waiting to see if Dr. Levinson remembered her name. "And since this is a post-wedding Sheva Brachot, I should mention my own search for an eligible man with a keen interest in desert life and the arts. My two grown kids are financially independent, and I love to cook. Kosher optional!"

Everyone clapped, and Cantor Bentov started singing "*Here comes the bride,*" which broke whatever ice was still in the room.

I was seated next to Rabbi Doctor Yosef Schlumacher, who had arrived later than the others and seemed more like a lawyer or a banker than a rabbi—clean shaven, full head of salt-and-pepper hair, a Brooks Brothers suit over a blue shirt and a cherry tie. He placed his Blackberry by his fork and extended his hand, which had the long fingers of a pianist. "It's an honor to meet you, Dr. Dinwall."

"Please," I said, "call me Christian."

"And you can call me Joe." He didn't let go of my hand. "You know, in my opinion, being a physician is second only to Hashem, because when God wants to spare a sick man's life, who does He rely on to do the actual saving?"

Before I had a chance to respond to this lofty compliment, Debra and Mordechai arrived from the city, and the room erupted with singing, "Mazal Tov and Siman Tov," which literally meant "*Good luck and a good omen,*" but with the clapping and the repetition attained an inspiring effect much greater than the simple words themselves. The men got up and began to advance around the table in slow, step-after-step dance. Debra and Mordechai sat at the head of the table, smiling. When the trotting dance brought me near her, I bent over Debra and kissed the red wool cap she was wearing. She looked up and gave me a beautiful smile.

We washed our hands, and after the blessing over the bread, the meal commenced. The maid and the cook went back and forth to the kitchen, clearing plates and delivering loaded dishes under the supervision of Mrs. Levinson, who stayed on her feet and pointed here and there with her finger like a conductor of a gastronomical orchestra.

My new friend Joe was charming. We nibbled at the appetizers while discussing mental injuries that continued to inflict veterans even decades after combat. He surprised me with his up-to-date knowledge of the VA system's shortcomings in mental healthcare. When the main dishes arrived, he was eager to taste my Pork Apricot à la Crème, spooning it off my plate with easy familiarity. He had never eaten pork and was curious to know whether the taste was authentic, which I assured him it was.

When Mrs. Levinson coordinated the delivery of various pies and sweets on silver trays, accompanied by coffee and tea, Joe and I were embroiled in an argument over the heart-brain division of human physicality and emotionality. He cited a recent study that had identified distinct chemicals released from the heart muscle of mice when confronted with danger or when shown a piece of cheese, and a third chemical that appeared in the blood exiting the heart in conjunction with sexual arousal of the male mice.

"There's no question," I argued, "that the heart reacts chemically to various stimulations, but the source of emotions is not in the heart. The chemicals are produced in response to the messages from the brain, which is the only intelligent organ we have that can feel and think. The heart is purely a physical machine, and all its reactions are directed by the brain through the nerves by electrical signals."

"Is that so?" He pointed at Debra, who was whispering something in Mordechai's ear. "When you look at her, don't you feel a distinct reaction in your heart?"

I looked at my daughter and felt a tightening in my chest. She was lovely and happy and in love. My eyes moistened. "Following this logic," I argued, "tear ducts are centers of emotional activity as well."

"Maybe they are."

"But it's the brain that tells us to cry, to break into a run, to hide, or to eat. Those particular reactions are localized to each organ."

"Isn't our brain's activity also a series of chemical and electrical reactions? How is it different from the reactions that happen in other parts of the body? Is there really a difference between the brain and the heart or the tear ducts?"

I didn't have an answer to that.

"I believe our body experiences emotions in every organ and every limb. Because the heart is the main pump, it's a center of emotional response, just like the brain."

"What about heart transplants?" I looked at him.

"What about them?"

"Based on your theory, a person's emotional disposition would change to that of the donor."

"On the contrary." Schlumacher sipped his coffee. "Our emotions are a web of chemical actions and reactions that are expressed physically in every part of our bodies, but what dictates them? Are emotions driven by the physical workings and chemical components of our human machine, or does our emotional response to any particular event come from something completely—"

"Spiritual?"

He shrugged. "As a psychologist, I'd say that our emotional responses are determined by the complex set of traits, created by a process of preconditioning that formed our individual mental engine over a lifetime of experiences, together with our genetic heritage. But as a rabbi, I'd call it something else: a soul."

I wanted to counter with the theoretical possibility of a brain implant, which is not yet possible, but with time and scientific progress would one day become a reality. We already know that a stroke or a brain injury causes personality changes. Wouldn't a new brain cause a complete change of the individual's soul?

Dr. Levinson stood and announced, "Let us now begin with the blessings!"

We filled our glasses with sweet red wine—mine was poured by Schlumacher—and Dr. Levinson recited the first of the seven blessings. "*Boreh pri hagafen…Blessed be He, creator of the fruit of the vines.*"

Three of the black-garbed men were honored with reciting the next blessings, and Schlumacher recited the fifth, which expressed gratitude to God for rejoicing a barren woman with sons, a reference to the matriarch Sarah, who was blessed with a son when she was over a hundred years old.

I realized that Dr. Levinson was looking at me. I gestured at Aaron, and he did an excellent job reciting the next blessing in Hebrew, which everyone repeated in singing, "*May God rejoice this beloved pair as You once rejoiced the first creations who lived in Eden; blessed be Adonai, who rejoices bride and groom.*"

The seventh blessing went to Cantor Bentov, who filled the room with his sonorous voice, slowly building up pace with this long blessing until he had everyone on their feet, dancing and singing, "*Soon, our God, Adonai, may it be heard in the cities of Judea and the outskirts of Jerusalem, sounds of joy and voices of happiness!*"

The women stood aside, clapping rhythmically, and the young couple remained seated at the head of the table while we danced around in a lumbering, step-after-step pace. I caught Debra's eye, and we blew kisses to each other. She was still wearing the wool cap, similar to the one worn by Rebecca out of respect for the other women, who followed the strict Orthodox rule that a woman's hair is like her private parts. Surely Debra wasn't going to keep her hair covered always, was she? I wanted to ask Rebecca if she knew, but my wife was standing with the other women.

Debra prodded Mordechai to get up and join the procession. He squeezed between me and Dr. Levinson, and we sang the Hebrew words while proceeding slowly around the long table. And so, finally, the two fathers flanked the groom. We were not walking him down the aisle to the chuppah, a joy I would never be allowed to experience, but at least we locked arms in celebration of their union.

After the Orthodox men departed, the rest of us migrated to the living room, where Dr. Levinson poured kosher whiskey for everyone and asked me to give a toast.

I thanked our hosts and turned to address Debra and Mordechai directly. "Tonight is very special," I said. "It is the conclusion of your first day as a married couple. Now that I've met Mrs. and Dr. Levinson, I know that Mordechai comes from a solid and happy home that has provided him with a good example. And you, Debra?"

My daughter gave me a little wave with her hand, which returned to her lap. I wondered why she wasn't holding Mordechai's hand. Telling by the way they looked at each other, intimacy wasn't a problem. Did Halacha forbid husband and wife from holding hands in public?

I dismissed the issue from my mind and continued, "Your mother and I are leaving for Arizona tomorrow to prepare for the Sheva Brachot dinner party we're throwing on Thursday. And we feel like partying, because we have a sense of accomplishment. When it comes to marriage, ours has been the one you've experienced closely throughout your childhood and adolescence. Now, all grown up, you're launching your own marriage, and we hope that our example has prepared you for success."

"It's been a wonderful example," Debra said, "except for your long working hours."

Everyone laughed, and I said, "When it's time for Mordechai to choose his specialty, make sure he goes into dermatology."

He shook his head and made a slicing motion with his hand.

"What," I asked, "you want to be a *mohel?*"

This earned a collective "*Oy!*"

"Joking aside," I continued, "we are each different and unique. Hashem made us in His image, but threw in enough variations to make it interesting and challenging. For example, He made me a Christian and my wife Jewish. He made me an only child of a hard-scrubbing young widow, Rebecca an only daughter of Holocaust survivors. Before we met, Hashem had taken each of us through an individual path that shaped and reshaped us distinctively. Until we met and fell in love, and even afterwards, we had each grown through different experiences, scarred by different hurts, and moved by different memories. And sometimes, when conflicts erupt, we jump onto our own high horse or climb atop our own mountain. We announce the truth as we see it and refuse to come down from our perch of righteousness until love brings us down to the lush valley of compromise and growth. And what do you call this amorphous mess that dictates our peaks and valleys? Is it our character? Our personality? Our soul?"

Rabbi Doctor Schlumacher smiled at me.

"Whatever it's called, it sometimes leads us to conflict with those we love." I raised my glass at Debra and Mordechai. "Those differences attract us to each other. But they also have the potential to break us apart."

Rebecca came over and stood next to me.

"Therefore," I said, "I want to wish you not only love, but also the strength to continue to love even when embroiled in conflict or when facing a crisis. I wish you spirited arguments and passionate reconciliations, strength in your individual beliefs, and the ability to find common grounds and, more than anything, mutual respect while you build together the foundations of a true and equal partnership. As we recited in the seventh blessing today, may you enjoy all four: love, camaraderie, peace, and friendship."

We drank to that, and Dr. Levinson insisted that I try the Bechstein. I accompanied Cantor Bentov on the piano while he sang *"Hineh mah tov u'mah naim – How good and pleasant, sitting together as brothers..."*

When the song ended, Rabbi Doctor Schlumacher sat beside me on the bench. Rather than a Jewish melody, he began to play Wagner's *Ride of the Valkyries*. He did it from memory, and I was shocked, not only because it wasn't written for a piano, presenting the player with a complicated challenge of technique and adaptation, but also because Wagner's Nazi sympathies had made the composer objectionable to Jewish audiences. We looked at each other, and Schlumacher grinned while playing masterfully. I wondered why he chose to play this music, which had inspired *Apocalypse Now*, during a celebration for the newlyweds. Considering that Schlumacher came alone tonight, perhaps his own marriage was apocalyptic?

But the music was beautiful, and its use in popular culture had made it familiar to everyone in the room. When the piece was over and the clapping subsided, my fingers began playing *The Flying Dutchman*. The hands beside mine joined in, and we played Wagner together to a room full of mesmerized Jews in Brooklyn. Go figure!

It was 1 a.m. when we said our good-byes in the foyer. Schlumacher shook my hand and then, as if overcome with emotions, hugged me tightly. "Christian," he said, "you're a very special person. I'm blessed to have met you!"

"I feel the same, Joe."

"We must complete our heart-versus-mind discussion." He glanced at his watch. "I know it's late, but how about meeting for an early breakfast? I can come to the Muse Hotel at, let's say, seven-thirty a.m.?"

Our flight wasn't leaving until mid-morning, so I accepted.

Dr. Levinson, who was shaking hands with Cantor Bentov nearby, heard the exchange and offered to join us.

"Of course," I said. "Why not?"

We left for Manhattan in a limousine arranged by the Levinsons. Debra and Mordechai stayed over in Brooklyn.

Part Four
Tuesday, December 22

Frosty the Snowman

Rebecca pulled open the window curtains, letting in the brightness of a sunny morning. I glanced at my watch. It was ten past seven. "Hurry up," she said, "you'll be late for breakfast."

"I don't need twenty minutes to get ready." I pulled her back into bed.

"Hey!"

"Come on." I held her. "It'll be quick."

She rolled away and threw a pillow at me.

"*Pleeeeeze!*"

Rebecca giggled, looking very young. "Those two rabbis are going to smell it on you."

"What two rabbis?" I dropped my feet to the floor, sitting on the side of the bed. "At most, they add up to half a rabbi plus a doctor and a half."

"Yes, *Doctor* Dinwall." She came over and sat in my lap, her arm bent around my neck. "And you are my one and a half world, you know?" She kissed me on the ear.

"Does that mean—"

"Shower. Dress. Eat." She jumped off my lap.

"And love? What about love?"

She pushed me into the bathroom.

The showerhead was one of those UFOs the size of a dinner plate, with a million tiny nozzles that created an illusion of standing naked in hot rain. I hummed Wagner's *The Flying Dutchman* while soaping my body with a hand towel.

Rebecca was brushing her teeth at the sink. She said, "You're jolly this morning."

"After the nightmare at the Pillars of Joy, last night's dinner was a fairytale."

"You liked the dancing around the table?"

"It was a whirlwind of ecstasy." I stomped my feet on the bottom of the shower, one thump after the other, imitating the slow procession of the men around the dining table.

She gurgled and spat. "Was that pork stew good?"

"It was the real thing. Incredible, considering there wasn't a shred of swine in it."

Her face appeared beside the shower curtain. "Did it make you feel special?" She had a naughty smile on, but I knew what she was asking.

"It was a touching gesture," I said. "But the pain's still there. At least I'm not as worried about Debra as I was when I left Pillars of Joy, convinced that she had just married into a bunch of primitive, heartless fanatics whose fundamental religion was nothing like ours."

She made a face. "That's a bit harsh."

"I was angry, and I feared for her, becoming part of a family whose obedience to Rabbi Mintzberg is absolute, no matter the cost and pain to others. He's an old fanatic, like the Eastern European rabbis who rejected Zionism and excommunicated anyone who suggested modern changes."

"But you changed your mind, right?"

"My phone conversation with Dr. Levinson yesterday morning showed me that he wasn't a fanatic like Rabbi Mintzberg. He shared my sense of humor and was straightforward in expressing regret about what had happened, implying that he was in the same boat as me, that he had no choice but to comply with those conditions or cancel the wedding. He practically disinvited Rabbi Mintzberg so I could attend the Sheva Brachot dinner and brought in Schlumacher, who is Orthodox yet modern, someone I could speak with as a contemporary, hold a normal conversation with. He accepted me the way I am, was open to my different point of view, and was interested enough to ask me to meet for breakfast to finish our discussion."

"Even though you made everyone call you Christian?"

"Maybe because of that. I tested them, and they did the right thing."

Rebecca held out a towel for me. "They're good people."

R abbi Doctor Yosef Schlumacher entered the lobby just as I came out of the elevator. He looked very different than last night, wearing a Yankees cap and a sweat suit that showed a runner's body. He saw me and waved. "Christian!"

"Out for a morning jog?"

"I try," he said cheerfully, "and it hurts!"

"I know what you mean." I gestured at the restaurant, where Aaron and Miriam were already sitting at our regular table. "Shall we?"

He glanced over his shoulder toward the doors to the street. "Actually, Dr. Levinson suggested we eat at Mendy's. It's a kosher deli not far from here."

"Of course." I should have thought of it myself. An Orthodox rabbi could not eat at a non-kosher hotel restaurant. "Let's go!"

Despite the early sun, the wind was frosty. We kept a healthy pace down to the traffic light at Sixth Avenue and continued up to Forty-eighth Street, which we crossed in the last moment before the light changed.

An NYPD squad car was parked in front of Mendy's Kosher Delicatessen. Two officers leaned against the car, chewing on bagels in wax paper, their plastic coffee cups resting on the hood.

We entered the deli, passing through the powerful downdraft of hot air from a vent over the door. I was out of breath, but not Schlumacher, who rubbed his hands with a big smile and declared, "I'm famished!"

Mordechai's dad sat at a corner table, engaged in a phone conversation, sipping coffee. We ordered at the counter and carried our cups and bagels to his table just as he was finishing the call in Yiddish. "*Zy gezunt,*" he said, which I knew meant something like "*All the best.*"

We shook hands, and I said, "Thanks again for last night."

"Our pleasure. It's the least we could do."

Schlumacher recited a blessing, and we ate.

"It's a crazy week," Dr. Levinson said. "The staff disappears in the middle of the day to do their Christmas shopping, and the patients are upset because they're missing the best deals. And when the nurses screw up because they're distracted, God forbid you express irritation and spoil their," he made the sign for quotation marks, "*holiday spirit.*"

"It's incredible," Schlumacher said, "how they have turned this historically solemn holiday into a meaningless frenzy of consumerism and silly jingles."

"And hard work for me," Dr. Levinson said. "I'll be working nonstop at the hospital to cover for my gentile colleagues from Christmas Eve to Monday morning. That's four days!"

"I usually do the same," I said, "but this year I'm off so we can spend time with Debra and Mordechai. We really look forward to getting to know your son and introducing him to our community. Rebecca and I also come from starkly different backgrounds. Her parents were strictly observant Jews, as you know, and I had no clue about Judaism. But we compromised and have built a wonderful life together."

He nodded but didn't say anything.

"This visit," I continued, "should help Mordechai understand how Debra grew up, how she formed her views and ideas. We're very excited about it!"

Dr. Levinson looked at Schlumacher, who smiled and said, "Knowledge and understanding are essential, if one is to make wise choices in life."

"And compromises," I said, "which are also essential." My Blackberry rang and I held it up to see the display. *Aaron Brutsky.* I answered.

"I saw you leave the hotel," he said without preamble. "Are you still with that psycho-rabbi?"

I laughed. "Good morning to you too, Aaron. We're at Mendy's. It's a little kosher place."

"I know it," he said. "Do you need me to come over?"

"Need you?"

Sitting across from me, Dr. Levinson crumpled his empty coffee cup.

"To give you reinforcement," Aaron said. "I Googled your new friend. Rabbi Yosef Schlumacher, Ph.D."

"And?"

Papers rustled on Aaron's end of the line. "You want to hear the titles of his recent books? One is: *Torn Apart – The Troubled Psychology of Children of Interfaith Marriages.* Another is: *Half-Baked Solutions – The Ticking Bomb of Non-Orthodox Conversions from Religious, Psychological, and Marital Perspectives.* And the most recent, co-authored with Rabbi Mintzberg: *Original Sin Exonerated – Why Orthodox Conversions Heal the Soul and Ensure Passage to Heaven.* His Ph.D. dissertation, later published by the *Journal of Psychology and Faith,* was titled: *Reform Judaism as a Stepping Stone to Heretical Atheism and Successive Generational Assimilation.*"

I pressed the phone to my ear. "Anything else?"

"There's a plan behind his efforts to ingratiate himself to you."

"Go ahead."

"Schlumacher is the mental health and counseling coordinator for the Rabbinical Board of Halachic Conversions, as well as chair of the Conversion Support Section of the Association of Orthodox Synagogues of America."

I thumbed the red button and put down my Blackberry.

"Christian," Schlumacher said, resting his hand on my forearm, "this isn't some kind of an ambush. You're facing a tough decision, and we're here to assist you in every way we can. There's no harm in talking, right?"

It was hard not to be impressed with his cool nerves. He guessed why Aaron had called, saw my expression, and hit the nail on the head.

Dr. Levinson caught on quickly. "We only want what's best for Debra and Mordechai. You want the same, don't you?"

My urge to stand up and leave was hampered by a weakness that came from feeling physically sick. I'd been duped! The charming phone call yesterday morning, the withdrawal of the ancient Rabbi Mintzberg in favor of Jogging Joe Schlumacher, the faux pork dish of my childhood, and even Wagner on the Bechstein! All of their gestures had not been signs of respect and acceptance but a coordinated attack, a honey trap, intended to soften me up and lure me into an Orthodox conversion, into becoming a *real* Jew.

"The Spanish Inquisition," Schlumacher said, "hunted down devout Catholics whose Jewish parents or grandparents had converted to Christianity."

I watched him speak, feeling numb.

"They arrested those decent people and tortured them into confessing that their Catholic faith wasn't sincere, that they secretly practiced Jewish rituals. And when a confession wasn't forthcoming, the inquisitors continued to stretch them on the wheel, pull out their fingernails, burn their genitalia, and comb their flesh with iron rakes." He shrugged. "No one held up forever. Every single victim eventually told his or her inquisitors what they wanted to hear. Physical pain impacts the mind like a pressure build-up inside a balloon. Eventually, it pops."

Exhaling, I said, "And your point?"

"The inquisitors knew that their victims' faith was honest and sincere, that many of those men and women wanted to be good Catholics. Everyone throughout the Catholic Church hierarchy knew that confessions generated by torture had no value or veracity. But the pope himself authorized the burnings at the stake—tens of thousands of former Jews and their descendants, decent people who genuinely aspired to be faithful followers of Jesus Christ, were murdered like this over several centuries. Why?"

"Evil hearts," I said.

"I don't think so. Clergymen who spent their days praying and studying would not knowingly commit sin, especially not the sin of torturous murders." Rabbi Doctor Schlumacher adjusted his Yankees cap. "Rather, they believed in decimating the Jews based on the absolutist concept of *limpieza de sangre.*"

"Purity of blood," Dr. Levinson said.

"Just like the Nazis," Schlumacher said, "and the Muslim fundamentalists today, the root of anti-Semitism is planted in the ideology of race, that Jews are a hateful race, physically corrupt. That's why the inquisition killed honest Catholics whose family origins were Jewish. They were cleansing Christianity, just like the Nazis."

I finished my coffee. "What's that got to do with me?"

"Two things. First, your daughter is Jewish by her mother, and therefore your grandchildren will be Jewish, which places them among the people of Torah, but also makes them subject to anti-Semitism. Second, and more important for you to understand, is that Judaism views conversions completely differently than Christianity and its inquisition. We don't share the racist beliefs of popes and imams. Rather, our Torah says that every human being is created in the image of God, disregarding religion, ethnicity, or skin color. And being Jewish is a matter of the soul, not the body."

"So?"

"It's simple," Schlumacher said. "Once you convert properly under Orthodox supervision, no one will ever question your status as a good and complete Jew. Judaism doesn't care about *limpieza de sangre*. Rather, purity of heart and compliance with Halacha is what Torah cares about."

"But I converted to Judaism over two decades ago. My heart is pure."

"We don't question your heart," Dr. Levinson said in a conciliatory tone. "You have good intentions, love for the Torah, and much more. But to truly become a Jew, there's a process, which begins with one's strict observance of the rules of Halacha. You must keep the Sabbath, follow kosher dietary rules, study the scriptures, and so on."

"It's not so complicated," Schumacher said. "I've worked with many converts over the years. Once you embrace a life of Halacha—"

"You want me to become Orthodox?"

They both nodded.

"Are you crazy?"

"Your wife was raised Orthodox," Schlumacher said.

"She grew out of it *obviously*. And we live in Arizona, for God's sake!"

"There are several Orthodox synagogues in the Phoenix area. I'll put you in touch with Rabbi Pinkhas—"

"It's out of the question!" I got up and collected my empty cup and paper plate. "I'm the president of a Reform synagogue. All our friends are Reform Jews. That's who we are! Who *I* am!"

Dr. Levinson stood up. "Don't you care about Debra?"

"She was raised Reform, and I hope she keeps our values of tolerance and acceptance. And if she decides to observe some elements of Halacha, we'll treat her the way we expect to be treated—with the same tolerance and acceptance, which you have pretended to show me while plotting behind my back!"

My new in-law was red in the face. "You really believe that my Mordechai's wife will be able to *tolerate and accept* that her parents eat non-kosher food and violate the Sabbath?"

"We don't violate the Sabbath—the Torah doesn't forbid turning on the lights and driving a car, does it?"

"Not explicitly," he conceded, "but the sages, whose words are God's words, just like Torah itself, forbid driving and cooking on the Sabbath. You do cook during the holy Sabbath, don't you?"

"We do," I said, "because we no longer need to start a fire to cook, which was the reason it was forbidden in the first place."

"You claim to know better than hundreds of generations of rabbis why God forbade cooking on the Sabbath?"

"Gentlemen," Schlumacher said, "let's not argue about theology when your children's future is the real issue."

"That's right," I said. "We raised our daughter not to judge other people's beliefs. We believe that God doesn't care if we drive a car and turn on the lights on the Sabbath, or if we cook meat and dairy together as long as it's not a calf in its mother's milk."

Dr. Levinson made a visible effort to control his voice. "Your daughter has changed. She now believes that God does care, that He does forbid the things that you do in violation of His Torah, that He will punish you for those sins."

"Debra will never stop loving us." I turned to leave.

Schlumacher held on to my arm. "What about your grandchildren?"

"*Our* grandchildren!" Dr. Levinson came around the table and stood with us in the middle of the deli, surrounded by Orthodox businessmen eating breakfast while reading newspapers or checking their e-mails. He didn't seem to mind the lack of privacy. "Think about the next generation! There will be births, circumcision ceremonies, Bar Mitzvahs, weddings. How would you feel to be excluded from all family events? How would your daughter feel? Or are you going to ask others to lie to her again and again?"

I found a chair and dropped into it.

"Christian, please listen." Schlumacher sat next to me and put his arm around my shoulder. "My heart and soul go out to you. I'm here to help you, that's all."

Taking shallow, quick breaths was all I could do.

"You must think long-term," he said. "How can you *not* become a complete Jew?"

Barely able to speak, I said, "But I *am* a complete Jew."

"Not in the eyes of Halacha, not in the eyes of your daughter and son-in-law, and not in the eyes of their future children."

"We're family now." Dr. Levinson crouched by my side, his tone pleading. "Our children are starting a family together. And one day, our grandchildren will ask you tough questions: Grandpa, why do you drive on the Sabbath? Grandpa, why do you eat non-kosher food? Grandpa, are you a shaygetz?"

———

Put One Foot In Front Of The Other

Aaron showed up at Mendy's without a coat or a hat, his cheeks red and his fists clenched. He pulled me up and guided me out the door. Dr. Levinson and Rabbi Doctor Schlumacher tagged along until we reached Sixth Avenue. Aaron looked over his shoulder and said something in Yiddish, and they walked away.

"Not feeling well," I said.

He pressed the crossing button repeatedly. "Can you believe these schmucks?"

"I need to sit down."

"You're fine." The light changed and Aaron pulled me across the avenue. "Let's get back to the hotel."

The sidewalk was full of people, rushing to work. We made slow progress along the shop windows.

Grandpa, are you a shaygetz?

"I'm going to be sick."

"Keep walking." He lifted my arm and rested it on his shoulder, but he was too short for me to lean on him, or I'd fall over. "Inhale. The cold air will do you good."

"They told me—"

"Screw those black hats!"

"But they're right. I've lost Debra." I turned away, bent over, and vomited.

Aaron ran into a store and came back with a fistful of napkins. He wiped my lips and chin. "Here. That's better. Breathe!"

I gagged but kept it down.

"It's the kosher coffee." He patted me on the back. "Doesn't agree with Christians."

His attempt at humor was endearing, but I was beyond comforting. My knees buckled and I sat on the pavement, my back to the wall of a building as hundreds of men and women walked by, unaware that my world had collapsed. "Go...get Rebecca..."

Aaron crouched next to me. "Come on, get a grip on yourself."

"We lost...Debra..."

"That's nonsense. Debra is married, that's all. She'll give you grandkids and—"

"They'll call me...Grandpa Shaygetz...wash their hands... after touching me."

Black shoes approached us, with thick rubber soles. My eyes rose and I saw dark-blue pants and a heavy belt, loaded with various holsters and pouches. I looked all the way up to see the lovely face of an Asian woman under an NYPD cap.

"Had too much to drink?" She reached for her shoulder communication piece.

Aaron forced me to my feet. "I'm Dr. Brutsky. This is my colleague. He's not drunk. We just came from breakfast, and he must have ingested spoiled food."

She lowered her hand. "You sure about that?"

"Feeling better...already." I forced myself to walk down the avenue.

With each step I felt better. The cold breeze needled my face, and Aaron kept me going. We turned onto Forty-sixth Street and approached the Muse. The bellman saw us and adjusted his red Santa hat with the fuzzy white brim and the top pom, which he tossed from side to side playfully. A taxi stopped at the curb, and his attention was diverted.

At the revolving door, I examined myself in the glass, brushing a few crumbs from my chin and the front of my coat. "Don't say a word to Rebecca. I need to think about what just happened before we discuss it."

"Nothing to discuss." Aaron pushed the door with its rustling wreath. "Forget about these clowns, you hear me? Debra is coming home on Wednesday. We'll have our own Sheva Brachot party on Thursday plus a whole week to snap her out of all that Orthodox bullshit. Before you know it, we'll have Mordechai driving her in your convertible to a Diamondbacks game on Sabbath afternoons."

I nodded, but knew we had no chance against Mordechai, his family, and their tradition-rich world, which Debra had vowed to join as she stood under the chuppah, not even noticing that her father was excluded. Her new world was ruled by Halacha, which branded me a pariah and forbade its adherents from embracing me as a father or a grandfather—unless I succumbed and allowed Schlumacher to launder me into a kosher Jew through the Orthodox conversion process, requiring me to turn my back on my faith, my friends, and my way of life. It was an impossible choice, and the sweet prospect of having Debra and Mordechai spend their honeymoon with us had just turned sour.

My concern for upsetting Rebecca with a report of the breakfast ambush was unfounded. She was seated in the lounge next to a burning fireplace decorated with red-and-white stockings. Flanking her, in matching high-backed chairs, were Mrs. Levinson and a woman I hadn't met but immediately guessed who she was. The three of them were laughing out loud at something Mrs. Levinson said.

As I approached, their laughter died down.

Rebecca stood. "That was a short breakfast. What happened?"

"Tell you later." I turned to Mrs. Levinson. "Thanks again for last night's dinner. It was an enchanting evening. Truly unreal!"

"We enjoyed your piano playing," she said, pretending to miss my sarcasm. "You're very talented."

"My mother made me practice for an hour every day." I smiled. "Except on Sundays, of course, when I played at our church."

"I love Sheva Brachot dinners," the third woman said, "always so festive and optimistic." She was dressed in a long skirt and a tailored jacket, her face lightly made up, her glasses frameless, and her stud earrings carried sizeable, flawless diamonds.

"And you," I said, "must be Mrs. Schlumacher."

"Dr. Zelma Cohen-Schlumacher." She curtsied and smiled with perfect teeth. "You're very perceptive."

"Not always. Your husband managed to fool me."

Rebecca grabbed my elbow. "*Rusty!*"

"Christian," I corrected her.

She groaned.

"Ladies, please excuse us." I pointed at the ceiling. "Our packing isn't done yet, and we're leaving for home in an hour— and not a moment too soon."

I could feel their eyes in my back on the way to the elevator. As the doors began to close, Rebecca joined me.

A song came from hidden speakers. "*If you want to change your direction—*"

"There's a thought," she said.

"But I like my direction." Looking up, I saw my face reflected in the black glass ball that housed the security camera, making my nose appear huge.

"*Put one foot in front of the other,*" the band sang, "*and soon you'll be walking across the floor.*"

The doors opened on our floor, and Rebecca stepped out.

"I like where I am," I followed her. "Why should I cross over?"

———

I'll Be Home for Christmas

Christmas week at JFK Airport wasn't a merry time. The curbside check-in lines were long, and when snow began to fall, Rebecca and I went into the terminal and joined a queue whose beginning was out of sight. We treated each other with the awkward politeness of a couple tiptoeing around a combustible conflict. The hordes of passengers and crew members around us were similarly on edge, being pressed into this anxious bottleneck of modern travel.

Almost two hours later, with our luggage checked in and our shoes off and on at security, we finally arrived at the crowded gate area. None of our friends was flying with us, having made different plans, but it seemed that every New Yorker had decided to leave the winter behind.

My Blackberry chirped. I looked at the display. *Jonathan Warnick.*

It took me a moment to focus.

Mat Warnick's brother. *VetBestMate.com*

I hit the green button. "Jonathan? How are you?"

"Still kicking," he said, "thanks to you. Sorry I didn't respond to your Happy Rosh Hashanah call—just had the craziest three months of my life."

"Welcome to the club."

"I heard from Mat that your daughter was getting married. Mazal Tov!"

"Thank you. How are things in the dating business?"

"We went public on Nasdaq."

"Congratulations. Now you can afford a gym membership, yes?"

"I can buy a gym if I want to, but I don't have time to exercise. It was the best IPO of the year, and our stock keeps going up. I think your New Year wishes helped."

"And a bit of your hard work, I'm sure. How's your lovely wife?"

"She's well, thanks. How're things with you?"

Rebecca rubbed her finger and thumb and mouthed, "Ask him!"

"We're fine, but the synagogue is struggling financially, as Mat must have told you. Could use a new AC system, if you're interested in donating."

"Actually, I'm thinking of something bigger."

The loudspeakers announced a series of boarding calls, gate changes, and delays. I sheltered the Blackberry and my mouth. "How big?"

His voice was garbled.

"Hold on!" I headed for the restroom. Inside, I took a position against the wall between the urinals and the wash sinks. "That's better. Say again?"

"I'd like to give a substantial donation so that you won't have to waste time worrying about how to pay the bills."

"That's nice, but don't do it for me. I'm just a volunteer. Tomorrow there will be someone else running the board and harassing your brother to fix the AC."

"Mat told me how you have to beg the members for money to keep the place going. It's a shame. If I give a good chunk of change, the synagogue will be able to function in perpetuity."

It took me a moment to digest what he'd said. "That will require a very large sum."

"How much?"

"Enough to throw off half a million a year in interest." I chuckled at this pie-in-the-sky.

He didn't respond.

"I'm kidding. We'll be grateful for whatever you can give." I moved aside to let a man in a motorized scooter pass by toward the last toilet stall. "Are you still there?"

"I was just calculating," Jonathan said. "It's doable."

The scooter guy couldn't drive into the stall. He struggled to get up. I went over and held his arm until he stood and managed to grip the doorframe.

"What if I set up a ten million dollar endowment?"

With the Blackberry switched to my other ear, I asked, "Are you joking?"

The disabled man looked at me, thinking I'd spoken to him, and I pointed at the Blackberry. He raised his eyebrows and closed the stall door.

"It's not enough? I'll supplement it later."

A pilot came out of another stall, wheeled his bag over the tips of my shoes, and contorted his face in pantomimed apology.

"Dr. Dinwall? You still there?"

"Ten million dollars?" I used a paper towel to wipe my shoes. "Can you give away that much dough?"

"My share of the company is worth fifty times that. And I also got a lot of cash out of the IPO."

The scooter guy passed gas.

Jonathan asked, "What was that?"

"Nothing you should worry about, now that you can afford a private jet." I relocated to my original spot near the wall.

"Fractional ownership. Best way to fly. Anyway, I'll have my lawyers draw the necessary documents as soon as you tell me that the board accepts my conditions."

"Conditions?" The word stabbed my ears, bringing memories of standing against another wall, watching my daughter's wedding proceed without me. "What conditions?"

"I'd like to commemorate my parents."

What sounds too good to be true, is too good to be true. But still, I hoped he didn't want what I thought he wanted. "You'd like us to put their names on the wall?"

"Put their names on everything that currently has *King Solomon*."

I sighed. "Everything?"

"As the new name of the congregation—on the building, the Sunday school, the website, letterhead, books, and so on. Scratch off 'King Solomon Synagogue' and replace it with 'Golda and

Leo Warnick Synagogue.' I want my parents' memory carried forward." He paused. "They were decent and hard-working people. They deserve it."

"True." His father, a World War II veteran, had been my patient, and I had kept his weak heart beating until the rest of his body lost a long battle with prostate cancer. Mrs. Warnick had died last year, ending her long reign over the synagogue's mah-jongg club.

The scooter guy unlocked the stall door and cleared his throat.

"Someone needs help here," I said, "so I have to hang up, but I can't tell you how excited I am about your offer. Would you send me something by e-mail? Just a couple of lines that I can forward to the others in confidence. We're having the board's annual meeting tomorrow night. I'll present it for a vote and… we'll move forward!"

By the time I had the disabled gentleman back in his scooter, his hands washed and his travel bag secured in his lap, my Blackberry vibrated to indicate receipt of Jonathan's e-mail.

Stepping outside into the bustle of the terminal, I read the message:

DR. DINWALL, AS WE DISCUSSED, I WILL MAKE A DONATION TO SET UP AN ENDOWMENT OF $10 MILLION, PROVIDED THAT THE BOARD VOTES TO CHANGE THE NAME TO THE GOLDA AND LEO WARNICK SYNAGOGUE. JONATHAN.

I chuckled at his casual tone. Ten million dollars! The annual meeting was going to be a lot more interesting than anyone was expecting. Instead of painful downsizing, we would be preparing for growth. I looked up and saw Rebecca standing in line to board our plane. She beckoned me to hurry up.

The plane was filled to capacity, the weather was worsening by the minute, and the crew's nerves seemed pulled to the max. Our assigned seats were far from each other, but we didn't bother to solicit the flight attendant's help in finding someone willing to switch.

While there was still time, I used my thumbs to type a short e-mail to the members of the synagogue board—Aaron Brutsky, Judy Levy, Larry Emanuel, Mat Warnick, Cantor Bentov, and Rabbi Rachel:

> DEAR FELLOW TRUSTEES, PLEASE SEE ATTACHED E-MAIL FROM JONATHAN WARNICK, WHICH SPEAKS FOR ITSELF. OUR PRAYERS HAVE BEEN ANSWERED! IMAGINE – NO DEFICIT BUT PLENTY OF SURPLUS MONEY TO RENOVATE, EXPAND, HIRE STAFF, DO MARKETING, GROW… HOW EXCITING! SEE YOU AT TOMORROW EVENING'S ANNUAL BOARD MEETING. YOURS, CHRISTIAN DINWALL, PRESIDENT.

I sent it to them with a copy of Jonathan's e-mail. Through the window I could see the deicing machines spray the wings while snow kept falling. Delay seemed inevitable, but to everyone's relief, the plane pulled back from the gate on time, and we were airborne within minutes.

I must have fallen asleep, because the next thing I saw was a sunny sky and the sprawl of metro Phoenix below.

The man sitting next to me shifted his heavy girth. "Gee, it's like we flew from hell to paradise."

"In more ways than one." I rubbed my eyes.

"Can't wait to hit some golf balls, soak in the Jacuzzi, and down a few beers." He put up his tray and tightened his seatbelt. "How 'bout you?"

"I live here."

"Let me guess: You don't own a snow shovel, do you?" He roared in laughter, and his wife looked up from her Kindle and smiled.

"No. I don't own one, even though we get a bit of snow every few years."

While we waited for the doors to open, I turned on my Blackberry and found that all six recipients of my earlier e-mail had replied:

Aaron Brutsky: JONATHAN HAS A GOOD HEART :-)

Larry Emanuel: DITTO.

Mat Warnick: PER MY BROTHER, HE'S DOING IT BECAUSE OF DR. DINWALL.

Cantor Bentov: HALLELUIAH! HALLELUIAH! HALLELUIAH!

Judy Levy: HURRAY! (DO YOU THINK HE'S READY TO ALSO SPEND MONEY ON ART?)

Rabbi Rachel: GOD TESTS US WITH GIFTS. (CAN WE KEEP KING SOLOMON NAME?)

I assumed the rabbi's cryptic response was in jest, as was Judy's, so I didn't bother replying. We would have plenty of time to joke and celebrate at the board meeting.

We exited the plane into a packed terminal. Sky Harbor airport was always under construction, struggling to keep up with the rapid growth in passenger traffic. But two days before Christmas, things were beyond capacity. Our bags took over an hour to reach the luggage carousel, and the taxi line was another forty minutes. Once we were on our way, I showed Rebecca the correspondence on my Blackberry.

She read it. "Oh my God!"

I laughed. "Impressed?"

"And you think this is a coincidence?"

"What do you mean?"

"Just when we need it! A light at the end of the tunnel!"

I holstered my Blackberry. "The synagogue isn't exactly in a tunnel—"

"Who's talking about the synagogue? I'm talking about us. Once the money is in, you can walk away with a clear conscience."

"Walk away?"

"That's right. Pass the presidency to Aaron and be done with this headache."

I was taken aback. "You want me to leave the leadership just when there's finally enough money to do things? Why?"

"Because we have our own problems."

"We have challenges, not problems."

"We have both." She looked out the window. "And no room for the synagogue's problems. Thank God for Jonathan Warnick and his dating service!"

"I agree with that. Perhaps I should ask for a commission."

She laughed and rested her head on my shoulder. I took her hand, and we remained silent for the rest of the ride home.

We entered our house with the last rays of the sun.

Raiding the freezer, Rebecca fished out a package of Costco Atlantic Salmon, corn on the cob, and garlic bread. She whipped up a nice dinner while I unpacked our bags. We ate with a bottle of red wine and the local TV news—the usual sequence of crime, disaster, politics, sports, and the weather. The crime was a murder-suicide, with breathless neighbors attesting to the shooter's otherwise good nature. The disaster was a pool drowning, reported from a roving helicopter with dramatic aerial footage of a beautiful back yard in Mesa. Politics involved the recent anti-immigration law, dramatized with a street protest over the fatal shooting of a Mexican laborer who attempted to flee the police. A spokeswoman for the sheriff's department explained that "the roundup of suspected illegal immigrants was done in compliance with applicable laws in order to free up paying jobs for law-abiding Americans." A sports update offered comic relief with a few clips of piled-up football players, basketball dunking by black athletes who dwarfed the tremulous hoops, and a token soccer goalie leaping in the wrong direction from an incoming ball. We were spooning off a shared bowl of frozen yogurt when a tanned weatherman gloated in comparing the Phoenix sunshine to the sodden rest of the country.

Rebecca turned off the TV. "Are you ready to talk?"

"About Levinson, Mintzberg, Schlumacher, and Company?"

"What else?"

"Not by a long shot." I pulled her into my arms. "Some fat guy on the plane told me that this is a good place for soaking in the Jacuzzi and getting drunk. What do you say?"

Rebecca sighed. I took it for a yes, lifted her while gripping the wine bottle, and carried both of them to the patio outside, silently complimenting myself on the foresight that had prompted me to switch on the Jacuzzi heater earlier.

———

Part Five
Wednesday, December 23

Rockin' Around the Christmas Tree

Having opened all the windows to let the fresh morning air into the house, Rebecca started the vacuum cleaner, which made the neighbors' dog bark incessantly. I set up the extra bed in Debra's room and brought in the mattress from the storage closet. A quick call to the hospital verified that all was well. Aaron had already finished morning rounds and started on the first surgery of the day. Expecting me to call, he had left a message with Nina: "You're on vacation. Don't call us. We'll call you if we need you."

With my duties done, I topped off the air in my bicycle tires and went for a long ride.

On the way back, I stopped at the Coffee Bean on Scottsdale Road for a large latte and a toasted bagel and sat outside in the sun. My achy muscles absorbed the warmth, and my sweaty shirt slowly dried. I watched the regulars stop for their morning coffee in a parade of luxury vehicles and classic sports cars, some of them pricier than a new cardiopulmonary bypass machine.

Before leaving, I picked up a cup for Rebecca, which I balanced in one hand while riding my bike—not an easy task, but worth the effort to show her my appreciation for last night. It was a relief to be back to our normal life, and with the sun shining warmly, I realized that Aaron had been right. Things would work out just fine. Debra would arrive tonight with Mordechai, back to her own environment and roots. She would loosen up about all that Orthodox observance that her love for Mordechai has generated, and together we would find ways to bridge the gap between us and his family.

W hen I entered the house, the vacuum cleaner was no longer howling. I looked for Rebecca in the kitchen and living room, finally finding her in the study, seated in front of the computer.

She turned, startled.

"Sorry," I said, "didn't mean to scare you." I put the coffee cup before her and looked at the screen. It was a Google search page. The words she was searching were:

JEWISH ORTHODOX CONVERSION ADULT PROCESS TIMELINE

"You forgot the word shaygetz." I crossed the room and dropped into a leather loveseat.

"Why are you making it into such a big deal? What if we start observing a few rules? It's not the end of the world."

I didn't respond, my mind still digesting this shocking discovery that, while I had optimistically assumed that life was good again and that we would show the newlyweds a united front, secure in our happy way of life here in Arizona, my wife was surfing the Net with an agenda altogether different than mine.

Misinterpreting my silence, she browsed a notebook in which she had summarized her findings so far. "The first thing they require is that you demonstrate a sincere commitment to becoming a Jew. I think we got that one down solid, with you being president of the synagogue, no less." She looked at me expectantly.

"President schmesident," I said.

"Next, they would require you—I mean, require *us*—to adopt an Orthodox lifestyle, keep the rules of Halacha, and promise to remain observant even after the conversion."

Clearing my throat, I gestured vaguely with my hand.

"We'll need to make only a few changes." Rebecca counted on her fingers. "Eat kosher food, which I can take care of. It's good I've kept my mom's recipe notebooks."

"Lucky," I said.

"We'll have to observe the basic rules of Sabbath, such as not drive, turn on lights, or watch TV, which isn't too bad. Attending prayers at an Orthodox synagogue three times a day isn't required when you're working, so that leaves only Friday nights and Saturdays. Again, no big deal. And I can help you study the rules of Halacha about food, Sabbath, prayers, holidays, and personal hygiene."

"You mean *inter*-personal hygiene."

"That's right." She shrugged. "Couples can't be together during the woman's monthly period. It's about the hygiene of intimacy."

"Is it hygienic to get clean by dipping in the mikvah, a pool of standing water in which a hundred other women have also immersed?"

"That's just a symbolic act of cleansing. Everyone showers before and after the mikvah. The main thing is to avoid contact with menstrual discharge."

"For two weeks every month?"

"It's a bit long, but the principle makes sense."

"It made sense in biblical times, before tampons, absorbent pads, and indoor showers with hot water and lots of soap."

"Nobody is going to police us in the bedroom, okay?"

I raised my hands in surrender. "Just making a point."

"Point taken." She scanned the rest of her notes. "After the completion of study and the period of observance of the rules, you'll qualify for an examination—assuming there are no problems."

"Problems?"

"Such as wise-ass comments that piss off the rabbis."

"Ah, right."

"They'll bring you before a panel of rabbis for questions about your studies and your commitment to observe Halacha for the rest of your life. If you pass, there will be another period of studying, followed by a hearing before a rabbinical court of conversions. Once they approve you as a Jew, you'll dip in the mikvah and have a circumcision." Rebecca held up her hand to stop me from protesting. "You're already circumcised, so a *mohel* will only nick your precious dingo."

"Ouch!"

"To draw a drop of blood, that's all. Purely symbolic."

"Symbolic emasculation, that's what this whole thing is about."

"And after the circumcision, you'll be one hundred percent Jewish even according to the most religious black hat in Brooklyn. That's it!"

"*That's it?*" I kept my voice down even though I was ready to shout.

"Why can't you just listen?" She held up the notebook. "Judaism doesn't solicit converts. There are no Jewish missionaries. In fact, Mrs. Schlumacher told me that they try to convince people not to convert. But for us, because we're already Jewish in every other respect, they'll do everything to smooth out the process and make it easy."

"Easy?" It was my turn to count on my fingers. "We'll need to get rid of our dishes, pots and pans, silverware, kitchen appliances, and buy all new stuff. We'll have to leave King Solomon and join some Orthodox synagogue. We must stay home on Saturdays and do what? No *Sixty Minutes*, no bike rides, no Jacuzzi dips, no going out with friends to see a movie. And speaking of friends, we won't be able to ever again share a good steak at a restaurant or enjoy dinner at the Brutskys or at anyone else's house for that matter. And no vacations where there's no kosher food and a synagogue. We could vacation in Brooklyn, I suppose."

"Orthodox Jews go on vacations. There are kosher hotels, kosher cruises, even kosher National Geographic trips."

"So we can go to the Amazon on a kosher safari. That's great. But what about the rest of the year?"

"I don't care about vacations." Her shoulders slumped, and her eyes moistened. "We have only one daughter."

"Please don't cry. I won't have this discussion if you're going to cry."

"I'm not crying, okay?" Rebecca blew her nose. "This whole thing is not about humiliating you. It's about our happiness as a family, going forward."

"Caving in to religious arm-twisting will make us happy?"

"Who's twisting arms? It's a genuine difference of opinion about what it means to live a Jewish life. You and I made our compromise years ago, and I've honored my part, haven't I? Have I ever tried to pull you toward the way I grew up?"

I shook my head.

"I didn't, even though I missed some of my childhood's traditions, because Reform life worked for us. It was a good compromise. But now we have to deal with the fact that Debra has made a different choice."

"Has she?" I stood up, unable to remain seated. "She hasn't been home since before she met him. This is our chance to refresh her memory about our way of being Jewish, of being tolerant and flexible, of letting go of anachronistic customs that make no sense in the modern world."

"What's anachronistic to you is fresh and beautiful to Debra."

"Nonsense! The only fresh thing is a boy with big teeth—"

"You want to break up her marriage? Is that what you want?"

"No." I took a deep breath, exhaling slowly. "Of course not. But after Debra swung all the way to his family's extreme observance, it's time for the pendulum to swing back. Their visit is our chance! She's been their captive, now she'll be free to return to normal here, at home, while Mordechai is *our* captive. Don't you see it? Let him make sacrifices for love, just like Debra has done for him!"

Rebecca shook her head, sighed, and looked at me at length before saying, "I'm sorry to tell you this, but you really don't understand your daughter. She wasn't anyone's captive. She made no sacrifices. She really believes in living according to Halacha."

"Not true. You're the one who doesn't understand her. Debra is obeying Halacha for him, for love. Now it's his turn to give up some Halacha for love."

"He's in love with her, not with you."

"So what? Can't he adjust a bit in our direction? I understand that he has to respect his father, on whom he's dependent, but he can give me some respect too. I'm not a leper."

"It's not only about you!" Rebecca stood, facing me. "It's about how we—you and I—live in a way that's already causing a rift between us and them."

"Is it?"

"Yes! Do you really think they want to spend their honeymoon here?"

"What do you mean?"

"They're doing us a favor!" Her voice broke, but she quickly recovered. "Debra and Mordechai and their future children are going to be strictly Orthodox."

"Not if we insist—"

"We are irrelevant! They'll be following the traditions of hundreds of Jewish generations, traditions that our Debra loves and enjoys and doesn't view as *anachronistic.* Our lifestyle, as well as your religious status, are two strikes against us. We're incompatible with our own daughter. That's what Mrs. Levinson and Dr. Cohen-Schlumacher came to talk to me about yesterday morning. That's what their husbands were trying to communicate to you over breakfast, before Aaron dragged you away."

"It was a double ambush—like a pincer, squeezing you and me at the same time."

"You're paranoid!"

"And you're naive!"

Rebecca held her hands forward, as if pleading. "Can't you accept that they're only trying to help us remain part of Debra's life? That they want to be family with us? That they actually *like* us?"

"As long as we agree to adopt their way of life."

"What's so important? A steak once a month? TV on Saturdays?"

"Our way of life isn't important? Our faith in a God who doesn't dwell on technicalities that were relevant for tent-dwellers in ancient Canaan? Our loyalty to the synagogue, to our friends and community? Aren't they important to you?"

"They're all important." Rebecca sighed. "But not as important as my only child and not as important as the prospect of enjoying my grandkids."

There was something comical about the idea of Rebecca as a grandmother. I chuckled. "It's not a black-and-white choice. We can work with Debra and Mordechai, give a little, take a little."

"That won't do."

Her stubbornness was frustrating. "This whole concept is crazy," I said. "How could I start living by religious rules that make no sense to me?"

"But you expect Debra and Mordechai to violate religious rules they do believe in? To commit sins to accommodate you?"

I could see her point, but still, my heart told me that Debra couldn't actually believe in all that Halacha business. Soon Rebecca would realize it as well. But right now, my goal was to get my wife off this conversion idea. "Tell me," I said, "how would I go to work and look at Aaron's face every day? What am I going to say to my best friend of twenty-five years? Sorry, pal, but I can't socialize with you anymore because, according to Halacha, you're a sinner?"

"Then don't go to work."

"What do you mean?"

"We can move away from here."

That statement shocked me more than everything else. "Move away?"

"Back to New York." Rebecca's tone revealed that this wasn't a shot from the hip but an idea that had fermented in her mind for some time. "Why not? We both love New York, and you're entitled to retire from the VA with a pension, right?"

"A very small pension. Not enough to live on in Manhattan."

"Dr. Levinson can get you another job, doing the same kind of surgeries you do here, but for a lot more money."

"He said that?"

"Mrs. Levinson told me. And for what this house is worth, we can buy an apartment on the Upper West Side and make a new life." She came over and held my hands. "We'll be close to Debra, close to Broadway theaters and the best museums, close to *civilization!*"

Taking a deep breath, I asked, "You really want to do this? Leave Arizona? Start all over?"

She nodded. "I'm going to return to school, get a master's degree, maybe a Ph.D."

"You could do that right here, at ASU."

"But isn't Columbia University better?" She pressed my hands to her heart. "Think about it. That's all I'm asking. We'll be back in New York City, a new chapter, a new adventure!"

Having just returned from there, I couldn't deny that walking the streets of the city, its sounds and smells, had felt familiar. Our student years had been the happiest, but could we recapture that youthful energy now, over two decades later? "There's a contradiction here," I said. "We'll be returning to our student locales to prepare for becoming grandparents."

Her eyes glistened. "I knew you'd come around!"

"I didn't say that. I still don't like the way they treated me in the wedding and the manipulations that followed. *Scottish Pork Apricot à la Crème!* Give me a break!"

She laughed. "You said it was good."

"It was tasty, but it was designed to lower my guard and lure me into an ambush. For them, I'm still a shaygetz."

"A very handsome shaygetz." She reached up and kissed my lips. "So you'll think about it?"

Would I consider caving in and converting, becoming Orthodox, observing all those rules I believed to be nonsensical? It was a theoretical question, because Rebecca was wrong about Debra's belief in the validity of Halacha. Starting tonight, my mission would be to prove it, to get my daughter back from the religious abyss, with her young and malleable husband in tow.

Rebecca took my hand and repeated her question. "Will you think about it?"

"Thinking," I said, "isn't a problem. But don't expect me to—"

"That's good enough for me." Rebecca glanced at her watch. "I'm meeting the kosher caterer at the synagogue to plan for tomorrow night's party. But Debra and Mordechai are taking the latest flight from La Guardia, so you and I will still have plenty of time to talk before they arrive."

"You want to tell them tonight?"

She nodded.

"Too soon." I shook my head. "It's not a decision we should make in a day, committing to observe an Orthodox lifestyle for the rest of our lives. It's a question of faith, not something to be done for expediency, when we don't even know that we have to do it, depending on where Debra really stands in the long term."

"Don't fool yourself," Rebecca said. "She's committed to an Orthodox life."

"If you're so sure, let's discuss the whole situation with them. Open it up. Stir the pot, so to speak."

Rebecca looked down at her feet. "I would, but—"

"What?"

"There's one issue that might come up. It could be embarrassing." She exhaled. "For a mixed couple like us, once the non-Jewish spouse has completed the conversion process, there must be a new marriage ceremony, performed by an Orthodox rabbi."

I let go of her hands. "What are you saying? That we've cohabitated all these years? Like roommates?"

"Technically, under Halacha, but we know it's not like that."

"It's exactly like that! If we must get married again, it means we haven't been married properly!"

"A technicality, that's all." She tried to hold my hand.

"If we agree to such a ceremony, it would amount to an admission that everything we have together, our life here, our family, has been wrong." I gestured at the bookshelves and the myriad family photos. "All this is wrong?"

"A small ceremony, in private, and the problem will be fixed."

"Is our marriage broken, that it needs fixing?"

"From the point of view of Halacha, yes, it's broken."

"And from your point of view?"

Rebecca hesitated.

"Well?"

"It is broken…from Debra's point of view."

"Why are you speaking for her?"

"I don't want to argue about it. Dr. Cohen-Schlumacher told me that her husband can expedite things, shorten the conversion process to six months, make it less burdensome for us as a couple."

I saw the redness spreading on Rebecca's face and realized what she meant. "They want us to stay apart from each other during the conversion? Is that it?"

"They didn't make the rules. Halacha is what it is."

"*Unbelievable!*"

"It's only temporary," she said meekly.

"It's intrusive to a grotesque degree! Don't you see it?"

"Why are you taking it so personally? Under the rules of Halacha, a couple like us is technically—"

"Living in sin?" It suddenly occurred to me that last night had been her way of giving me a parting gift, something to look forward to while I went through the conversion process. Still, it was hard for me to believe that Levinson and Schlumacher had so quickly managed to inject a wedge between us, fracture our marital base of unity and trust. "You'll agree to be apart from me for six months? Or even longer?"

"It's not like we won't be able to see each other, to talk and do all the things we enjoy doing together." She shrugged. "It will be like dating, except that we won't be allowed to have sex, that's all."

"That's all?" Not waiting for her response, I walked out of the study.

"Rusty!" Rebecca's voice chased me. "*Please!*"

Snatching my car keys from the kitchen, I ran out of the house, got in the Volvo, and drove off. Only then, gripping the wheel with my chest pressed in a vise of agonizing heartache, I exploded with a long string of expletives.

Every fall, at the corner of Cactus Road and Fifty-sixth Street, a pumpkin patch would spring up. Until she left for college, Debra and I used to come here every October to prepare for Halloween. It was an annual family ritual, decorating the front yard with pumpkins in various sizes, some of them carved to accommodate candles. We added spider webs and clanking skeletons among the oleander bushes and mesquite trees. After nightfall, we donned scary costumes and leaped at every trick-or-treater with fists full of candy.

In December, however, the pumpkin patch always turned into a dense forest of firs, guarded by a giant Santa floater.

I wasn't planning to drive there. It just happened at the end of an hour of fuming behind the wheel. Perhaps it was my subconscious GPS. But after sitting in the car for a few minutes, I made a conscious decision to turn off the engine, get out of the car, and walk by Santa's grinding air pump toward the rows of rootless trees.

Standing aside to let a couple drag a tree out the gate, I watched their happy faces—much younger than mine—and envied what seemed like a happy-go-lucky relationship, free of unnecessary conflict. But then the wife dropped her end of the tree, the husband gave her a look that could have passed for the word *stupid*, and I felt better.

"Merry Christmas." A thin man with black hair and tanned complexion approached me from the shadows. He was holding a small book, which he closed and slipped into his pocket. "May I help you?"

"I'm thinking of buying a tree," I said.

"Natural or artificial?"

This question caught me off guard. "I didn't know there's a choice."

He smiled, his teeth yellowed from smoking. "How long since you last shopped for a Christmas tree?"

"Never." Seeing the doubt on his face, I added, "We're Jewish. It's a long story."

"No problem. I have a blue-and-white tree if you want."

"Green would be fine. Something modest."

My mother had always managed to bring home a tree on Christmas Eve—small, misshapen, more a bush than a tree, often an undesired new growth that didn't fit some mansion owner's overall landscape vision. But it fit our tiny apartment, and every year we decorated our tree together with old trinkets and my art projects from school. And each of us placed a gift for the other under the tree. The rest of her rare vacation day would be spent cooking, attending church, and taking me to visit relatives.

"Let me show you around." He took me down a path that was barely wide enough for one person. "On the right, these are all traditional trees—good American evergreens, grown on farms and harvested specifically for Christmas. We have Douglas fir, Noble fir, Norway spruce, a few hybrid pines. Prices are one to five hundred dollars, depending on size."

I grunted, depriving him of an indication of my price range, which I didn't know either. My presence here must be a rare phenomenon in consumer statistics. Who else would go impulse-shopping for a Christmas tree?

He pointed at another section. "This area is for the designer trees."

"Excuse me?"

"Genetically engineered for perfection," he said with obvious pride. "Look at the shape, perfectly symmetrical as it tapers to the pointy top."

"They're nice," I admitted.

"You can see the color, deep green, lush with vitality." He pulled on a branch, showing me. "These needles will stay green for two weeks, healthy and aromatic like the day it was harvested. You won't have to worry about watering it."

"Impressive. How much are these?"

"Around a thousand, but I'll give you a discount because Christmas is almost here and you're a first-time buyer."

"And Jewish," I said. "We are bound by tradition to pay wholesale prices, never retail."

He smiled and beckoned me to follow. "The artificial trees are ready for use, with built-in lights and decorations."

"Plug-and-play Christmas trees?"

"This one is the original and still very popular." He reached into a box and pulled out a cylindrical plastic tube. With rapid, practiced movements he extended it to twice my height, released the branches in a system resembling multiple umbrellas attached to a single pole, each bough covered with thousands of green needles. A four-legged base opened up, and he placed it on the floor. An electrical wire emerged from the tube that served as the tree trunk, and once it was plugged into an outlet, the faux tree lit up in multiple colors that blinked like faraway rainbow stars.

Stepping back, I clapped. "This is incredible. Who invented this?"

"The Adis Toilet Brush Company." He unplugged and packed up the tree. "Back in the thirties, they basically made a big foldable toilet brush and called it Silver Pine. It was made of scrap metal at first, then aluminum, and later plastic. Now it's made of recycled water bottles. In China, of course."

"How much?"

"It depends." He pointed at a row of boxes. "You can get a basic one for under a hundred dollars. But most people like something that doesn't look like a poor imitation of an evergreen."

"Let me guess," I said. "They want both tradition and revolution, something that evokes old memories while striking a fashion statement."

"That's good," he said, tapping his head, "I must remember this line."

"Feel free to use it."

"Thank you." He led me down the line. "Such customers go with a black tree or pink, blue, yellow, or red. Or a combination— you could alternate the modular branches. And this one has feathers instead of needles."

"Feathers?" I touched it, impressed with the sensation—like petting a dead bird.

"Or you can get one that's inverted, the wide base up and the summit tip down."

"That's how my world feels right now. But really, do people buy an upside-down Christmas tree?"

"We sell a few every year."

"I'm all for individualism, but there's something genuine about a real, natural, green tree, don't you think?"

"It's more traditional." He nodded thoughtfully. "But then you'll need to buy the lighting separately."

"What are the options?"

"We used to have small bulbs on a string, but if one burnt out, the whole thing would go dark and you had to search along the wires for the bad bulb." He proceeded to a set of shelves with boxes. "Fiber optic lights are affordable, and we carry all colors. But the best is the 'Stay-Lit' technology, which is affordable and effective, second only to LED, which doesn't get hot like regular lighting. It can be controlled by a computer chip with different blinking patterns, which you can synchronize with holiday music from your iPod."

I moved on to a line of trees that seemed cut in half lengthwise. "What's this?"

"Let's say you want to set up a tree in a small room." He patted the wall. "You set up this half-tree flat against the wall, plug it in, and you're done. Some people like it in the hallway or the bathroom."

"A Christmas tree in the bathroom?"

"Houses in Scottsdale sometimes have very big bathrooms, with a couch and even a television set."

He was right. I had been to a few of those.

"Artificial trees are very practical," he continued. "No dry needles all over the place, no strings of lights in messy knots, no need to buy a new tree every year. Also, less global warming."

I was overwhelmed. Coming in here on a whim, my general idea was to buy a tree and bring it home—a bit dramatic perhaps, but a good way to assert my identity. If Rebecca was pulling back toward her Orthodox roots, then I had the right to pull back toward my Christian roots. That would surely get her off the conversion idea. Also, a tree could demonstrate to Debra and Mordechai that I wasn't ashamed of my upbringing. The tree's presence in our living room would instigate an honest discussion and allow me to share memories from Christmases in Tarrytown. But which tree? Natural ones do make a mess, which Rebecca wouldn't appreciate, but an artificial one just didn't do it for me. A toilet brush turning into a Christmas tree? LED lighting synchronized with my iPod? No, all this was too far removed from my childhood memories. But the natural trees seemed too big and healthy, nothing like the ones we used to have.

"Difficult choices?" The man smiled, smoothing his black hair over a thinning top.

"What about you?" I looked around at the natural firs and plastic trees. "You can have anything you want, right? So what kind of a tree do you take home to your family?"

"No tree."

"Excuse me?"

He pulled the small book from his pocket and showed me the cover. Under a title in Arabic letters, the English translation appeared: THE HOLY KORAN.

———

All I Want for Christmas is You

Jerusalem Arts & Books was Rebecca's favorite gift store for any Bar Mitzvah, wedding, baby naming, or house warming. I parked a few storefronts down in order to avoid questions about the full-bodied Douglas fir growing from the back seat of my convertible while I shopped for Judaic trinkets.

My work was made easier by a discount table up front, loaded with leftovers from Hanukkah, which had ended almost a month earlier. I picked up a handful of glitzy Jewish star pendants, tiny menorahs, super-hero figures wearing beards and yarmulkes, and play soldiers in IDF uniform. On my way to the cashier, I noticed a shelf of items featuring the pattern of the Israeli flag—socks, wool hats, headbands, gloves, scarves, and even a funeral wreath with a combination of the Israeli and American flags. I took two pairs of socks, a wool hat, gloves, a scarf, and the wreath.

The cashier, an elderly woman sitting on a tall stool, ran everything through the scanner without a comment. But the wreath was too much for her. "Who died?"

"Joshua," I said. "Haven't you heard?"

"Oh, really?" Her hand went to her mouth. "Joshua Leibowitz is dead?"

The name was familiar—a lawyer and one-time president of the Jewish Federation. "Not that Joshua," I said. "The dead one is Joshua of Nazareth."

"Don't know him. What happened?"

"He was crucified." I handed her my credit card. "It's on the front page of the *Jewish News.*"

"You are naughty." She giggled like a girl comprehending a dirty joke. "Joshua of Nazareth. *Oy vey!* May God protect us from the evil eye!"

On the way home, I called Rebecca's mobile. It went straight into her voicemail. I knew she was at the synagogue, preparing the Gathering Hall for our Sheva Brachot party tomorrow night, so I left a short message: "It's me. Sorry for storming out this morning, but I was really upset. Anyway, I found a way to better clarify my feelings. You'll see when you come home. Good luck with the caterer."

Spreading a blue tarp on the driveway, I pulled the tree out of the car and used the tarp to drag it through the front door into the house and down the hallway to the living room. With the metal base set up between the fireplace and the piano, it was time for the most challenging part of doing this alone—raising the tree to an upright position. After a few futile attempts, I managed to prop the tree up by crouching as I lifted it off the tarp. With a loud groan I aligned the bottom of the trunk with the hollow base and slipped it in. This awkward maneuver caused a nasty cramp in my left arm and shoulder, and I dropped on the sofa, panting, waiting for the pain to pass.

The rest was easy. I spent an hour among the needling branches, threading the fiber optic lights and hanging little menorahs, Hasidic superheroes, IDF toy soldiers, and blue stars. The Israeli socks stood in for stockings along the fireplace mantle, and Debra's old teddy bear donned the Israeli-style wool hat, scarf, and gloves. I had to use a stepladder to reach high enough to attach the wreath onto the mirror above the mantle.

Satisfied, I plugged in the lights, stretched on the sofa, and basked in my glowing handiwork. It was lovely.

The twilight in the windows revealed how long I had napped. The ceiling above me blinked continuously with the blue-and-white lights from my Christmas tree. I heard Rebecca's voice in the kitchen. Her voice verged on crying as she told someone what an awful thing I had done on the day our daughter was coming home with her new husband.

I swung my legs over to the floor and sat up. The cramp in my left arm shot through my neck and down into my chest. It hurt, and I waited for a temporary dizziness to pass. Hearing Rebecca's upset voice was also hurtful, but I had to make her understand where I was coming from.

"He's up," she said, her steps approaching thought the hallway. "Why don't you talk to him?"

Standing up, I felt sick. Fighting with Rebecca was rare. We've always managed to agree on all the important things, or compromise on what was more important for one of us than the other. But I knew that this situation would challenge us like nothing else.

"Here he is, Rabbi," Rebecca said.

I shook my finger, but she handed me the phone anyway.

"If you meant it as a joke," Rabbi Rachel said, "I don't think Rebecca got it."

"No joke," I said. "It's a beautiful thing. You should see it. Want to come by?"

Now it was Rebecca's turn to shake her finger, but it was too late.

"Sure," the rabbi said. "I'll be over in ten minutes."

Rebecca left the room without looking at my tree. I assumed she had seen enough of it, coming home when I had been asleep. I followed her to the hallway, but she entered the powder room and shut the door.

I knocked.

"Go away," she said.

"What's the big deal? The whole world is celebrating Christmas."

"Not in my house!"

"It's my house too. And how can this be so offensive to you? Everywhere you shop there are decorated trees and Santa impersonators yelling *Ho! Ho! Ho!*"

"The more reason I don't want to see it here!"

"But I do. I decorated a tree every year until I met you. Why can't I do it in my own home?"

"Leave me alone."

"We're together, not alone."

She didn't respond.

Arguing through a bathroom door was not what I had hoped for, but I couldn't stop myself from pressing on. "What about fairness? I've shared all the Jewish holidays with you every year since college. Why don't you share one of my holidays? Just once?"

No answer.

I tried the door handle. It was locked. "Why can't we discuss it like adults?"

Inside, the toilet flushed and the vent fan turned on, making enough noise to drown my voice.

Back in the living room, I switched on the sound system and searched the channels until I found Mariah Carey singing *"I don't want a lot for Christmas..."*

How appropriate!

I turned up the volume until it hurt my ears. Carey sang the familiar lines, and I paced back and forth from my tree to the opposite wall and back, the words pulsating through me like a current. *"I don't even wish for snow..."*

I peeked into the hallway. The powder room door was still closed, but there was no way Rebecca wasn't hearing the song at this decibel, which made the words reverberate through the walls. When Carey reached the last line, I sang with her at the top of my voice, *"Baby, all I want for Christmas is...youuuuuuuuuuu!"*

Rabbi Rachel found me in the driveway, where I had relocated after the musical tornado failed to dislodge Rebecca from the powder room. We hugged.

"Thanks for coming," I said.

"What are friends for?" She paused at the doorway and kissed the mezuzah scroll on the doorpost. "I've been thinking about the Warnick donation. The concern is that we'll be the envy of Jewish institutions in all of Arizona. It's too—"

"We'll be paying our bills." I closed the door. "That's what I'm thinking about."

"Money isn't everything. We must consider all the ramifications. I've prepared discussion points for tonight's board meeting."

"I think we're meeting at Judy's house, right?"

"At seven-thirty. But perhaps you and I should discuss things beforehand so we're on the same page during the meeting?"

"Let's deal with one crisis at a time." I showed her into the living room, now eerily quiet.

Rabbi Rachel stood there, contemplating my decorated Douglas fir. She sighed and asked, "Where's Rebecca?"

"The rabbi's here," I yelled down the hallway. "You can come out now."

She joined us, wiping her eyes with a trail of toilet paper.

Rabbi Rachel hugged her.

"Can you believe this?" Rebecca gestured at the tree without looking at it.

"Aaron told me," the rabbi said, "about the exclusion from the wedding ceremony." She turned to me. "Rusty, I've never been angrier in my life!"

"Call me Christian," I said.

"You see?" Rebecca pointed at me. "He's punishing me for what that old rabbi did to him in Brooklyn. And he wants to change his name to Christian."

"It's not a change," I said. "It's a restoration. Christian is my real name."

"Then it's more of a reversion than a restoration, right?" The rabbi passed a hand through her curly hair. The roots were gray above her creased forehead. "Considering what they did to you, we're all sympathetic. We understand that you're filled with resentment and want to make a point about your heritage and past."

"You bet I do!"

"It's only natural. But to insist on being called Christian? And to force a Christmas tree on Rebecca? Of all things, a Christmas tree, which is a pagan symbol? Isn't it an overreaction?"

"You'll also overreact when you hear how they've launched a campaign to convert me. They want us to become Orthodox."

Rabbi Rachel adjusted her black-framed glasses. "Tell me more."

"Maybe Rebecca should tell you. She's all for it. She wants us to leave the King Solomon Synagogue, sell our house, and move to New York, where I can operate on rich, kosher patients."

"That can't be true! Is it?"

My wife, who stood with her back to the fireplace, pressed the toilet paper into a ball and threw it at me. "That was a private conversation!"

"You called the rabbi," I said. "How can she help if she's not aware of all the facts?"

"I called her about the contamination of our home with paganism, not to discuss our private family problems!" Rebecca held her hands forward as if fending off both of us. "I'm really sorry, Rabbi Rachel. I made a mistake calling you."

"My dear, please." The rabbi touched Rebecca's arm. "We've been friends long enough. You can discuss anything with me. I'm here for you."

Rebecca took the tissue I held out to her and blew her nose. "This was supposed to be the happiest time of my life." Her voice broke. "Now look at me!"

Seeing her so upset, I was flooded with regrets. "Maybe that's your punishment for marrying a shaygetz."

She looked at me with teary eyes. "There shouldn't be a punishment for marrying the man you loved."

Loved. Her use of past tense jabbed my chest. "I still love you," I said, "as much as I did on that afternoon in your parents' apartment."

She looked down at the carpet in silence that hurt me more than any words.

"Look," Rabbi Rachel said, "you're both angry now, but if you take a step back and accept the bigger picture—"

"I'm not angry," I said.

"But I am," Rebecca said.

"Because I won't continue on the path of appeasement?"

"Because you're turning into a different person!"

"The opposite is true. I'm finally trying to be true to who I really am. And I'm tired of continuously proving myself as a Jew. I'm the same guy you've been married to since college—a Jew named Christian, a Jew who grew up a Christian, who loved his Christian mother and missed his Christian father."

Every time I said the word "Christian," Rebecca flinched. "Are you done?" she asked.

"Christian is my name, and it's too bad that you've so conveniently forgotten it. I'm a Jew whose Christian childhood's few wonderful memories revolved around Christmas. Why can't I reminisce, not in secret, but out in the open with those I love? I want to cherish my Christian memories, even as a Jew, and share the experience with my wife, my newly married daughter, and her husband. Is it so difficult to understand?"

"You know," Rabbi Rachel said, "this situation reminds me of—"

"What kind of nonsense is this?" Rebecca glared at me. "You've never, ever, not even once in twenty-five years, mentioned this rubbish about cherished Christmas memories. Not even once! So either you're lying about your longings or you've kept it secret, hiding something so emotional from me, which is even worse!"

"I was in denial, okay? I was afraid of your reaction! Afraid to upset you!" I realized I was yelling but didn't care. "Haven't I done enough to prove my Jewishness? Haven't I celebrated Rosh Hashanah, Yom Kippur, Sukkoth, Simchat Torah, Purim, Hanukkah? Have I ever missed any of those?"

Rebecca shook her head. "But Debra—"

"What about Debra? Have I not taught her to recite *Shema Israel* before falling asleep? And danced with her on my shoulders in the synagogue? And built a Sukkah and spun a dreidel with her? And practiced the Hebrew scriptures for her Bat Mitzvah? And snuck a glass of water to her during the day of fasting?"

The two women watched me in silence. I rarely lost my temper.

"Haven't I done it all?" I kept my eyes on Rebecca, determined to make her respond.

"You have," she said. "You were the best father."

"The best *Jewish* father," I said, "and a pretty good husband too."

"That's why I'm upset now. After everything we've been through, how can you do this to me? And worse, to Debra?" Rebecca threw her thumb behind her back. "*This tree!*"

"Is that really fair?" Rabbi Rachel's voice was pacifying, like an adult addressing a distraught youth. "Your daughter is an adult now, intelligent and educated. A married woman. Isn't she capable of dealing with her father's more complex feelings about Judaism and Christmas?" Rebecca looked at the rabbi, not replying.

"The Debra I know will manage just fine."

"I don't want her to manage," Rebecca said. "I want her to be happy."

"Really, Rebecca," the rabbi smiled, "aren't you over-protecting your daughter?"

My wife glared at our rabbi and said, "You wouldn't understand."

This brief retort, which lasted for only three words, was enough to chase the blood away from our childless rabbi's face. She straightened up to her modest height and walked out of our house.

———

Santa Claus is Coming to Town

Judy Levy's house rested on the northern shoulder of Camelback Mountain. Her late husband, a much older man, had passed away a decade ago. To get there after dark, a driver had to possess the strong nerves of a tightrope artist and the best set of headlights. My nerves were better trained for the more civilized environment of a bloody operating room, but the Volvo's Xenon headlights threw off veritable sunlight that chased away much of the desert eeriness. I steered carefully up the narrow gravel path, which weaved between giant boulders, pinched a hairpin turn around overgrown cacti, and rattled over a drain wash strewn with pebbles.

A coyote leaped from the bushes and paused in front of my car, observing the intrusion. I hit the brakes. Three more coyotes joined in. They had raggedy tails, wolf-like snouts, and a casual trot that exuded the cockiness earned by reaching the top of the food chain. I sat behind the wheel of my open-top car, a cool breeze rustling the dry weeds around me, and for a moment I was no longer in the very center of the fifth-largest metropolis in America, but alone in the wilderness, auditioning for a role in these carnivores' dinner.

The moment passed when a pair of headlights appeared in my rearview mirror, and the coyotes ambled into the darkness.

Two more turns and a few hundred yards up the hill, the path ended in a carport, occupied by Judy's old Jeep Wrangler and piles of scrap metal. There was just enough flat area to accommodate a few more vehicles.

Cantor Bentov and Aaron arrived a moment later, parked their cars, and joined me.

Aaron whistled. "You are the man! Ten million dollars!"

I locked my car. "Not bad, eh?"

"It's incredible," Cantor Bentov bellowed. "The best Christmas gift Santa has ever delivered to a bunch of Jews!"

"You better watch out," Aaron said, slapping my shoulder, "way things are going, we'll appoint you president for life."

Another car came up the hill. The dust from our arrival still lingered in its headlights. It was Mat Warnick's service van, which must have been a real challenge to drive up here. When the doors opened, the interior lights showed Rabbi Rachel in the passenger seat. They spoke for a few minutes while we waited, then joined us. We said hello, and I was relieved to be in a group, giving me time to figure out what to say to the rabbi. It had been my fault that Rebecca was fuming to the point of insulting her. Should I have discussed my Christmas tree idea before bringing it into the house? Most likely Rebecca's crying would have dissuaded me. But facing Rabbi Rachel, I wanted to apologize to her on behalf of both Rebecca and myself, but the truth was that I hadn't spoken with my angry wife since the rabbi had stormed out, and not because I didn't try. Somehow, the presence of that tree in our living room had pushed Rebecca over the edge of rational discussion and made her treat me with open hostility, which had never happened before in all our years together. It was as if she stopped loving me, though I knew it couldn't be the case. Had she been so infuriated because of the combination of a Christmas tree and my insistence on being called Christian? Or the risk of alienation from Debra unless I converted in accordance with the Orthodox rabbis' requirements? Whatever it was, Rebecca had hurt Rabbi Rachel's feelings, and I had caused it.

But the rabbi didn't wait for me to break the ice. She pulled me down to peck my cheek. "I was wrong to leave your home in anger. Please forgive me. Rebecca already has."

"You spoke with her?"

"Of course. She was right. My understanding of parents' anxieties about their children is limited to theory. It wasn't my place to patronize her. Debra is the most important person in the world for your wife."

"For me too, which is why I want to protect Debra from the Orthodox fundamentalist misinterpretation of Judaism and show her *and* Mordechai that—"

"Look at those suckers!" Mat Warnick pointed to Judy's front door handles. "They look alive!"

The intertwined rattlesnakes did appear alive, their sparkling scales giving an illusion of movement, which Judy had probably intended. Only a closer look in the dim light revealed the mounting hardware and the thin coat of hardened silicon over the open jaws and sharp fangs.

"Ring the bell," Aaron urged Mat, who was the newest board member and had never been to Judy's place.

Before I managed to yell a warning, Mat complied, only to find his finger pressing on the arched spine of a black scorpion. The dangling stinger sprung up when the body was pressed in, stinging his finger. Mat cursed and fell backward, where Aaron was ready to catch him.

We all had a big laugh, and Judy opened the door. "Who's the sucker now?"

"You're a sick human being!" Mat walked in with his hand in the air, examining it against the foyer light. "It stung me!"

"It's dead," Aaron said, still laughing.

"So what?" Mat was panicking. "The venom stays active! They can sting after they're dead!"

"It's fake," Judy said. "I made it out of rubber, paperclips, and foil." She took his stung hand and led him back to the door. "Look at it. The stinger is dull, won't penetrate the skin. It's just for fun."

"Some fun," Mat said. "I see them every day on the AC machines, inside electrical boxes, in the attics. Scorpions, black widows, rattlesnakes. I hate them!"

Aaron put his arm around Mat's shoulder. "Don't pout. It's a big night, ten million greenbacks, all because of you!"

"It's my brother's money, not mine." Mat rubbed his hand, still unsure about the scorpion. "And anyway, as I wrote in my e-mail, Jonathan is giving the money because of Dr. Dinwall."

We entered Judy's living room, and Rabbi Rachel said, "A lot of patients are grateful to their doctors, but they don't give away millions of dollars to an institution unless they believe in its strength and future."

Mat checked the armchair before sitting in it. "He's not giving the money out of gratitude to his doctor."

Judy, who was carrying a refreshments tray, stopped midway from the open kitchen. "You're not making sense. He's giving it because of Dr. Dinwall, but not out of gratitude?"

"Correct," Mat said.

Rabbi Rachel carried a straight, carved-wood chair from a dining table and positioned it across from the sofa. "Can you explain?"

"Jonathan told me that Dr. Dinwall inspired him, not only because of how he cares for his patients, but also because he has served the synagogue for so long as a volunteer president, managed the affairs of the congregation, and worked so hard without asking for anything in return." Mat glanced at the rabbi. "He's the hardest-working employee, but we don't pay him a salary."

I sighed inwardly. She was being talked down to again because of me.

"My brother," Mat continued, "started VetBestMate.com in the hospital, working on his laptop in bed, because he wanted to help people. He learned it from Dr. Dinwall. And the business success was only a byproduct of Jonathan's dedication to helping single veterans find love. It's still the company's slogan: *Be Good For Goodness Sake!*"

"Then how come I didn't get any shares?" I spoke casually, as if I didn't really believe Mat. "Or would this defeat the whole idea?"

"It's never too late," Aaron said.

We laughed and sat down to start our business. Judy phoned Larry Emanuel, who was at the hospital, and we heard his voice on the speaker. "I'm at work," Larry said, "unlike some other doctors."

"That's why they pay you the big bucks," I said.

"Yeah, right!" He blew air into the phone, which on our end sounded like spitting.

"Let's start." Judy picked up her drawing pad, which she also used to take notes. "This is the annual meeting of the board of trustees of the King Solomon Synagogue. We have all the trustees present in person or by phone, so we have a quorum for valid voting. I'm chairing the meeting as secretary. The agenda includes two items: Financial reports and the Warnick offer. But first, the rabbi will open with a word from the Torah."

"Thank you." Rabbi Rachel was sitting on the straight chair, which placed her at an elevated position to the rest of us. She opened a book. "Let me quote from Deuteronomy: '*And God elevated you today to be His chosen nation, as He had promised, and entrust his laws to you, to make you supreme among all the gentiles, for His glory.*'"

She looked up and met my eyes. "But who does God speak to? Who are the 'Chosen People,' the beneficiaries of His divine promise of supremacy above all others?" She flipped through the pages to another spot. "The earliest mention of this promise appears in Genesis, chapter seventeen, where God promises Abraham the land of Canaan: '*And you shall honor my Covenant, and your seed after you for all future generations.*' The question is: Did God limit the Covenant to the biological descendants of Abraham?"

No one tried to answer.

"The solution," she continued, "appears in the next sentence, when God explains that the Covenant shall be open not only to Abraham's seed, but also for newcomers to the faith: '*The sons of gentiles who are not from your seed.*' In other words, we, the Jewish people, are not a defined ethnic group or a race, but an open faith to all those who join in the Covenant. By adopting the faith in Adonai our God, Adonai the one and only, they too become chosen. Unfortunately, some so-called rabbis have erected artificial, technical barriers to prevent righteous gentiles from joining the Jewish faith. I believe those rabbis are violating the divine Covenant, which they pretend to protect."

"Well put," Aaron said and winked at me.

"Let us pray," the rabbi concluded, "that the God of Abraham, the Almighty, who can see into human hearts and tell good from evil, that He shall bless us and the rest of the people of Israel, and we say, Amen."

"Amen," Judy Levy said, and raised a glass of lemonade. "To the open Covenant!"

Everyone sipped lemonade, and I smiled at Rabbi Rachel, wishing things were that simple.

Larry Emanuel, who served as treasurer, had e-mailed Judy a summary of the financial report. She handed it out. It showed the synagogue operating on the brink of insolvency. But it seemed clear to everyone that the second item on the agenda made any further discussion of the financial report superfluous. Cantor Bentov made a motion to approve the report, I seconded the motion, and we voted unanimously to approve it.

"About the offer from Jonathan Warnick." I looked around. "The only thing we are asked to do in exchange for the money is to adopt a new name, which shall be 'Golda and Leo Warnick Synagogue.' Are there any questions before we vote?"

Rabbi Rachel looked at Aaron, and he said, "No doubt that this is a wonderful opportunity. The main concern is that the congregation has been known by its current name for so long. People have donated money over the years to King Solomon, a name that connotes communal ownership. The new name might imply a private ownership."

The rabbi nodded and smiled at Aaron. He glanced at me and shrugged.

"That's a ridiculous concern," Judy said. "No one would think that a synagogue is a private enterprise owned by Jonathan's dead parents. Lots of public institutions carry names of private donors."

"They're my parents too," Mat said, "and I feel awkward about this, almost like being pretentious, even though it's not my money. I won't say anything to Jonathan because I don't want to spoil the deal, but a person who wants to give to charity should do it because it's the right thing to do, because God will reward his righteousness in the next world. Charity loses its virtue when it's given in exchange for personal benefits in this world."

From the way Rabbi Rachel watched Mat speak, I suspected he was repeating what she had told him in the van on the way up the mountain. Also, the words he used did not sound like Mat's words.

"That's Jonathan's prerogative," Aaron said. "As Judy said, naming rights are often given to donors. But there could be resentment among our congregants if we completely dispose of King Solomon." He glanced up at Rabbi Rachel, perched high on her chair.

"A few grumblings," Larry said, "are a small price to pay for this huge donation."

"Mat and Aaron" the rabbi said, "raised important issues. I am deeply concerned about the demand to change the name of our synagogue."

"Better to shut it down altogether?" Judy picked up a fistful of nuts. "I can make a beautiful plaque that will say: *On this spot until recently stood the King Solomon Synagogue.* I'll use singed brass. It's very commemorative."

"What are we talking about here?" Larry's voice creaked from the speakerphone. "We have no choice. We need the money ASAP. Desperate situations require drastic solutions."

"We're not desperate, and we're not shutting down." Rabbi Rachel held up the book. "As Mat has said, the Torah is clear that charity should be given without conditions or worldly rewards."

"Jonathan was very clear," I said. "He wants the new name of the synagogue to replace King Solomon everywhere. He was specific—put the new name on the building, the Hebrew school, the website, and so on."

"That's correct," Mat said. "He wants our parents' names to become known in association with a successful institution, and he's willing to spend the money to make it successful."

"*Make* it successful?" The rabbi's voice was sharp, almost angry. "Why? Isn't it successful already?"

No one responded.

"Let there be no question," Rabbi Rachel said, "That the King Solomon Synagogue is a beautiful community of faith and learning, which I've built from nothing over a lifetime of dedicated labor of love. Don't you agree? Isn't our congregation successful already—in every respect other than money?"

On the speakerphone, Larry chuckled. "It's like the dying man in the desert telling his camel, 'Don't we have everything we need—other than water?'"

"Jonathan wants to make it *more* successful," Mat clarified.

Rabbi Rachel didn't seem convinced. "In what way? We're entitled to know what changes he has in mind, what other demands he might raise later on."

"The name change," I said, "was the only condition."

"For now. But what's coming next?" The rabbi looked from face to face. "A wealthy person giving such a sum isn't going to sit back and let us do as we like, correct? Money talks—and talks and talks and talks!"

"Money is good," Judy said. "We'll have funds to renovate the building, put in a proper sound system, add educational programs. Look at the Gathering Hall, for example. It's musty!"

"Hey!" I shook a finger at her. "We're having a Sheva Brachot dinner there tomorrow!"

"Who cares," Larry said, "about future demands? We'll have the money in the bank, and if Jonathan has ideas about improving the synagogue, we'll hear him respectfully and decide then."

"The demand for a name change," Rabbi Rachel declared, her voice rising, "is an ominous sign! It implies the donor's insistence that, in exchange for the money, we discard everything that the King Solomon Synagogue has stood for, everything that we identify with as a community."

"Then call my brother," Mat said, "and tell him how you feel about the name change. Explain to him how Torah treats genuine charity. Maybe he'll give up the name change, or agree to some kind of a compromise—"

Larry must have knocked on the phone in his office, which on our end sounded like gunshots. "Are you people drunk? A guy wants to give us ten million dollars, and all he's asking is that we put a different name on the place? I wish he wanted to rename the VA hospital for Golda and Leo—tell me where to sign!"

"My parents were good people," Mat said.

"Of course," Rabbi Rachel said, her tone calmer, conciliatory. "We all loved your parents and are happy to acknowledge their memory. But I think Rusty should talk to Jonathan about keeping King Solomon, which is the name everyone associates with our congregation." She smiled to soften the hard-sell. "After all, King Solomon was a pillar of wisdom and culture in our national history, a figure of historic greatness."

"And lots of wives," Aaron said.

"Exactly," the rabbi said. "And we can commemorate Golda and Leo in a more modest way." She looked at me. "Will you talk to Jonathan?"

"Excuse me," Judy said, "but I don't think that's a good idea."

I wanted to hug her.

"Just think about it," Judy said. "How could Jonathan say no to him?"

"That's the whole point," Rabbi Rachel said. "It's important to set boundaries for such a donor, or he'll think that we will cave in to his every demand, cater to his every whim, and accommodate his every capricious idea forever. And if Rusty calls him, our chances are good that he won't refuse."

"He won't say no," Judy persisted. "He'll just find an excuse to scrap the whole thing, and a month later we'll hear that the Silicon Valley Museum of Computer Chips and Salsa will be renamed the Golda and Leo Warnick Museum."

Cantor Bentov, who had not spoken yet, raised his hand. "Beggars can't be choosers—or bargainers. We need this money."

"The name change," Aaron said, "is unfortunate. But it creates a long-term commitment, because he won't allow the place to fall apart while his parents' names are on it. He'll put in more money later on if it's needed."

"Good point." I breathed in relief. The wind was blowing in the right direction.

"My opinion is unchanged," the rabbi said, "I think Rusty should try to pressure him to give up the name change, not only because a spiritual community shouldn't be up for sale, but because this is who we are, the King Solomon Synagogue. If Jonathan really wants to help his late parents' congregation and do them honor, he should support us rather than force us to change who we are."

"Then you better not cry later," Larry said, "because I'm telling you now that Judy's right. He'll politely withdraw the offer and give the money elsewhere."

"That's a valid concern," I said, "which is why it won't be me calling him. But if one of you wants to reach out to Jonathan and try to negotiate a concession on the name change, please go ahead. We'll need to vote, though, to give you the authority to speak for the board. Anyone?"

No one volunteered. It was clear that such a call would put the whole donation at risk. Everyone in the room understood it, except for the rabbi. Or did she also understand the risk yet for some reason wanted to take it?

Rabbi Rachel had a piece of paper in her hand. She folded it and put it away.

"Okay," Judy said, "I'm making a motion to vote on the offer."

"I second the motion," the cantor announced.

"Wait a minute!" The rabbi stood. "We are a Jewish congregation, not some business corporation where money talks louder than anything else. With all due respect to your assistance as volunteer trustees and lay leaders, I am the rabbi! I am the spiritual leader of the King Solomon Synagogue! I am the final authority on all matters of Judaism and worship, and I've made it clear to you that I object to the name change. I therefore object to the acceptance of the offer. Haven't I made it clear?"

"Excuse me," Judy said, "I'm sorry to interrupt you, Rabbi, but under the by-laws, once a vote has been called and seconded, the board must vote."

I was impressed with Judy's wise choice to make a mild technical argument rather than try to explain to Rabbi Rachel that her spiritual leadership role did not change the fact that she was an employee of the synagogue and that the board had the ultimate authority to make all decisions about synagogue business, including the rabbi's own employment. It was an unpleasant conflict, but she was wrong to throw her weight around or try to block the board from voting, especially in this case, when every business-minded person would know that we had no choice but to accept the offer.

The rabbi sat down.

No one spoke.

Judy broke the silence. "Everyone in favor of accepting the offer as is, including the name change, raise your hand."

Everyone did, except for Rabbi Rachel. On the phone, Larry said, "My hand is up."

"Those opposing, raise your hand," Judy said.

The rabbi raised her hand.

"The Warnick offer is accepted by majority. So voted."

There was a long silence while Judy scribbled on her pad.

"As president of the board," I said, "I want to thank you all, especially Rabbi Rachel for leading a thorough discussion of this critical decision in the life of the synagogue. Our disagreement is regrettable, but I know that we all share a dedication to do what's best for the congregation."

The rabbi looked away.

Judy finished recording the vote as if nothing unusual had happened and announced that the meeting was adjourned.

To deflect the tension, Judy invited us to her studio. The space used to be an open balcony, perched on the mountainside with open views of the northeast valley. Windows had been installed around, but otherwise it was maintained as an outdoor space, with a floor of rough wooden planks and whitewashed walls. The lighting was very bright. Half-finished projects, mainly wood carvings and metal sculptures, filled the space. She led us to the end and tugged at a stained cloth sheet, exposing a large, convoluted maze of steel and wood.

The cantor gazed at it. "What in the world is this?"

"The basic structure is a cross." I gestured at the two pieces of railway tracks, which Judy had welded to form a cross taller than any NBA player. "The rest seems to be a bent-up candelabra." I traced the seven branches, one pointing up, tied with barbed wire to the upper part of the cross, three bent sideways, tied to the left arm of the cross, and three to the right. I crouched to look closely at the base of the candelabra, which was carved as a human face, its mouth agape in a silent scream. It was bound to the bottom beam of the cross with several rounds of barbed wire that formed a thorny crown on the forehead.

"It's not a candelabra." Still crouching, I turned to look at Judy. "You crucified a menorah?"

"Correct," she said. "Menorah is the national symbol of Israel, and I feel that the world is continuing to crucify the Jewish people for our one sin—bringing light to the world."

"There was a painter," Cantor Bentov said, "who did something similar."

"A fictional painter," Aaron said. "Asher Lev, the main character in a Chaim Potok novel."

"But unlike Judy," I said, "Asher Lev depicted the crucifixion of his mother."

———

Silent Night

Aaron and Cantor Bentov asked me to have a drink after the board meeting, and we gorged on iced tea and lemon slices at Houston's while discussing all the things we could do for the synagogue with the money.

I didn't realize how late it was until I saw the rental Malibu cooling its tires in my driveway. It was after 11 p.m.

With access to the garage blocked off, I parked at the curb, turned off the engine, and sat there, looking at the bright windows, especially the living room. I should have been home earlier to reconcile with Rebecca and greet Debra and Mordechai when they arrived. And I should have stood by my Christmas tree and delivered a speech about love and memories and respect for different traditions. But I was late, and now my daughter and her husband must be confused and upset, while Rebecca was delivering her own speech, which could not be very complimentary of me.

Drawing my Blackberry from its holster, I checked for new e-mails. Nothing. I opened Jonathan's note from yesterday, which had communicated his offer, and typed a reply:

DEAR JONATHAN, I'M HAPPY TO REPORT THAT THE BOARD OF TRUSTEES VOTED EARLIER TO ACCEPT YOUR OFFER. WE ARE EXCITED, HUMBLED, AND GRATEFUL. WE LOOK FORWARD TO WORKING TOGETHER WITH YOU TO BRING SUCCESS AND

GROWTH TO THE GOLDA AND LEO WARNICK SYNAGOGUE. WARM REGARDS, CHRISTIAN DINWALL, BOARD PRESIDENT.

Despite the late hour, he responded within seconds with one word: GREAT!

With this final task out of the way, I considered driving off. It was a tempting option—I wouldn't have to deal with the accusations and tears that awaited me inside. On the other hand, dodging a confrontation would imply guilt, and even though a contentious family row was unappealing, it was the only opportunity I would ever have to shock Debra out of her enamored state of mind, breach the fortifications of rigid Halacha, and reach my daughter's true self. And even if Debra was too far down the path of observant lifestyle, I had to bring her to my side so that we could find a modus of co-existence with Mordechai's Orthodox universe, a begrudging acceptance that would enable Rebecca and me to remain active participants in Debra's life and the family she was starting.

At the front door, my heart beat harder against my chest at the prospect of unpleasantness, yet I was struck by hearing nothing but the chirping of a nearby cricket. The night was completely calm, none of the acrimonious voices I had expected to hear from inside.

I turned the knob and walked in.

"Daddy's home!" Debra ran to me and threw her arms around my neck in a tight hug. "We've been waiting for you!"

"Board meetings," I said, "you remember how long they can go."

"Do I!" She had her hair in a ponytail, thankfully not covered by a cap or a wig. I took it as a positive sign.

Mordechai appeared, holding a paper plate with a piece of cake. "Hello, Dr. Dinwall." He balanced the plate in one hand and shook mine with the other. "We heard the news about the big donation. Congratulations!"

"Thank you." I glanced at the doorway leading into the living room. "Great to have you here, kids."

Rebecca yelled from the kitchen, "How did it go?"

"Pretty well," I said. "We've accepted the offer, but the rabbi is not happy."

"Why not?"

"I'm not sure. The name change upsets her and she's worried that other conditions will follow. It's odd, like this influx of cash scares her for some reason. I bet she'll change her mind when the money comes in and we can do good things with it."

Rebecca came into the foyer wearing her cooking apron and a big smile as if all was well. "Are they paying you a commission?"

"The reward of a mitzvah," Mordechai said, "is the mitzvah itself, as Talmud tells us, because every good deed is counted by God toward our salvation."

I took advantage of this opening. "You believe God will reward me for saving a Reform synagogue?"

He grinned as if had I caught him with his fork in a piece of bacon. "Who knows what God will do? But Rabbi Mintzberg says that God judges us by our intentions, not by the results of our actions."

"That's comforting," I said. "Shall we sit in the living room?"

"Why not?" Rebecca raised her eyebrows in a mocking expression and led the way.

Following her, I expected to see the tree gone, the fireplace mantle cleared off. Had she stuffed it all in the garage or thrown it away altogether? And how could I say anything now, with these two having just arrived for their honeymoon?

"Dad, you're such a comedian," Debra said as we entered the living room. "Won't they be insulted by this?"

"Insulted?" I paused, looking at my tree, its blue-and-white lights blinking, its decorations undisturbed, looking exactly as I had arranged them earlier. "Who's going to be insulted?"

"I told Debra," Rebecca said, toughing one of the branches, "that you wanted to do something for the hospital staff."

"Do something?"

"Since we couldn't invite them to the wedding or the Sheva Brachot dinner."

"Yes?"

"Did you forget the brunch on Sunday?" Rebecca spoke in a tone of a wife mothering her absentminded husband. "Bagels, lox, and hot cider to toast their Christmas."

"Ah." I looked at her in disbelief. "How nice."

"I spoke with Nina," Rebecca said, "told her you've already decorated the living room all by yourself. She was so impressed!"

"Really? Did she like the idea of bagels and lox for Christmas?"

"With all the garnishes," Rebecca smirked, "who wouldn't?"

"Of course. But keep out the capers—too bitter for Christmas."

"Good point. We don't want to pickle the holiday spirit."

"Right." I watched Debra lift up her old teddy bear and show it to Mordechai, who tugged at the blue-and-white scarf. "Will they come?"

"She'll ask the other nurses and let me know," Rebecca said. "Most of them have family in town for the holiday weekend, so it might not work out, unfortunately."

"Too bad."

"Don't be so disappointed." She tapped a Jewish star on a string, making it spin. "It's the intent that counts."

We went to the kitchen and sat around the table. I was still in shock at Rebecca's devious maneuver. She had pulled the rug from under my whole effort to confront Debra and Mordechai with the duality of my Jewish faith and Christian traditions. I had thought that staying under one roof with a Christmas tree would stimulate a passionate discussion about prejudice, xenophobia, and the destructive forces of extreme religiousness. But Rebecca had turned the whole thing into a benign effort at workplace harmony—a Jewish doctor making a last-minute, half-hearted, condescending effort to acknowledge the hospital workers and their holiday.

For a moment I was fuming, ready to blow up and tell all. But the cake was excellent, and my daughter was home for the first time since last summer, telling us about the beginning of her married life, about the new apartment and the first breakfast they had together as a couple—singed wheat toast and Mordechai's version of scrambled eggs, which included cottage cheese, ketchup, and a few shards of eggshell. We laughed, and Rebecca brought me a cup of herbal tea, seeming completely happy and loving, though I could see the victorious glint in her eyes.

There was a headdress on the table, folded up. I picked it up. "Is this yours?"

Debra nodded. "You want to try it on?"

I did, and they found it very funny.

Touching his yarmulke, Mordechai asked, "Do you want to try mine?"

"I'm not kosher yet." I handed the headdress to Debra. "Are you going to keep your hair covered like the Orthodox women?"

"I *am* an Orthodox woman."

I gestured at her hair. "How come it's not covered now?"

"Inside a woman's own home," Mordechai answered for her, "or even her parents' home, she may remove her headdress, unless there are strangers around. It's a special dispensation, according to Rabbi Mintzberg."

"*Mean-Zeh-Berg*." I sipped from my tea. "*Mount Mean*."

"Not *mean*," Debra said. "*Mints*. He makes me think of those little chocolate mints you find on the pillow in a good hotel, you know? Dark on the outside, but kind of sweet inside, with a sharp bite."

"A sharp bite," I said. "That's him."

"The cake is excellent." Mordechai put his yarmulke back on, glancing at me and looking away. He clearly was terrified of the moment of truth, when Debra would find out what had happened at the ketubah room at the Pillars of Joy.

"Here." Rebecca sliced off pieces and placed them on Mordechai's and Debra's plates.

"I'm full." Debra pushed it away. "Didn't you like our rabbi, Dad?"

"Just playing with words." I wondered how Mordechai had been able to keep from telling her the truth. Spoiling her wedding night had been my concern, the reason I had demanded that they lie to her about me feeling sick. But keeping this secret for much longer was risky for Mordechai, who had the most to lose should Debra find out and feel deceived. Was he too young to understand this risk? Or was he hoping the secret would remain undisclosed?

"He's a famous rabbi." Debra's voice had a defensive pitch to it. "People come from all over to ask him questions of Torah. I feel fortunate to have had him officiate at our wedding."

"Speaking of the wedding," I said, "it's been three days already, and if you don't mind me asking, did Debbie do a grandbaby for Daddy?"

"*Dad!*" Debra threw a cake crumb at me, and Mordechai turned red.

"I'm sorry, but your mother is worried."

"Am not!" Rebecca sat down and pulled Debra into her lap, cradling her like a mother would a small child, which looked funny with Debra being much taller than her petite mother. "If you have to know, Dr. Dinwall, then after the wedding night a bride is forbidden to her husband for a period of time."

"That's right." Mordechai smiled with those big, white teeth. "I'm dying here."

The boy had a sense of humor, which delighted me with hope. In a way, I liked the idea that he couldn't touch my daughter, but I also felt sorry for him. "A little bit of abstinence," I said, "is good preparation for the harsh realities of marital coexistence."

"Okay." Debra got off Rebecca's lap. "We're going to sleep now."

"Wait," I held her arm. "What's the update on your med school applications?"

She shrugged. "I'm only applying in the New York area—"

"My dad is on the board at Albert Einstein," Mordechai said. "We're hoping to end up there together."

"Great," Rebecca said. "Ask for a two-for-one discount."

"It's a good school," he said, "and they're very accommodating to observant students."

Debra nodded, and I held back my disappointment that she wouldn't be attending medical school at Columbia, as I had done.

We said our goodnights, and they were gone into Debra's old room.

At the door to our bedroom, I asked Rebecca, "Did you really call Nina?"

"Of course. I wouldn't lie to Debra. But don't worry. No one is available. We can take the kids to Sedona on Sunday as planned."

"The staff must be laughing all over Facebook." I sighed. "Bagels and lox for Christmas?"

"Are you looking for another fight?"

"Hell, no!" I laughed. "You're a clever woman."

"Exactly." She handed me linen, a towel, and my toothbrush. "Go sleep with your tree."

Have Yourself a Merry Little Christmas

Going to sleep alone was a new experience for me. It had happened occasionally that Rebecca was already asleep by the time I got home from the hospital. But her presence in bed next to me would invariably have a calming effect, enabling me to get over the nervous rush of surgery and fall asleep. Still, I was on vacation now, and the jovial time we had just spent together gave me a good reason to be optimistic about turning Rebecca around. By tomorrow night, I expected to be back in the master bedroom upstairs, our pillow talk dedicated to a united effort of pushing back the tide of Orthodoxy that was threatening our relationship with Debra and the boy she had married.

I pulled the plug and the tree lights went off. Lying down on the living room sofa, I recited the night prayer, another calming ritual I had adopted years ago: "*Hear, O Israel, Adonai is our God, Adonai is One...*"

The sofa was plump and cushy. At first, the luxurious, body-forming leather under the linen embraced me comfortably. But soon, instead of lying on the sofa, I was lying *in* it. My eyes wide but seeing little in the darkness, I slowly sank into the soft cushions like a silent victim of warm quicksand. I stretched out to my full height, turned on my side, moved closer to the firmer edge, but with every new position the sinking sensation soon resumed.

Suddenly, I was overwhelmed by the onslaught of suffocation. *Air!*

I kicked off the covers, leaped from the sofa, and opened the window, gulping in the night air. My heart was racing, and I chided myself for consuming all that iced tea so late in the evening, loading up on caffeine.

After a few minutes, my breathing slowed down. I turned on the lights and sat on the sofa. The pain in my left arm seemed worse. I rotated it, trying to loosen up the shoulder. I should have bought a smaller tree, perhaps an artificial one that required no heavy lifting.

Looking at my Christmas corner, I felt that something was odd about it. At first I attributed it to the Judaic decorations, which most people would consider out of place but to me seemed appropriate in light of my particular personal history. The oddity went beyond the decorations, and it took me a few minutes to pin down the cause: *No gifts!*

The checkout lines at Wal-Mart defied the late hour or, more accurately, the *early* hour. It was almost 3 a.m. when I finished my shopping spree and pushed the cart through a parking lot full of cars and SUVs. Everything fit in the trunk of the Volvo, except for the set of Callaway golf clubs and the elongated box of gift-wrap paper, which I dropped in the back seat through the open top. I zipped up my windbreaker and drove home. The rushing air felt fresh and invigorating.

I brought in the goods without waking up anyone. The stepladder was trickier, but I managed not to bang it against the walls on the way from the garage. It wasn't quite as tall as the highest bough, but I reached up to the top of the tree and tied the star-shaped balloon, which was painted in gold with shining letters: Golden Days Are Here Again! It was probably intended for a retirement party, but my choices were limited to items that were not explicitly for Christmas, or there would be trouble when Rebecca got up.

It took me almost an hour to write the three cards. Then, armed with scissors and tape, I sat on the carpet and began to wrap the gifts.

———

Part Six
Thursday, December 24 – Christmas Eve

We Wish You a Merry Christmas

By 8 a.m., I could tell from the sounds of toilets flushing and showers running that everyone was up. When Rebecca's hair dryer quieted down, I sat at the piano and pounded the keys with the basic notes of "We Wish You a Merry Christmas."

The sound drew the three of them to the living room, where they found me playing the familiar Christmas tune. Before my wife had a chance to hit me with a heavy object, I started singing the revised lyrics that I had written at dawn:

"We wish you a merry marriage,
We wish you a merry marriage,
We wish you a merry marriage,
And a baby next year!

God's blessings to Mordechai,
And to all of your kin,
God's blessings to Debra,
And a baby next year!"

The big smiles on Debra's and Mordechai's faces encouraged me, and I continued to the next part:

"Oh, bring us a cutie munchkin,
Oh, bring us a cutie munchkin,
Oh, bring us a cutie munchkin,
Or twins for good cheer!

God's blessings to Mordechai,
And to all of your kin,
God's blessings to Debra,
And a baby next year!"

By the encore, the young couple was singing with me, "*We wish you a merry marriage!*" Rebecca took a little longer, but Debra forced her into it, and they sang together, "*We wish you a merry marriage,*" and giggled at each other as the last line came around, "*And a baby next year!*"

Setting the mood so successfully with music, I found no resistance to my invitation to open the gifts. I had arranged the wrapped packages on the coffee table rather than under the tree so as not to trigger Rebecca's wrath.

Mordechai went first. He removed his card from the box of golf clubs and read it.

TO OUR NEW SON-IN-LAW, MAY YOU ENJOY MANY MORE VISITS TO THE CITY WITH THE MOST GOLF COURSES IN THE UNIVERSE, AND MAY YOUR GAME BE AS SHARP AS YOUR NEW WIFE. LOVE, YOUR IN-LAWS

"Nice," Rebecca said, reading over his shoulder.

I handed her a gift. "And this is for you."

She tore the wrapping. It was a picture frame. The photo I had chosen to insert showed me flanked by Rebecca and my mother. It was a bit comical, as Rebecca was much shorter than my mother, and I was even taller. But most important was the fourth participant, my mother's dwarfish Christmas tree, under which she had placed a single gift for me and my Jewish girlfriend—a box of kosher Elite chocolate, made in Israel. I still don't know where she had found it, but Rebecca had been touched by the gesture. The photo was taken with my camera, set on a short timer, capturing one of very few occasions that Rebecca spent time with my mother, who died a couple of years later, shortly before her fiftieth birthday.

On that particular Christmas Eve, after my mother had fed us, I wheeled the old kerosene stove to the porch, and we sat in wicker chairs, our coats buttoned up, to watch the barges navigate between chunks of ice on the Hudson River. We drank hot cider, spiced up with rum, and listened to my mother talk about her childhood in Scotland, the terrifying Atlantic crossing, and her teenage years of hardship in the new country. She spoke of my father, whose family had been in America for several generations yet maintained its Scottish pride. He courted her with teenage enthusiasm, and by the end of their senior year in high school, they knew that God had meant for them to share a life.

He was drafted at eighteen, and they saw each other during brief leaves. They tied the knot before a county clerk near the base, and a week later he shipped to Vietnam. I was born nine months later, and he chose my name during a phone call, patched through a field radio. His choice—Christian—surprised her as he wasn't prone to expressions of devoutness. In his next letter he said: THERE ARE NO ATHEISTS IN THIS JUNGLE. He wrote weekly, and she wrote back and sent photos. She could sense his longing, but men back then thought it unseemly to whine. His letters spoke of a happy future once he completed his service. He would be entitled to attend college on Uncle Sam's dime and planned to become a doctor. Between his Scottish stubbornness and his American optimism, my mother explained, there was no question that he would accomplish his goal. But then a rocket hit his boat, and it was all over.

I touched Rebecca's hand. "Do you remember?"

She put the photo down on the coffee table and nodded. "We were so young."

"Read my card," I said.

It was a white card, with no pre-printed graphics or poems. I looked over her shoulder at my own handwriting: WILL YOU MEET ME HALFWAY?

Rebecca got up and went to the kitchen.

Debra and Mordechai looked at me, unsure what to say. I wasn't sure either. But a moment later Rebecca returned and tossed the card in my lap. I looked at it and saw a sentence she had penciled underneath: I HAVE MET YOU HALFWAY FROM THE BRONX. BUT NOW WE HAVE TO MEET DEBRA HALFWAY TO BROOKLYN!

Debra reached for the card. "Isn't this supposed to be a family event? No secrets!"

Before I had a chance to respond, Rebecca snatched the card from my hand and added a sentence: AND DON'T MAKE ME CHOOSE BETWEEN YOU AND HER!

I looked at her and shook my head. There was so much I wanted to say, but it would have to wait until we were alone.

"Thank you for the clubs," Mordechai said. "I don't mean to be rude, but I'm really not comfortable with this." He gestured at the tree.

"Why not?" I was ready for the discussion. "Tell me."

"It's their ritual, celebrating that false messiah of theirs."

"A common misconception," I said mildly. "The Christmas tree is not a religious symbol. It comes from feudal Europe, where they celebrated the new year by lighting a fire under a tree and dancing around it. Later on, people started hanging fruit on the tree before the celebration. With the passing centuries, it evolved into a tradition of cutting down a small tree and decorating it indoors, mainly because the season is so cold. And these days, everyone celebrates the holidays with a Christmas tree even if they're not religious."

Mordechai looked at Debra for help, but it was Rebecca who jumped in. "Don't be an idiot, Rusty. It's a Christmas tree. *Christ-mas!*"

I kept my voice even, not succumbing to her provocation. "Over the years, the New Year tree took on the name of the Christmas holiday, which relates to the birthday of Jesus. That's true. But I did an Internet search that really surprised me. Historically, many Jews in Europe brought a Christmas tree into their homes, first as a gesture to their household employees, but later it spread as an independent holiday custom, with gifts for everyone. Sometimes it was combined with Hanukkah, but the Jewish calendar changes every year—like this year, for example, that we celebrated Hanukkah a month ago. But the tree is not about religion."

"So let me summarize your scholarly research," Rebecca said. "Christmas trees aren't about Jesus Christ. Rather, Christmas is a celebration of trees, just like Easter is a celebration of eggs, Thanksgiving is a celebration of turkeys, and July Fourth is a celebration of fireworks. Did I get it right?"

"The Christmas holiday is about Jesus Christ," I conceded. "But the tree isn't."

"Where do you read this stuff? *The Christian Science Monitor?*"

Pulling out a page I had printed off Wikipedia, I showed her the highlighted paragraph. "Even Theodore Herzl, the visionary of modern Zionism, entertained the chief rabbi of Vienna at his home while the kids played under the holiday tree."

"It's not a holiday tree." Rebecca brushed away the paper. "It's a Christmas tree!"

"Whose side are you on?" I said it lightly, but inside I was seething.

"I'm on the side of the truth." She pointed at me. "And you're on the wrong side!"

I gestured at her and me. "We're on the same side."

"Then you should know that Jews don't celebrate Christmas!"

I picked up the Wikipedia printout and pressed it to my achy chest, taking shallow breaths, struggling to speak through the fog of frustration. "Herzl wasn't Jewish?"

"Hold on," Debra said, "before you two kill each other, can I open my gift?"

The wrapping on her gift was a rainbow of vivid colors, and the card had a matching pattern on the outside. There was also a pre-printed, saccharine Hallmark holiday message inside, which I had covered with stickers of parrots. My message was written by hand on the blank, left side of the card:

TO OUR PRECIOUS DEBRA: ALWAYS REMEMBER THAT LIFE ISN'T TIDY. BEING DIFFERENT IS OK. KNOW WHO YOU ARE, AND DON'T BE AFRAID TO STAY THE WAY YOU ARE, EVEN IN BROOKLYN. LOVE, MOM AND DAD.

My daughter looked up from the card, her forehead creased.

"Look at your gift," I said.

She took the paperback out of the torn gift wrap. It was my dog-eared copy of Kosinski's novel *The Painted Bird*.

"My mother gave it to me." I slumped back in my seat, trying to calm down. "You never met her, but there's much about you that reminds me of your grandmother, especially your strength and determination. And loyalty."

"Thanks, Dad." She hugged me. "I'll read the book on the flight back to New York tomorrow."

Through the comfort of my daughter's physical affection, I struggled to digest what she had just said. "Tomorrow?"

"I'm sorry," she smiled, sitting back next to Mordechai. "We forgot to tell you last night, but we decided to go back on Friday so we can be in New York before Sabbath starts."

"But I ordered kosher meals," Rebecca said. "It's all arranged!"

Debra shrugged. "It's not just the food, Mom. We also like to attend services on Friday night and on Saturday morning."

"You can join us," I said. "We don't have to drive. I measured the distance to King Solomon. It's just over one mile."

"We'll walk together," Rebecca said. "The weather is perfect for walking, and everyone was looking forward to seeing you at the synagogue on Saturday."

"We'll see them tonight," Debra said meekly, "at the Sheva Brachot dinner."

Rebecca bit her lips and looked at me. All my anger at my wife had now turned to sympathy. I reached over to take her hand, but she pulled away and stood. "But why? I don't understand!"

Mordechai also stood up. "Please don't be upset with us. We wanted to stay, but Rabbi Mintzberg ruled that we may not attend Sabbath services at a Reform synagogue, where the lights are turned on and off, microphones and loudspeakers are in use, music is played, and the rabbi is a woman. Every one of these things is a violation of the holy Sabbath and the rules of Halacha."

Rather than argue with him, Rebecca looked down at me, her expression saying, "What did I tell you?"

And I was facing a fork in the road. One option was to express anger, to attack, the other was to reason and cajole. I took the second, but allowed my voice to express indignation as I gripped his arm and made sure he looked at me. "Listen, before your wedding I was a stranger to you. And being as young and as dependent on your parents as you are, it was understandable that in any conflict you would side completely with them and their rabbi. But now we are your family too. My wife and I would like nothing more than to treat you with the generosity and love that we would have shown our own son had we been blessed with one."

"It's true, "Rebecca said.

"But with that," I continued, "comes the expectation of some respect. All you needed to do was pick up the phone and share with us the dilemma presented by your rabbi's anti-Reform ruling, and we would have suggested a solution to make everyone happy, you agree?"

He nodded. "I was afraid that when you heard what Rabbi Mintzberg said—"

"There's no issue here." I controlled my urge to curse the old rabbi, but Debra had no clue about what had happened at the wedding. "You have the right to follow Halacha just like we have the right to practice Reform Judaism and its inclusiveness." I glanced at my Christmas tree. "We respect your choices, and as hosts, we must accommodate you."

Sighing with relief, Mordechai looked at Debra, who smiled back at him.

"So here's the solution," I continued. "There are several Orthodox synagogues in the area. We'll all stay at a hotel near one of them." Anticipating Rebecca's concerns, I added, "We'll get a suite with a kitchenette and have the kosher food ready in the hotel. We'll dine together in the room after walking back from the synagogue. How's that?"

"Perfect," Rebecca said. "Let's do it!"

"Maybe next time," Debra said. "We already changed our airline tickets, and Mordechai's family is hosting a kiddush lunch at their synagogue on Saturday."

"We'll change back the tickets," I said, ignoring the part about Mordechai's family—they could host a kiddush lunch another time. "Any airline change fees are on us. After the Sabbath, on Sunday, we have a reservation for a Jeep rental in Sedona so we can explore the red rocks. And one of my patients, who owns an air touring company, offered to take us on a flight over the Grand Canyon and up the Colorado River to Lake Powell, including a stopover at the Navaho Tribe's heritage center. Then, on Tuesday—"

"Daddy, please!" Debra put her hand on my mouth. "We are going home tomorrow."

"But why?" I waved my hands around. "This is also your home!"

"Not anymore. I'm married now."

"Yes, you are married, and it's wonderful, but you're still our daughter, aren't you?"

She looked at her mother for support, but Rebecca was as distraught as I.

"Dr. Dinwall," Mordechai said, "please accept our decision. We can't stay here for Sabbath. We have to leave tomorrow and make it home to New York before sunset. But we are excited to spend today with you and meet everyone tonight."

The finality in his tone left no room for further discussion. Clearly he could be assertive when he had to. This discovery was surprising, but also very good news, because I now had much less time to adjust his worldview and loyalties, which meant resorting to shock therapy. "Okay," I said. "Let's enjoy the day together."

Rebecca groaned.

I patted his shoulder, indicating there were no hard feelings. "What would you like to do?"

"Debra told me there are great places to hike around here," Mordechai said, visibly relieved. "And it's so nice outside."

Rudolph the Red-Nosed Reindeer

R ebecca's phone rang as we were getting out of the car at the foot of Pinnacle Peak in north Scottsdale. It was the kosher caterer, asking for a final count for tonight's dinner party. "I'm not sure," Rebecca said. "We invited all the members of the congregation. Usually only friends and relatives attend these events, but my husband is the president of the synagogue, so others might feel obliged to come."

"Tell her a hundred people," I said. "I doubt there will be more."

"Set up tables for two hundred," Rebecca said. "And keep plenty of extras to refill the buffet trays if more people show up." After a brief pause, she added, "That's fine. We'll pay for everything you bring, even what you'll have to throw away."

I sighed.

The path was busy with hikers as if it were a weekend. With the night coolness still lingering in the morning air, some people wore red-and-white wool hats and matching coats. The younger kids had reindeer antlers growing from their caps, and one teenager had a large cross attached to his back, the horizontal beam wider than his shoulders. Up close, I could tell it was made of foam, painted a patchy brown to look like wood.

Halfway up the mountain, Mordechai stopped to take in the view, which was fine with me. After a sleepless night, my muscles ached and I was out of breath.

"Look at these houses!" He pointed downward. "They're huge!"

"In this area," Rebecca said, "anything under five thousand square feet is considered a small house. But usually they're seven or eight, maybe even ten thousand square feet."

"It's not just the houses." He sheltered his eyes from the sun. "Look at that pool. It's got waterfalls! They also have a tennis court, and over there, their own putting green! And baseball batting cage!"

"This is nothing." I rotated my left arm, which seemed to help with the ache. "A few miles up the road there's a group of mansions with their own airstrip. They land their private planes and taxi them into attached hangars the way we drive our car into the garage."

Mordechai whistled. "I have a feeling we're not in Brooklyn anymore."

An hour later, the top of the trail offered a magnificent view of the brown desert landscape, patched up with green golf courses surrounded by red roofs. Rebecca pointed out different locations for Mordechai, beginning with the barren cliffs of the McDowell Mountains. "It's a huge nature preserve," she explained, "full of wildlife. Sometimes the animals come down into town—foxes, coyotes, javelinas, which are wild pigs that move in packs, and even bears and mountain lions."

I had to sit on a rock and contend with a stitch that stabbed my ribs. My Blackberry vibrated against my hip. There was a new e-mail from Judy Levy, sent to all the members of the King Solomon Synagogue:

DEAR FELLOW CONGREGANTS: I'M DELIGHTED TO ANNOUNCE THAT LAST NIGHT THE BOARD OF TRUSTEES VOTED TO ACCEPT A SUBSTANTIAL DONATION FROM JONATHAN WARNICK. THIS GENEROUS GIFT, WHICH IS THE RESULT OF EFFORTS BY OUR LONG-TIME VOLUNTEER PRESIDENT, DR. DINWALL, WILL RESOLVE THE SYNAGOGUE'S FINANCIAL DEFICIT AND ENABLE

US TO ADD EDUCATIONAL AND SPIRITUAL PROGRAMS FOR THE BENEFIT OF EVERYONE. ALSO, AS MANY OF YOU KNOW, THE WARNICK FAMILY HAS BEEN PART OF OUR COMMUNITY FOR MANY YEARS. THEREFORE WE ARE HONORED TO RENAME THE SYNAGOGUE FOR GOLDA AND LEO WARNICK. WITH GOD'S BLESSINGS, JUDY LEVY, BOARD SECRETARY.

P.S. TONIGHT AT 7 IS THE DINWALL FAMILY'S SHEVA BRACHOT DINNER.

I forwarded Judy's e-mail to Jonathan Warnick with a brief note:

JONATHAN, FYI. AGAIN, ON BEHALF OF THE BOARD, THE MEMBERS, AND THE STUDENTS OF OUR HEBREW SCHOOL, THANK YOU AND GOD'S SPEED! CHRISTIAN DINWALL, BOARD PRESIDENT.

"Are you okay?" Debra crouched next to me while Rebecca continued pointing out the sights to Mordechai.

"With you around, life is good." I holstered my Blackberry and leaned on her as I stood up.

"You don't look well."

"Not enough sleep. And I'm still recovering from New York."

"Oh, about that, Mrs. Levinson was going to ask the photographer to paste your image into the chuppah photos. He could use the images he got earlier, when you stood near the entrance."

"He'll doctor the photos to add a doctor?"

"It's a simple operation, easy to do with digital images."

I chuckled. "What did you tell her?"

"That you wouldn't like it."

"Why not?"

"Because I don't believe the upset stomach story." Debra paused, looking at the distant mountains, waiting for me to protest, which I didn't. What could I say?

"You would have been there, right next to me, correct?"

I remained silent. How could I deny it?

"If it was only a physical thing, a sickness, you would have dragged yourself over somehow or had Aaron give you a piggyback ride."

"He's too short. My hands would drag on the floor."

"Then you would have sat on the floor under the chuppah or in a chair next to me. You would have put on diapers if you had to, no matter what anyone said. You wouldn't miss it for anything!"

The last few words Debra cried out, causing Rebecca to stop her tour-guide routine and turn.

I caressed Debra's cheek. "It's better that you keep thinking of it as an upset stomach."

"My dad taught me that it's always better to tell the truth."

"Yes." I sighed. "It is."

"Then tell me the truth!"

"I'd rather let Mordechai tell you what happened."

When he stood before his bride, I could see that Mordechai was as nervous as he had been in the ketubah room. The boy had a lot to explain, and I felt sorry for him. But it was their marriage he now had to save, and I had enough trouble with my own wife. I threaded my arm in Rebecca's, and we started on the path downhill.

No one spoke as we drove away from Pinnacle Peak. I put down the top to let in the sun but kept the windows up to shelter us from the wind. In the back seat, Debra looked out the window, sniffling, and Mordechai sat with his face in his hands. The atmosphere resembled the ketubah room, only now I was in the driver's seat.

Instead of turning south on Pima Road toward home, I headed north to Desert Mountain in the hope that the beautiful scenery and sunny weather would somehow elevate everyone's mood.

After a while, the sniffling stopped, though Debra kept facing away from Mordechai. I was preparing to say something that would instigate a discussion, but Rebecca, who was still getting lost regularly despite having lived here for so long, somehow recognized my meandering and asked, "Where are you going?"

"A little detour." I pointed at the hills of Carefree. "It's a beautiful drive."

"Get us home please!"

"That's what I'm doing," I said innocently. "It's just a little longer."

"*Rusty!*"

There was my opening. "Christian is my name."

"I won't call you by that name."

"Why not? It's my given name. Christian. You want to see my driver's license?"

"No."

"How about our State of New York marriage license? Says it right there next to Rebecca Greenbaum. *Christian Dinwall.*"

"Don't be a smart ass!"

"Facts are facts."

Behind me, Debra blew her nose.

Rebecca took off her sunglasses and glared at me. "Will you stop this idiotic name-change campaign? You were Rusty when I met you, and you've been Rusty ever since. I will never, never, never call you by that name!"

In the rearview mirror I saw expressions of alarm on both Debra's and Mordechai's faces. But I wasn't going to drop the argument, not now that I got Rebecca to discuss it. "Tell me why?"

"You know why."

"*Azoi?*" I assumed the nasal, accented voice of Rabbi Mintzberg: "But why not, *Rey-bay-kah?*"

Mordechai chuckled behind me, but Rebecca didn't see the humor. "I won't address my own husband with an adjective that means *Non-Jewish! Goy! Shaygetz!*" She was yelling now, and tears flowed down her cheeks.

It was painful for me to do this, but I had to. "A word with multiple meanings only means what you want it to mean." Steering the car to the shoulder, I stopped, put on my hazards, and pressed the button that closed the power top. "The word 'Christian' could be used to describe someone who believes in Jesus Christ. That's true. But I don't believe that he was the Messiah, so I'm not a Christian and therefore the religious meaning does not apply to me. Rather, when I'm called Christian, it's just a name, not an adjective, okay?"

"Never!"

"What if my name was Mohammed? Or Buddha? Or Dick?" I checked the roofline above the windshield to make sure it closed properly. "Would you also refuse to—"

"Dick is fine," she said. "I'll call you Dick, because you are a dick!"

"At least I'm *your* dick."

Laughter came from the back seat.

"It's my right," I pressed on, "my unalienable human right to choose how people call me."

"You already chose Rusty. I like Rusty." Rebecca looked at me. "I even love Rusty."

Love. Present tense. That's good. "And I love you too," I said. "But I don't want to be Rusty anymore. Rusty is a redhead mechanic or a used-car salesman or a tattooed porn star. But I'm not Rusty. I'm Christian Dinwall, and I'll continue to correct you until you're too tired to resist."

"Fine," she said. "I'll call you Christian. Or Dick. Whichever you prefer."

That was too easy. "Will you? Really?"

"Yes. I will. *Christian. Christian. Christian.* Happy?"

"Very happy. What's the catch?"

"You can't call me Rebecca anymore. From now on, you must call me Satan. That's my name from now on: Satan Dinwall."

"You don't really mean that."

"Why not?"

"Because it's not the same."

"But it is," Rebecca said. "For me, if I have to call you Christian, then I might as well salute you." She raised her right hand. "*Heil Hitler!*"

"Mom, please!" Debra leaned forward between the backs of the front seats, the way she used to do as a little girl, and I almost yelled, *Buckle up, Debbie!*

"What?" Rebecca half-turned and realized that Mordechai was laughing into his hands. "What's so funny?"

"The Nazis," he said. "Every time an argument heats up between Jews, we accuse each other of being like the Nazis. It's sick!"

"Sick," Rebecca gestured at me, "is when a husband demands that his Jewish wife call him Christian. That's sick!"

"You're like two children," Debra said. "It's embarrassing. Enough already!"

"Don't be rude," Rebecca said.

"Then start calling Daddy by his real name. Call him Christian. Who cares?"

Rebecca was taken aback. "Don't you care?"

"No." Debra looked at Mordechai. "Do you?"

He eagerly shook his head. "It's just a name."

"Well," Rebecca turned and looked forward, her jaws set stubbornly, "I care!"

Even though Rebecca had not yet changed her mind, I drove on with the satisfaction that we had broken through the wall she had erected to prevent any discussion of the matter. Another achievement was Mordechai's clear indication that he was unfazed by my name, despite its secondary meaning. I knew that his acquiescence was owed in no small part to temporary circumstances. He was in the doghouse, and he would do anything to ingratiate himself to Debra and earn back her trust after failing to tell her the truth about why I had gone MIA from the wedding. It was a big challenge, and I decided to help him. Stopping at a traffic light, I said, "It was my insistence that no one told you the truth."

In my rearview mirror, Debra's nose was still red, but her eyes were dry. "It doesn't matter, Dad. It was still a lie."

"But I didn't lie," Mordechai said. "Your dad's friend, Dr. Brutsky, he told you."

"And you kept quiet," she said, "even though you knew how important it was for me to have my father next to me, or at least to know the truth about why he wasn't there."

Rebecca glanced at me, and I said, "He couldn't tell you. Part of the deal was that they promised not to tell you. The whole reason I caved in to *Mean-Zeh-Berg* was to prevent any disruption, to make sure that your wedding day remained happy."

"It was happy," Debra said. "But what's the point of a marriage if I can't trust my husband?"

"But we had to keep it from you!" Mordechai's voice sounded as if he was about to cry. "Making the bride happy is the biggest mitzvah, the most important thing under Halacha! How could I upset my own bride? And break a vow I'd made to her father? And violate my rabbi's instructions? How could I?"

"You could," Rebecca suddenly intervened. "And you should. Your wife comes first."

A car honked behind me, and I sped up to keep with traffic.

"Even your rabbi would know," Rebecca continued, "what Torah says about marriage: *And so a man shall leave his father and mother, and he shall come to his wife, and they shall become one flesh.* Have you studied this quote?"

Mordechai nodded, but Rebecca was looking at me, expecting me to also confirm that I felt bound by that rule of forgoing one's parents and home in favor of a wife.

"It's an interesting point," I said. "Does it apply to a wife also?"

"It does," Rebecca said. "That's why I stuck with you even though my parents cried and begged me to change my mind and find a Jewish guy."

Mordechai looked at Debra. "I wanted to tell you about it the next morning. But you were so happy, and I was afraid to spoil it."

"You should have," she said.

"You're right. I made a mistake. We're one flesh now. Everything I know, you have the right to know. I'll never hide anything from you, never betray your trust again." His voice cracked. "Please give me a chance."

Debra's face softened, and they smiled at each other, framed in my rearview mirror the same way I remembered their faces framed by the Skype screen on the eve of Rosh Hashanah. Had it only been three months?

We reached the house, and the two of them disappeared into Debra's room.

"Thank God." Rebecca said. "It was a close call, but Mordechai came through. I think they'll be alright."

"The real question is: Do you think they're going to obey Torah now and become one flesh in a more physical manner?"

"You could learn from him. About trust."

"Why do you say that? I've never betrayed your trust in any way whatsoever!"

"What you're doing to me now is the worst kind of betrayal."

"That's unfair." Rather than anger, I felt weak, deflated. But this was the discussion I had been waiting for, so I stuck with it. "You're the one who wants to change our whole life. You want to leave behind our friends and community, our home, even my job. You're the one who wants to change everything, turn us into Brooklyn black-hats."

"Don't exaggerate. We'll be modern Orthodox, wear normal clothes, live a normal life, work and study just like everyone else, but we'll also keep the Jewish traditions."

"Those rules aren't traditions. Traditions are optional, charming, heartwarming customs. Halacha rules aren't traditions, but constraints. They're invasive laws and regulations of every part of your life. They're meant to put you in a straight-jacket of arbitrary prohibitions."

"You're so wrong!" Rebecca came closer to me, her eyes focused on me intensely. "Why can't you see how much beauty exists in the observant lifestyle?"

"Beauty?" I almost laughed.

"Yes, beauty! The Sabbath is an incredible day—no phones, no e-mails, no TV, no business, no errands, no *to do* lists. Nothing is allowed to violate the purity of the Sabbath, so we can gather with friends for uplifting services, dine with family and friends at home with no interruptions. And the holidays? Think how nice it would be to celebrate each holiday with Debra and her family, to become part of a community of Jews who participate in synagogue life not only on Rosh Hashanah and Yom Kippur, but every holiday, every Sabbath, even every day. We will...*belong!*"

"You sound like a missionary." I paused, feeling lightheaded, as if the blood had drained down from my head, and my legs became heavy. "This idyllic picture of Orthodox life is painted by your nostalgic feelings. If that lifestyle was so wonderful, you wouldn't have left it to marry a shaygetz."

"I wouldn't have married you if I knew you'd betray me like this."

"What? Who's betraying whom?"

"When we married, you promised that we would have a Jewish home." She went into the living room and pointed at the tree. "This is a breach of our marriage vows!"

"Do you hear yourself?" I sat on the sofa, not only because my legs were wobbly, but in the hope of steering her toward a calmer discussion. "This stuff is nothing but a conversation piece."

"That's what you want? A conversation?" Instead of sitting down to discuss our differences, Rebecca crossed the room, grabbed a branch, and pulled as hard as she could, sending the whole tree crashing down. It hit the coffee table, breaking it in half.

I tried to speak, but a lump formed in my throat.

She tore the socks off the mantle and grabbed Debra's teddy bear, stripping it. The Israeli hat and scarf flew toward me.

Standing up, I held on to the wall while the room, blinking in blue and white, spun around me like a carousel.

"You're happy now?" Rebecca sobbed, hugging Debra's teddy bear to her chest. "Take all your…Christmas junk…and have a conversation…with the garbage dumpster!"

———

A Holly Jolly Christmas

Here I was again, driving with a tree in the back seat, aimed skyward like an anti-aircraft gun. The broken coffee table was strapped next to me in the passenger seat. Between the physical exertion of cleaning up and the crushing disappointment in Rebecca's rejection, I perspired heavily. It didn't help that the midday sun was baking me in slow traffic. The pain in my chest wasn't only mental, but a vacuous sensation that made me realize that I hadn't eaten yet today. Was I developing an ulcer? There was a bit of water left in a bottle between the seats, and I gulped it.

When I finally reached the 101 Freeway and could speed up, I stuck my head sideways into the wind and took in all the air my chest could hold. The indigestion discomfort passed, and I felt more optimistic. True, another round had ended in defeat. But the battle wasn't over. I had an idea that would blow everything out in the open.

Finding my destination on University Boulevard in Tempe, I was surprised by the size of the operation. *Lights4U* wasn't the cute little outfit its name implied. The warehouse had a row of loading docks, five of them occupied by medium-sized trucks that carried the company's name. I parked, carried the pieces of the coffee table to a large garbage bin, and went into the office.

Several desks, ringing phones, and at least ten people filled the office. A plastic partition cordoned off a corner, where a bearded man with a ponytail and tattooed arms examined a wall-mounted board with color-coded columns and numbers. When I entered, he turned to me, showing a hairy chest through his unbuttoned, sleeveless shirt.

"Like your tattoo. Marine corps?"

"Second battalion." He measured me up and down. "How about you?"

"VA Medical Center."

"You're a doc?"

"Christian Dinwall. I fix hearts." Noticing a Harley Davidson poster on the wall, I asked, "That's your ride?"

"Used to be." He limped around the desk and shook my hand. "I'm Roy. What can I do for you?"

"Christmas decorations. I need lots of lights. Massive. Colorful. Striking. The best you have."

"You want the works?"

"That's right."

"I'll put you down for next year."

"My party's tonight."

He pointed at the board. "It's Christmas Eve, for Santa's sake! We're struggling to finish the jobs we've already promised to folks."

I pointed at his leg. "Who took care of you?"

"The surgeon?" He scratched his beard. "Dr. Finestein."

"He was the best orthopedic surgeon we ever had."

"Was?"

"Parkinson's disease." I extended my hand, spreading my fingers. "Our worst enemy."

"That's too bad. He was a good doc."

"He still is, only he's limited to diagnostics and rehab work." I looked around. "Since I'm here already, can you show me the place?"

Roy beckoned me. "Come."

The content was predictable—boxes of wires, various lighting setups, balloons, wire mesh animals and sleighs, and fake trees in modular parts, pre-arranged with colorful stars and figurines. There was everything one would expect to see in a place specializing in Christmas decorations. But what shocked me was the enormity of it all. There were hundreds of boxes, sorted out with hand-written labels, as well as huge shipping containers on wood pallets. At least fifty employees worked in the warehouse, some driving forklifts, others loading the trucks with supplies while supervisors in company t-shirts marked off their packing lists.

"Impressive," I said. "Are all these guys family members?"

He shook his head. "I only hire veterans."

"*Caucasian* veterans."

"Not true. I got a couple of black guys." He pointed. "But no Mexicans. Nothing against them. Actually, Latinos are hard workers, good guys for the most part. But with the anti-immigration frenzy going on, I can't take the risk."

"You can hire documented Latinos, check their papers, make sure they're legal here." Even as I said it, I thought of Jose, our synagogue custodian. We'd never asked to see his papers, which he probably didn't have. Like many other employers in Arizona, we preferred to pay our Mexican laborer cash wages without payroll taxes while enjoying the dedication, the long hours, and the gratitude for the opportunity we gave him, a father of five who was determined to make a life for his kids, give them a chance at the American dream.

"I tried," Roy said, "hired only Mexicans with work permits. But one afternoon, the sheriff's department raided us and arrested a bunch of them. It took two or three days for my guys to prove that they're in this country legally, that their papers weren't fake or anything. Out of forty-three arrested, thirty-eight were eventually released. But I lost a fortune."

"That's too bad."

"Look, my business is labor intensive. With a bunch of employees suddenly taken off the job, I had to cancel deliveries, lose deals, lose customers, lose reputation, and my competitors picked up the business because I couldn't deliver. So, no more! Only an idiot hires Latinos these days. It's not worth it, you know?"

"Proves the law of unintended consequences."

"You bet."

I pointed at a truck that seemed almost ready to leave. "How big is this job, for example?"

"An insurance company on the west side of town. Standard stuff." He shrugged. "Our best customers want the glitz up at least a month before Christmas. But we always have a bunch of last-minute projects."

"Like this one?"

"Mostly corporate parties. They rent a place for the night and hire us to decorate. Stuff's up in the evening, down the next day. These are the last ones. We've been going full speed for a month now." He gestured around the warehouse. "That's why I need to stock up on inventory."

"How much is this job?" I pointed at another half-loaded truck. "I'm just curious."

Roy beckoned a woman from inside the back of the truck. "Pinky," he tapped on her writing board, "what's the total on this one?"

"Six thousand bucks," she said. "It's all external lighting and ornaments. I threw in some extras, you know, Christmas spirit and all."

They laughed, and I asked, "Is this a corporate party?"

"A law firm." She looked at her notes. "Berger Henkin Ginsberg and Strauss."

"I'll pay you double what they're paying."

They looked at me.

"Usually it's me who takes care of other people's emergencies." I glanced down at his leg. "But today it's my emergency."

"That's a new one," Pinky said. "A Christmas emergency?"

"It's a long story," I said, "but the bottom line is that this Christmas could save my family. Or destroy it."

Roy looked at me, and when he realized I wasn't joking, he said to Pinky, "Screw the lawyers. Do the doc first."

It was late in the afternoon when the little convoy, comprising my Volvo and the *Lights4U* truck, arrived at the synagogue. It was not an imposing building. Rather, its design aimed to complement the desert topography with soft, earthy tones, using sandy plaster, natural wood, and aged copper. On one side it bordered a rocky drainage wash that ran with flash floods only a few times a year, saving the neighboring golf course from turning into a grassy swamp. On the other side of the synagogue was a Montessori preschool and, next to it, a church that shared with us the good services of Jose, as well as a host of donated gardening and maintenance tools he used daily in both houses of worship. We also accommodated each other's overflow parking needs, which rarely fell on the same day, again thanks to Jose, who kept ADDITIONAL PARKING signs that he propped with the arrows pointing in this or that direction, depending on whether the particular holiday was Jewish or Christian. Tonight, for example, we planned to adjourn our Sheva Brachot dinner no later than 10:30 p.m. in order to accommodate the church's Midnight Mass.

Pinky and her crew of three stepped out of the truck and looked around, clearly confused by this surprise destination. She must have assumed the job was intended for my home, but correcting her mistaken assumption back at the warehouse would have required a great deal of explanation. It was a safe guess that Pinky and her crew had never put up Christmas decorations at a synagogue.

I honked a few times to alert Jose, got out of the car, and approached Pinky. "Pretty straightforward, isn't it? Our maintenance guy will show you the electrical hookups and anything else you need."

"Isn't this a Jewish temple?" Pinky came closer to me so she could speak out of her crew's earshot.

"That's right."

"What's going on, Doc?"

"Don't worry. It's all kosher."

"Hey, I don't want any trouble."

"No trouble. I'm the president of the congregation. And on top of it, I've rented the Gathering Hall for a party tonight. My daughter got married on Sunday."

"Congratulations." She didn't seem convinced. "You want me to dress this place up for Christmas?"

"Over here!" I beckoned Jose over and introduced him to Pinky.

They shook hands.

"How's the preparations for the party?"

"Food people are in back," he said, "making tables, plates, flowers. Very good."

Pinky asked him something in Spanish, which I didn't understand.

"*Si! Si!*" Jose pointed at me. "*El presidente!*" He waved his hands as if including the whole place and added in English, "Señor Doctor is boss here. Everything!"

"Okay," she said. "Got it. You're the boss. Now, I have enough stuff to make this place light up the whole neighborhood. I need to check your breakers for sufficient load."

"Come," Jose said, "I show you."

She rolled her hand in the air, and the three crew members sprang into action. They lowered two tall ladders from the roof, pulled down a ramp from the back of the truck, and began unloading.

"One thing," I said, catching up with Pinky, "don't put up any crosses."

"How about a nativity scene made of fiber optic lights? It's lovely."

"No Christian religious symbols. But Santa stuff is okay."

"We'll put the reindeer and sleigh on the roof." She pointed at the tree that protruded from the back of my car. "What about this one?"

"This one," I said, "you can set up inside the Gathering Hall. The big one you have in the truck can go next to the main entrance. And make them glow with everything you have— except crosses."

"Jewish stars okay?" She laughed at my expression. "I'm dating a Jewish guy. He's a biker, rides with a club called the Stars of Davidson."

"I read about them in the *Jewish News.*"

"He started it." She put her hands next to her mouth and yelled toward her crew, "Do the roof lights first! Triple color!"

Leaving them, I went into the synagogue. There was no one at the office. I sat at the computer and typed up song lyrics that had been composing themselves in the back of my mind for hours.

Relieved to find enough paper in the printer, I ran a bunch of copies.

Around the building, in the back, the caterer's unmarked van was backed up to the kitchen doors. I found her in the Gathering Hall, setting up the tables. She was a South African émigré, known in the valley for successfully balancing the strict demands of the rabbis who issued kosher certifications with the no-less arduous demands of her customers—mostly Scottsdale housewives who were determined to keep up with the Joneses. She could deliver a dairy spread with panache befitting a seven-course carnivorous meal. We had known each other for years—she had catered Debra's Bat Mitzvah party as well as the memorial services for both of Rebecca's parents.

I handed her the pile of printed lyrics and asked to have a folded copy placed under each plate. We chatted for a few more minutes, and I found an opportunity to mention casually the decoration project beginning outside. "I'm having a bunch of lights put up on the building. It's a surprise, so please don't mention it to Rebecca when she calls you."

B ack outside, as I passed by the caterer's van, my Blackberry rattled, startling me. I pulled it out, but the bright sun made the screen unreadable. I walked over to the shade of an old olive tree, its veins intertwined, hardened as rocks, yet giving birth to new sprouts. Under the thick canopy, the text on the screen came out clearly. It was an e-mail from Rabbi Rachel to the whole congregation:

DEAR MEMBERS OF THE KING SOLOMON SYNAGOGUE, I'M RESPONDING TO JUDY LEVY'S EARLIER E-MAIL. I'M AS SAD AND FRUSTRATED AS YOU MUST BE BY THE THREAT OF LOSING THE NAME AND IDENTITY OF OUR SYNAGOGUE. KING SOLOMON WAS ONE OF THE GREATEST KINGS IN JEWISH HISTORY. HIS WISDOM HAS INSPIRED OUR PEOPLE FOR THOUSANDS OF YEARS. TRUE, OUR CONGREGATION FACES FINANCIAL CHALLENGES FROM TIME TO TIME, BUT WE'VE MANAGED SUCCESSFULLY OVER THE YEARS, THANKS TO YOUR COLLECTIVE GENEROSITY. AS I

TOLD THE BOARD OF TRUSTEES LAST NIGHT, ACCEPTING A BAG OF MONEY FROM A DONOR IS TEMPTING, BUT THE SACRIFICE OF OUR CORE VALUES WOULD BE SINFUL. WHEN KING DAVID ANOINTED SOLOMON AS HIS HEIR, HE RECOUNTED GOD'S PROMISE: "IF YOUR SONS STAY ON THE RIGHTEOUS PATH, FAITHFUL IN HEARTS AND SOULS, THEN YOUR KINGDOM SHALL NEVER CEASE TO FLOURISH." KINGS I, 2(4). SIMILARLY, I BELIEVE GOD EXPECTS NO LESS FROM US. WITH FAITH IN OUR HEARTS AND SOULS, WE CAN CONTINUE TO FLOURISH WITHOUT SELLING OUT FOR THE PROVERBIAL THIRTY PIECES OF SILVER. WITH GOD'S BLESSING OF SHALOM, RABBI RAC

That's how it ended: RABBI RAC. I checked again for the origin of the e-mail. It had come from Rabbi Rachel's address. She must have been eager to send it out. Her words were nothing short of an electronic attack on the board. How could she ignore what it had taken for me and a few others to keep the synagogue functioning—and pay her salary! And what was she proposing as a practical alternative? The congregation's "COLLECTIVE GENEROSITY" had not stopped our decline so far, had it? True, some of our members were wealthy and generous to arts and culture institutions in Arizona, but not to the synagogue. Only weeks earlier I had shared with her a *Commentary* magazine piece about the discrepancy between how American Jews are exceedingly philanthropic in support of academic and civic institutions but give very little to Jewish causes. It was true nationwide, and it was true here.

It occurred to me that, because Judy's earlier e-mail clearly attributed Jonathan's gift to my efforts, the rabbi's e-mail could be construed as a personal attack as well.

Peering at my Blackberry, I read again the last sentence of her e-mail: "WITH FAITH IN OUR HEARTS AND SOULS, WE CAN CONTINUE TO FLOURISH WITHOUT SELLING OUT FOR THE PROVERBIAL THIRTY PIECES OF SILVER." Was her reference to this particular sum, which Judas Iscariot had purportedly accepted for betraying Jesus, merely coincidental? Or was she hinting, ever so subtly, at my non-Jewishness?

I scanned the text again, finding another suspect sentence: "As I told the board of trustees last night, accepting a bag of money from a donor is tempting, but the sacrifice of our core values would be sinful." Wasn't Judas Iscariot accused of accepting the thirty pieces of silver in a money bag?

My Blackberry vibrated suddenly, jolting me out of my intense contemplation of this disaster. In a flash of rage, I threw it away. The Blackberry hit the trunk of the olive tree and fell to the rocks in several pieces.

"*Damn!*"

The world started spinning faster than I'd seen it spin before. I bent over, my hands on my knees, my eyes shut, and breathed deeply. Staying in this folded position, I slowly shuffled to the caterer's van, determined not to collapse. Through the open back I found a bag of ice, tore the plastic, and scooped out a few ice cubes, which I pressed to my face and forehead. I continued to breathe deliberately, saturating my brain with oxygen, fighting off that ominous sensation of an approaching loss of consciousness.

———

Hark the Herald Angels Sing

I recovered well enough to go to the restroom, rinse my face and wet my hair. Feeling better, I checked on Pinky and her crew. They were on the roof, rolling out lines of electrical cords while Jose trimmed back the overgrown oleanders along the wall to provide better access for their ladders.

Satisfied that all was proceeding well, I walked down the street, past the Montessori preschool, to the church. I had never stepped into this church, which, like our building, was quite modest. The sign above said: THE HOLY NAME OF MARY CATHOLIC CHURCH.

Heavy doors led me into a dark vestibule. I heard faint voices singing somewhere in the building. The cool air carried a tangy aroma. The Saltillo tiles were uneven, lain with wide concrete grout. A statue of Christ, slightly taller than me, stood over a circle of fluttering candles, a book pressed to his chest. His kind eyes followed me as I walked over to another set of doors. I almost crossed myself, an old reflex that apparently wasn't completely gone.

When I entered the main sanctuary, the boys' choir was practicing under the guidance of a thin woman with big glasses who used a pencil to direct them. I leaned against a column to listen, but she cut off the singing with a slash of her pencil and berated them, "Not good! Dry as the Salt River! Where are your feelings?"

She fiddled with an old-fashioned CD player to restart the recording of the melancholic hymn. The boys started singing again, still showing little enthusiasm. I could see that some of them skipped many of the Latin words. Our old church services had been conducted in English, but I had taken Latin in high school and college in preparation for medicine, and it came back to me as the boys sang. They were practicing in order to lead their parents and relatives during the Midnight Mass. I translated in my mind and quietly chanted the English words of the hymn:

"*Father,*
Who makes this holy night aglow,
With the magnificence of Jesus Christ,
Whom we accept as our Lord, the truest light,
Convey us to eternal delight,
In Heaven's kingdom,
Where He lives with you and the Holy Spirit,
A God, forever, and ever."

She made them repeat it three more times, then inserted another CD into the old machine. A familiar tune came from the speakers, and the choir began to sing, "*Hark, the herald angels sing, Glory to the newborn king!*"

I joined them with quiet humming in the back of the church. It was just like the old days. But when they reached "*Pleased as man with man to dwell,*" the accompanying music gave a sharp screech and died. The woman's pencil dropped, and she pounded on top of the CD player, trying to revive it.

A few of the boys kept singing, "*Jesus, our Emmanuel, Hark, the herald angels sing.*" Others started laughing. I hurried up the aisle to the front, where an elderly organ stood by the side wall. I dropped into the seat and began playing, just as the last few voices completed the verse and sang the chorus, "*Glory to the newborn King.*"

I played catch for a few notes, sorely out of practice, but within a line or two, I caught up. At the end of the song, I returned to the beginning. By now, there was a perfect flow of synchrony between my fingers and the choir, which now sounded fuller, many voices joining back in the singing.

Not bothering to look at the woman, I played, and they sang, "*Hark! The herald angels sing...*" Their pronunciation matched with my tempo. I could tell that all of them were engaged now, intrigued by the stranger who had suddenly showed up to play for them, rewarding me with the heartfelt vocal effort that had eluded their pencil-wielding conductor.

During the third verse, their voices surged, shouting the word "*Hail!*" and continued, "*the heav'n-born Prince of Peace!*" I glanced over my shoulder and saw that all the boys' eyes were on me, all of them smiling as they shouted, "*Hail! The Son of Righteousness!*"

It made me shiver as I realized that these boys, whom I had never met before, were actually cheering me on at the tops of their voices, giving their own interpretation to the old lyrics. My fingers kept hitting the keys ever harder, the old organ reverberating through the sanctuary, the choir roaring with every ounce of air their lungs could expel, until the last line, which they practically screamed: "*Glory to the newborn king!*"

In the silence that followed, I heard clapping. My eyes searched the pews and found a man in a black robe. He stood in the rear and clapped, and soon the woman joined him, then the boys, row after row, until all hands were clapping. I made a theatrical bow and went to the front, where I shook hands with many of the boys and complimented them on their singing.

I'm Father Donne," the priest said. "I've never heard our choir sing like this. God has blessed you with divine talent."

"Hardly." I shook his hand, which was bony but warm. "Christian Dinwall. I used to play in our church, back in New York. It was a long time ago."

"Even more inspiring, then." He ushered me into his office and closed the door. "To play like this, one needs superb hand-eye coordination and a sensitive soul. And you managed to connect so well with our easily distracted boys."

"I don't know about the soul, but my hands get lots of practice. I'm a surgeon."

"Oh." He fiddled with the cross that hung from his neck. "I hope you're not here about one of my parishioners?"

"Nothing of the kind. In fact, I'm here as president of the synagogue down the road."

The look of puzzlement on his face was almost comical.

"I converted many years ago. My wife is Jewish."

"Ah."

I could see that he wasn't pleased. Church authorities used to burn people like me at the stake. "It's an interesting coincidence," I said, "that the music for *Hark the Herald Angels Sing* was composed by a born Jew, grandson of the great Jewish rabbi and philosopher Moses Mendelssohn. The composer, Felix Mendelssohn, went the opposite way from me, converting from Judaism to Christianity."

"We prefer that," Father Donne said with a hint of a smile. "But a woman's charm is a powerful allure. You're not the first man to give up the love of Christ for the lust of a woman."

The irony didn't escape me—he was accusing me of something similar to what I faulted Debra for. "My religious choice wasn't driven by love. Or by lust."

"There's no shame. God made us the way we are, weak and prone to sin. But still, He continues to grace us with His fatherly love."

I felt my face redden. "I do admire the lessons of Jesus as a man, the stories of his compassion and humility."

"Those were Godly qualities."

"Aren't all men created in God's image?" I smiled to soften my argument. My purpose here wasn't to debate theology, but still, he deserved an explanation. "Falling in love with Rebecca wasn't the reason I left the church. My faith had dissipated much earlier."

He gestured with open hands, inviting me to elaborate.

"As a young man devoted to math and science, the stories of immaculate conception, virginal birth, death, and resurrection, or the Holy Trinity, couldn't possibly remain believable. For me, the whole thing attained the quality of charming children stories."

The priest crossed himself and kissed his fingers.

"I don't mean any disrespect."

He nodded. "Please, go on."

"It's kind of simplistic logic, but if Jesus was really the son of God, then the story is self-contradictory. I mean, imagine going to a billionaire and asking him for a donation to save a starving family or to save your church from shutting down, and he throws you a quarter."

Father Donne chuckled, as if the experience was familiar to him.

"If Jesus was Lord," I continued, "with divine powers and a direct link to his father, God Almighty, then he was like an all-powerful billionaire who lived during an era of most terrible suffering, his fellowmen bent under Roman boots, countless innocents being crucified everywhere, children taken away for slavery, widespread starvation, bloodshed, and torture. But despite his supposed divine powers, all Jesus did was to enlighten a blind person and fix a couple of lepers, right?"

"He did more than that."

"Okay, let's say that he performed a few miracles to help a handful of sufferers, gave some inspiring speeches, kicked over the money changers' tables. But if he was God, why didn't he wave his hand and end all that horrific suffering? Why didn't he bring peace and brotherhood to the whole world, as Isaiah had predicted that the real Messiah would do?"

His eyes turned to a crucifix on the wall.

"And besides," I continued, unable to stop the flood of words, "the whole thing about Jesus dying for our sins makes no sense. A real God, by definition, never dies, does he? And a real God doesn't really suffer, does he? He's God, for God's sake! So if he can't suffer, how could he suffer for our sins? And if he can't die, how can he return to life? How could there be a second coming if there wasn't a going?"

"You're taking a very...technical view."

"Think about it, okay? Being God, Jesus could have clicked his finger and vaporize all those Romans. Therefore all his mythological suffering and dying was his choice, right? He chose to let them nail him on the cross. He chose to let himself be killed, rise to life, die again, and so on. How can we poor mortals identify with this kind of volunteer victimhood? Do we have such a choice? Can we choose whether to suffer or not to suffer? To die or not to die?" Out of breath, I shrugged and sat back, surprised at my own outburst.

Father Donne's mouth opened, but then it closed without a word.

"I'm sorry," I said, my voice much lower, controlled, "but there was no way for me to believe Christianity's illogical storyline. I saw only two options: Either Jesus had been a divine, all-powerful God who therefore could not really die, which meant that his crucifixion had been a sham and he had never *died for our sins*, or Jesus had been a mortal man—a wonderful person, for sure, much admirable, like Mahatma Gandhi and Anne Frank, a person with great dignity in the face of oppression and cruelty, a person whose life and death is an inspiration to every one of us, to be kind, charitable, and…human."

The last word, for some reason, jolted Father Donne, who shifted sharply in his seat. "For someone who claims to have no faith in His divinity, you seem to have quite a passion for our Lord Jesus Christ."

"As a myth—"

"It appears that He is quite real to you, and the gospels provide answers for all your doubts, if you only open your heart to accept the truth."

"Please." I held my hand up. "I respect your faith, and I'm familiar with the theories, which our priest spent many hours discussing with me. But these convoluted explanations only reinforced my opinion that Jesus was just a protagonist in an inspiring fable."

"Then let me ask you a question: Does Moses get the same mocking treatment from you? Or Samuel? Or Isaiah, for that matter?"

Keeping a straight face, I managed not to say what I thought, that Moses and Samuel and all the other Jewish prophets had not claimed to be God's divine sons but served him reluctantly as human messengers delivering His word.

"Well?"

"I'm no theologian," I said. "These were just my own ruminations as a young man, long before I met my wife. Even if technically I was still a Christian , my faith was gone, and as I learned about her faith and heritage, I discovered a more common-sense framework for worship."

He seemed surprised. "What does common sense have to do with it?"

"Judaism is logical. We believe in a sole and intangible almighty, a force for goodness and charity. Yet despite His all-powerfulness, God allows us to choose good or bad and suffer the consequences for our choices. As a Jew, I see God as a positive presence that I can personally relate to, communicate with, and not only in the synagogue, but wherever I am, directly, without mediators and sacraments and holy ghosts. And Reform Judaism in particular fits my feeling of tolerance and flexibility, of focusing on substance rather than on minute technicalities and anachronistic rituals. I love it. I really do."

"Judaism is the basis for our faith too," Father Donne said. "Have you considered joining Jews for Jesus?"

I laughed. "Jews for Jesus makes as much sense as Jews for Jihad."

"Why do you say that?"

"Because the main point of Judaism is the faith in a single God, Adonai, the divine creator who is everywhere, all the time, intangible and without the crude physicality of idols and the fantasy of ghosts."

"But Jews believe in the coming of the Messiah!"

"True. We wait for God to send us a human leader, born to normal parents, flesh and blood. Our Messiah will be a mortal man, a man like every other man, only that God will give him the gift of leadership and inspiration to liberate us from the Diaspora and lead us back to the land of our ancestors. Our Messiah will not be the product of a hocus pocus pregnancy or the instigator of a failed insurgency that gets him nailed to a cross. Our Messiah will bring salvation to the world through faith in God, rather than superstitions, illusions, and inquisitions."

"Okay." He sat forward, his elbows on his desk, his hands open, facing me like two stop signs. "I understand. But still, you've come here today."

"My life as a Jew has been good...until a few days ago."

He watched me as I suddenly struggled for the right words.

"It's been hard." I swallowed, determined to keep my composure. "Last Sunday, my daughter married a young man from a very religious family, and the way they treated me threw my whole world into terrible doubts."

His intertwined fingers under his chin, Father Donne waited for me to continue.

"What happened didn't make me doubt the Jewish faith itself. But I've come to doubt my place among Jews. It's about belonging, about being accepted." I took a deep breath, then another. "Being Jewish is my religion. It's who I am now. But the people around me? Have they accepted me as a Jew?" I looked up at the ceiling to fight off tears. "I'm not sure anymore."

"So you want to test them?"

It took me a moment to realize that he must have seen the truck and crew from *Lights4U* and drew his own conclusions. "Yes," I said. "Exactly. I want to challenge their tolerance. Which is why I'm here."

He nodded. "Go on."

"Tonight we're having a dinner party to celebrate my daughter's marriage." I hesitated, choosing my words carefully. "Since I'm paying for it, I've decided that it's going to be more than just another Jewish feast, more than just another *nosh*. Rather, it's going to be an interfaith celebration of my dual traditions."

"Do you play the guitar?"

Surprised by the question, I shook my head.

"I used to, many years ago." He gestured at the corner of his office, where a guitar in a soft case leaned on an umbrella stand. "The first thing my teacher told me was not to tighten the strings too much, or they would pop."

The image was potent, and I could almost hear the sound of it happening. "It's a risk worth taking," I said. "The true friends, those who love and accept me, will celebrate with me. And those who refuse? They're not true friends, and I will have to accept that painful fact."

His forehead creased. "It's a brave experiment."

"It's a celebration, but as the host, I've decided to part with tradition, to have a different kind of a celebration, and I'd like to invite you and the members of your church to this event at the synagogue."

"Event?"

"Please join us tonight." I cleared my throat. "It will be the first-ever *Christmas Nosh.*"

Let It Snow! Let It Snow! Let It Snow!

B ack in the synagogue, I unlocked the office and used the phone to call home. There was no answer, so I tried Rebecca's mobile. She picked up after three rings. "Hello?"

"May I speak with Paul Bunyan?"

"Excuse me?"

I whistled the Monty Python tune for "The Lumberjack Song."

After a moment, Rebecca recognized the tune and chortled. She sang a couple of lines: *"I'm a lumberjack and I'm okay..."*

"Good memory," I said.

"What are you doing at the synagogue?" She must have seen the caller ID on her phone.

"I stopped by to check on the caterer and do some repentance."

"Good. And?"

"Mission accomplished." I watched through the window as Pinky unloaded the artificial tree from the truck. "It's going to be a great dinner. Where are you now?"

"We're at Nordstrom's. Debra's in the fitting room. We found beautiful dresses with long sleeves that she can wear to classes during the week."

"And Mordechai?"

"He's at Starbucks, studying for an exam." She was quiet for a moment. "Sorry about your tree...and the coffee table. It's been such a rollercoaster, and seeing Debra so upset, I'm just... on edge."

"It's my fault too. I've let the patients and their surgeries take over my life, like an escape, head in the sand. I should have shared my feelings with you better, including how much I've missed Christmas all these years—"

"Again with the Christmas?"

"It's part of me. It's who I am. I want you to accept it, share it with me."

"Is this your midlife crisis or something? You're off your rocker, you know?"

"How can you say that?"

"Because it's got nothing to do with Christmas or with your childhood or with your true self. You've gone meshuga over what happened at the wedding. That's all!"

Too upset to respond, I only groaned.

"It was a shame," Rebecca went on, "cruel and unfair. That old rabbi shouldn't have done that. But you must get over it. Enough already! What happened, happened. It's in the past. We have to concentrate on the future, or we're going to lose our daughter."

"We won't."

"Good!"

"And I promise you one thing." I watched Pinky use a cart to wheel the Christmas tree toward the entrance of the synagogue. "I'll do a much better job communicating my feelings from now on." *Starting tonight*, I thought, my anger mixed with giddiness at the prospect of my unfolding Christmas Nosh.

"We should go on vacation," she said, "just you and me."

"A kosher vacation?"

"Not nice!" Her tone told me she was smiling now.

"We can go to Jerusalem. I hear they're offering specials on study retreats at black-hat yeshivas."

She laughed. "By the way, Nina called. As expected, no one can come on Sunday. I told Debra that you took away the tree because the staff isn't coming for the Christmas brunch."

"How convenient."

"You're not bringing it back home, are you?"

"*Home is where your heart is,*" I quoted an old song by The Sounds. "By the way, did you see the e-mail from Rabbi Rachel?"

"Yes. She tried to call you, and when you didn't answer, she called me."

"What did she say?"

I heard Debra in the background, and Rebecca declared, "It's gorgeous! Wait a minute, I'm talking to Daddy." Back on the phone, she said, "The rabbi was terribly embarrassed. She had written the e-mail earlier, but realized it was hostile and inappropriate. She wanted to delete it, but mistakenly pressed *Send*."

"A high-tech Freudian slip?"

"That's what she said. Didn't you see her follow-up e-mail?"

"Not yet." There was no point in trying to explain what had happened to my Blackberry.

"She sent a follow-up e-mail to everyone, apologizing for the error, but still insisted that the name change is a sellout and a forewarning for worse things to come, and asked members to call on the leadership to rise above the temptation of easy money."

"Rise above?"

"That's the phrase she used."

"Did her e-mail include any yeast?"

A series of hard knocks shook the office door.

"See you at home," I said and hung up.

When I opened the door, Jose was tripping all over his words, mixing Spanish and English. I followed him to the front of the synagogue and paused at the sight of a dump truck backing up to the curb. Pinky was directing it with hand motions while the other crew members watched from the roof. She saw me and yelled, "Surprise!"

"What's this?"

The answer came from the rear of the truck. As the box began to tilt upward, the hinged horizontal door cracked open, and snow poured out.

Snow!

It fell in thick globs, like egg beat pouring out from a baker's bowl. Pinky signaled the driver, and the box stopped rising. He came out of the cabin with a shovel and flattened the pile to create a wider base.

I finally found my voice. "What in the world is this?"

"Roy threw it in for you," Pinky said, turning her baseball cap with the visor backward. "It's part of our premium options. How can you celebrate Christmas without snow?"

"But…how?"

"We truck it down from Flagstaff. People love it. Nothing like a pile of fresh snow in the desert!"

"Won't it melt?"

"Slowly." Pinky gestured at the setting sun. "The temperature will be down in the fifties within an hour. You'll still have a pile here tomorrow morning."

A car horn sounded. I looked up and saw Rabbi Rachel's Honda stop at the curb. She got out and hurried over. "What's going on here?"

"Getting ready for the dinner party." I pointed at the snow. "How do you like this?"

But she was already looking at the bundled wires of fiber optic lights, the rows of figurines awaiting placement along the building, and the modular Christmas tree rising by the entrance. She beckoned Jose to come over, but he pretended not to notice, keeping busy with a rake. To preempt her next burst of questions, I said, "That was quite an e-mail you sent around."

"What's with these decorations?" Rabbi Rachel's voice was more bewildered than angry. "You're turning my synagogue into Macy's?"

The comparison was funny, except for the way she said it: *My synagogue.*

"The synagogue belongs to all of us," I said as Pinky stepped away and the driver climbed back into the cabin of the truck. "And it's our family's event tonight, so please bear with me—"

"A Christmas tree? And all these gentile trinkets?" She pointed at the *Lights4U* truck. "What are they doing here? Is this one of your jokes?"

"Not at all. We'll be celebrating tolerance tonight."

The truck's engine revved up, and the box began to tilt farther up.

"By propping up a pagan display in front of a Jewish place of worship? Are you crazy?"

"My mental capacity isn't impaired." I used my hand to fan away the fumes from the truck exhaust. Snow began to trickle down. "I'm following all those sermons you've given about respecting different points of view."

She shook her head, the mane of curls trembling. "Do you know what Christmas represents? Have you any idea how much hate this stunt could instigate?"

The snow was pouring out faster, and I took her arm to get her out of the way. But my touch caused the rabbi to react as if my hand carried a deadly electrical current. She bolted backward, her ankle caught on the edge of the pile, and she fell over.

Before either of us managed to move, the box of the truck reached its top angle, tilted all the way up with a bang and a shake, and let out an avalanche of snow that buried Rabbi Rachel completely.

"Hey!" Pinky ran to the front of the truck and waved her arms wildly, yelling to the driver, "Stop! Stop! Stop!"

I leaped forward and began to dig in. The three guys shouted at each other as they scrambled to get down from the roof. Another surge of snow fell on top of me, knocking me down. As I struggled to get free from the pressing, cold bulk, my left arm hurt sharply, and a jolt of pain shot through my shoulder, worse than when I had struggled to set up the tree in our living room yesterday.

By now, all of them were on top of us—the driver with his shovel, Jose with a rake, and Pinky and the three guys with their hands. I tried to help, but my left side hurt too much, and I could barely breathe. Within seconds they pulled Rabbi Rachel out and helped her sit up while she spat snow and moaned pitifully.

I crawled across the curb and sat on the ground, holding my left arm and catching my breath.

It was unclear who called the police, but someone had, and soon we heard sirens approaching.

Jose took off at a fast trot toward the church down the street.

Two cruisers arrived, followed by an ambulance. They concentrated on Rabbi Rachel, whose leg was bent unnaturally. One of the medics asked if I was hurt, and I assured him it was only a pulled muscle.

Concluding that the driver had done nothing wrong, the police officers left. The ambulance took off with Rabbi Rachel. My relief at getting rid of her was salted with a few grains of guilt, but I brushed it off and watched the rest of the Flagstaff snow pile up on the desert landscape in front of the synagogue.

It was half past five in the evening, and I decided to go home and spruce myself up in preparation for a most interesting night.

———

Home for the Holidays

Before leaving the synagogue, I sent one of Pinky's crewmen to fetch Jose from the church. Our custodian showed up, still holding the rake, his eyes scanning the street. "No worry," I said, "the police is long gone, okay?"

He nodded.

"You work for me tonight." I handed him a one hundred dollar bill. "Help these guys with the installation, get the caterer anything she needs, and when the guests start to arrive, direct the parking."

Jose kept looking away, grimacing, as if he didn't understand fully what was required of him. Pinky spoke to him in Spanish, translating my words, but I knew he wasn't confused. He was spooked by my open argument with the rabbi, followed by her injury. He revered the rabbi on a primal, superstitious level, perceiving her to be God's personal representative on earth, the long arm of the divine law. I wanted to explain to Jose that his reverence was misplaced. Unlike Catholic priests or Orthodox rabbis, a Reform Rabbi functioned not as God's personal representative, but rather as an employee of the synagogue, whose job was to lead services and officiate in life-cycle events such as circumcisions, Bar or Bat Mitzvahs, weddings, and burials. But this wasn't the right time to attempt such a discussion with our nervous custodian.

"You work for me," I repeated, my finger going between Jose and my own chest, back and forth. "Police and rabbi not coming back. *Comprender?*"

"Okay, Señor Doctor."

Pinky patted his shoulder.

Driving off, I felt sorry for causing Jose so much anxiety. With our tight budget, he alone had to handle every aspect of the building, equipment, and landscape. With Jonathan's donation, however, perhaps we could hire a lawyer to help Jose obtain legal immigration status and start paying him an appropriate salary and benefits. We could also hire more staff as well as a marketing person to drive up membership. But before I would commit myself to the next phase of rebuilding our congregation, there was tonight's test, which would determine not only the future of my marriage and relationship with Debra, but could redefine my past, exposing as illusory much of what I had believed about my place in this world.

The western sky went from a golden glow to embers red. The departure of sunshine brought an evening chill that made me shudder in my short-sleeved cotton shirt. Stopping at a red light, I pressed the button to close the roof.

On the radio, Perry Como sang, "*I met a man who lives in Tennessee, and he was headin' for Pennsylvania.*"

When we first moved here, I used to miss New York and its East Coast culture of intense pace and intellectual energy. This longing had gone away, taking with it any thought of leaving Arizona. But what if my Christmas Nosh turned sour? What if rejection confronted me on all fronts? Would I have the guts to accept reality, devastating as it might be? And the strength to start a new life someplace else?

Fear overcame me. Was I making a terrible mistake? Was I putting everyone to an extravagantly impossible trial of tolerance and approval?

Turning into my street, I brushed away the negative thoughts. This was my home, my family, and my community. I was loved and respected, especially after practically saving the synagogue from its prolonged cash shortage. Tonight everyone would come around to share my holiday spirit with good food, merry singing, and recitation of the traditional seven blessings in honor of my daughter's marriage.

I entered the house and declared, "Home sweet home!"

"We're here," Debra called.

I found the three of them in the kitchen. Debra wore a long turquoise dress with a white collar, white cuffs at the end of the long sleeves, and a white belt with a delicate silver buckle. Mordechai sat at the table with an open textbook in front of him and a pen between his teeth, but his eyes were on Debra, who pirouetted to show off the dress, its price tag dangling from the back zipper.

"Very nice," I said, catching her for a quick hug. "I like it."

"You should," Rebecca said, pulling another dress off a hanger, "you paid for it."

"Me and you, partner." I kissed her on the lips. "Do we have any money left?"

Rebecca, who handled all our banking and bills, could usually tell me the balance in our joint account within a few dollars. But now she only shrugged and said, "We have credit cards."

Debra and Mordechai laughed, mistaking her answer for humor. Rebecca and I looked at each other and also started laughing. We had always regretted our inability to have more children, but financially speaking, this wedding-wrapped-in-college-tuition, together with the prospect of Debra's med school costs, made me appreciate the single-child parenting experience.

Mordechai glanced at his watch. "Time for the evening prayer."

Debra followed him out of the kitchen.

I looked at Rebecca. "Where's she going?"

"They pray together." My wife seemed proud. "Three times a day in accordance with Halacha. It's very sweet, isn't it?"

"True love." Seeing my daughter follow her young husband to recite the evening prayer on a weekday, an excessive religious practice that we Reform Jews never followed, my strategy became clear: Rather than try to draw Debra away from *his* way of life, I should pull Mordechai to the middle, and she would happily follow him toward a more moderate level of observance. "Time for my evening shower," I said. "If you join me, we can pray together while soaping each other's back."

"Ha."

Upstairs in our bathroom, my arm and shoulder still hurting, I popped two orange Motrin pills into my mouth and swallowed them with tap water. As I reached into the shower to turn it on, I changed my mind and turned on the bath faucet instead, pressing down to engage the bath drain.

While the water ran, I peered at my face in the mirror. The whites of my eyes were pink, my face sallow, and a bruise adorned my forehead, probably from the avalanche that had buried Rabbi Rachel. Should I have accompanied her to the hospital? Probably, but there was too much on my plate already, and the rabbi hadn't exactly been considerate or thoughtful toward me either. Perhaps her snow accident was God's way of making things right.

Immersing in the hot water felt wonderful. I poured in liquid soap and left the faucet running until the water rose to cover my body with a layer of bubbles. I folded a towel and used it to cushion the back of my head against the rim of the bath. I exhaled, letting out all the pent-up stress that had built up inside me.

As my breathing slowed down, every muscle in my body began to relax. Despite several difficult days and sleep deprivation, I would need all my mental capacities tonight. I thought of the Gathering Hall with the dressed-up tables, the front of the synagogue with the half-assembled modular Christmas tree and wires running everywhere. It would all be cleaned up and glowing colorfully by the time we arrived. I could see it in my mind.

The banging on the door made me sit up in the bath, sending waves over the rim, splashing on the floor. There was more banging, and Rebecca yelled, "Rusty? Can you hear me?"

"Yes." The folded towel that had supported my head slipped into the bath. "I'm here."

"Oh, thank God!" She tried the door knob. "Let me in."

I stepped out of the bath, dripping all over the place, and unlocked the door. "What's wrong?"

"That's what I want to know." She pulled a towel off the rack and wrapped me. "You weren't answering. I thought something happened to you."

"I must've fallen asleep." Sitting on the side of the bath, I watched her spread another towel on the floor by the bathtub to absorb the spilled water. "I was very tired. But I feel a lot better."

"After giving me a heart attack!" She used a third towel to dry my hair and face. "I've been yelling and knocking on the door. Didn't you hear any of it?"

"Nothing."

She pulled her dryer from a drawer and turned it on. I shut my eyes and felt her fingers comb through my short hair, the air hot against my scalp, her thigh pressing against me. I bowed my head, surrendering to this unexpected yet sensuous grooming.

"That's better." She turned off the dryer. "The last thing you need is a bad cold."

"What about the *first* thing I need?" I put my arms around her waist, held her close, my face pressed to her bosom, and breathed in her familiar scent.

"A shave." She kissed my forehead. "That's what you need." Stepping out of my embrace, she replaced the dryer in the drawer. "And a nice suit."

The Christmas Blues

I was doing my tie in front of the hallway mirror, paying little attention to their kitchen table conversation, when Debra called, "Dad? Can you come here for a minute?"

They were dressed and ready to go, he in a black suit over white shirt, she in a wool cap that covered all her beautiful hair and matched her burgundy dress.

"We're talking about family history," Debra said, "and I couldn't remember what exactly happened to your father, only that you never met him."

"That's correct." I adjusted my tie, twisting it so that the knot lined up with my shirt buttons. "He was lost in Vietnam when I was only a few months old."

"I'm sorry," Mordechai said. "Where is he buried?"

"Hold on. I'll show you something interesting." I went to the study and pulled out the box of papers I had brought from my mother's house after she had passed. There was her dog-eared book of hymns. A dusty folder was marked by her handwriting: JOACHIM DINWALL – LIFE AND DEATH

There was their marriage certificate, the framed photo from his boot camp graduation, which my mother had kept by her bedside until she died, and some stuff from his high school days—report cards, basketball scores, a few class photos, and letters of reference from teachers, to be attached to his future college applications. I had read through the letters many years ago, and they left me with mixed feelings. The banality of the formulaic praise, garnished with superlatives about his *unmatchable* intellect, *unbeatable* motivation, and *unquestionable* academic potential, all of it took on a somber undertone considering the tragedy of his unrequited optimism.

But the letter I pulled out wasn't banal or optimistic. It was still in its original envelope, torn along the edge, but I knew its content by heart.

Back in the kitchen, I unfolded the brittle page and showed it to Mordechai. It was addressed to my mother and was very short, especially considering its long-term implications for her and the baby boy she was carrying when the letter was delivered by two fresh-faced officers in pressed uniforms, mirrored sunglasses, and a brown staff car that waited for them with the doors open, the engine running, and the radio playing.

Dear Mrs. Dinwall,

The navy department deeply regrets to inform you that your husband, Joachim Dinwall, seaman, first class, United States Marines, was lost during action in the performance of his duty and in the service of his country. Due to battle conditions in the area of naval operations, his remains could not be recovered without subjecting navy servicemen to unmitigated risks. Please accept our sincere condolences.

John H. Chafee, Secretary of the Navy

Debra, who was reading it over Mordechai's shoulder, became teary. She had a good heart, my daughter. Perhaps it would be better if she gave up the study of medicine and became a housewife, saving herself a lifetime of excruciating encounters with ailing patients and anxious families. I hugged her. "You're his only descendent, and I failed to tell you whatever little facts I knew about him."

"Joachim is a biblical name," Mordechai said. "King Joachim ruled over Judea. The Hebrew name is a combination of two words: *Jehovah* and *Raise*. Together, his name implies that God has elevated him to be king. It's a wonderful name."

"Thank you," I said. "It was also the name of Mary's father in the New Testament, which means Joachim was the grandfather of Jesus Christ."

"That man never existed," Mordechai said. "The name Joshua was very common, and I'm sure there were many religious and political figures named Joshua during Roman times. But the church stories about him are all imaginary, pure fiction. Those so-called apostles invented a bunch of miracles and resurrections, which often contradicted each other. They contrived fictional gospels about a son of God to justify committing sins against the holy Torah with impunity."

"Isn't faith an act of believing in things that can't be proven?"

"God gives each person free choice, and gullible fools can choose to believe in nonsense."

"That's a bit harsh," I said. "More than two billion people believe in Jesus Christ. Are they all fools?"

"Billions of people believe in all kinds of bogus ideas," Mordechai said with a level of confidence I had not seen before. "But the leaders of the church should know better. They grasp onto esoteric sentences in Isaiah, which they mistranslate from Hebrew to fit absurd interpretations, and claim it as evidence that Isaiah supposedly foresaw the arrival of their false messiah."

"Your father once told me," I said, "that in matters of faith, one man's cherished truth is another man's kidney stone."

Debra laughed. "That's clever."

"But it's not about faith," Mordechai insisted, still serious. "It's about the Christians distorting the Old Testament illogically. How could that man be the Messiah? Isaiah and the other prophets said clearly that the real Messiah would bring about a new world order, with peace and justice for all, especially for the Jewish people, who will gather back to Israel and rebuild God's temple in Jerusalem. But the exact opposite happened during and after his so-called arrival, so how could their Joshua be a messiah?"

"They believe he is their spiritual savior, that it takes time—"

"Savior?" Mordechai sneered. "Even according to their gospels, that poor schmuck couldn't even save himself. How could he save others, let along the whole of humanity?"

"The world still needed repairing. We weren't ready to accept him. I think that's the reason Christians believe that he died and awaits resurrection."

"We didn't accept him, so he gave up? What, he got scared of a bunch of quizzical Jews? Intimidated by how much repairing the world needed? It was too much for him?" Mordechai shook his head in mock regret. "Poor little savior. How sad!"

Rebecca entered the kitchen and took my breath away.

"Mom," Debra said, "you look incredible!"

"Oh, you don't have to." My wife flipped her hair playfully.

"Wow!" I found my voice. "Look at you!"

"What?" She turned in a full circle. "I just threw on something from the closet."

The *something* was a dress that came down to her ankles, with sleeves that covered her elbows, and a cleavage that barely showed her throat. But the straight, goody-two-shoes lines of this very traditional dress contrasted with its dramatic, fire-engine red color and satin-like material that glistened with her every move. Her body was slim, but years of weight lifting to counter the threat of brittle bones, which had killed her mother, gave Rebecca muscle tone that fit her intense personality and constant motion. Add to that her thick mane of hair, which had remained jet-black with the aid of modern cosmetology, and her sculpted facial bones, covered with skin that was kept tight and glowing with the best Lancôme had to offer, and the result was my petite-yet-fierce wife, stunning and ready for battle.

Mordechai handed the letter back to me. "Thank you for sharing it," he said gravely.

"What's this?" Rebecca glanced at the letter. "Oh, I remember. You took it out once, when my parents were visiting."

"That was memorable." I folded it.

Debra asked, "What happened?"

"Nothing," Rebecca said.

"My father's name," I said, "reminded Grandpa Greenbaum of Joachim von Ribbentrop, the Nazi foreign minister who was hanged as a war criminal after the Nuremberg trials."

"Oy." Debra cradled her cheek in a manner that seemed too old for her years. "He really said that?"

I slipped the letter back into the envelope. "Grandpa Greenbaum's world was divided into two camps. The tiny camp of plucky Jews, who had survived for centuries despite constant attacks, and the huge camp of the worldwide gentile mob whose thirst for Jewish blood has been unquenchable. And guess in which camp I belonged according to your grandpa?"

"That's not true." Rebecca collected her purse and phone. "You were always paranoid about my parents, but they really loved you."

"They *tolerated* me. There's a big difference."

I went to the study and kneeled by the filing cabinet to return the letter to the file. I lingered there, consumed by doubts. Was Rebecca right? Was I paranoid about the people around me, seeing rejection where love existed? In a little while, we would drive up to the synagogue, where the three people who constituted my whole family were expecting to celebrate a time-honored Sheva Brachot dinner. But in addition to the happy friends, elaborate dishes of kosher food, and predictable congratulations, they would find a synagogue decorated for Christmas, plus a church delegation headed by Father Donne.

Standing up, I held on to the cabinet, my legs weary under the weight of physical fatigue and mental stress. I opened the window and rested my elbows on the sill, a light breeze cooling my face. Clearly the power nap in the bathtub hadn't done the job. If I could only get a good night's sleep, everything would clear up. I needed to think!

But my train had already left the station, my Jeep had crossed the Rubicon, and my water had gone under the bridge. All these clichés applied to my situation. I had made a choice to act, based on the limited information available to me, same as I had done with countless medial patients. In my profession, you didn't recede into indecision when the patient was already prostrated on the table, his chest open, his heart iced, waiting for new veins—or death.

My mind flipped through the images of the past few days. I thought of Pinky and her crew and Jose's apprehension. They had surely finished all the installations, lit every bulb, and hung every trinket on the green boughs. The tables were set, the food steaming on the trays, and the rabbi in the hospital. How could I back down now? I had taken it all too far for chickening out. Was I making the biggest mistake of my life? Only if I lose my nerves and optimism! It was up to me whether tonight's Christmas Nosh would succeed or not. I could lie down on the floor and fall asleep right now. But how could I let all my efforts go to naught?

I filled my lungs with air and shut the window. It was time.

The three of them followed me down the hallway, high heels clicking on the tiles, Mordechai buttoning his jacket. I held the front door open for them. "Ladies and gentleman, start your engines!"

"You're chirpy all of a sudden," Rebecca said, waiting for me to unlock the car.

I thumbed the key fob, and the Volvo's lights blinked. "What's a team without a cheerleader?"

———

The Little Drummer Boy

We drove down Scottsdale Road, the hardtop closed to protect Rebecca's hairdo. I became apprehensive. A few more turns, and we would arrive at the synagogue. How would they react? My heart beat faster, and the interior of the car grew smaller, closing in on me. I turned up the AC and directed the vents at my face.

Rebecca looked at me. "Are you ill?"

"I'm fine. Why?"

"You don't look fine." She touched my forehead. "No fever, but your skin color—"

"Must be the long bath." I checked myself in the mirror and saw Debra's face in the back. "Are you excited?"

"Nervous," Debra said. "I hope Rabbi Rachel isn't angry with me."

"Not with you." I chuckled, remembering the rabbi's reaction to my touch, her back-flip, and the snow avalanche burying her.

Rebecca didn't miss it. "What's so funny?"

"Our rabbi," I said, "she's in quite a state."

"She won't start arguing about the Warnick donation tonight, will she?"

"Probably not." I glanced at the mirror again, finding Debra. "Have you come to terms with what happened at the wedding?"

"We phoned Mordechai's parents earlier." She looked across at her husband. "I wanted them to know how upset I am about your exclusion from the chuppah and even more about keeping me in the dark. I know we can't go back and make it right, but I wanted to hear from them that something like this will never happen again."

Pride filled me. That's my girl!

"It's not so simple," Rebecca said.

"Actually, it's pretty simple." I made another turn and slowed down. "Respect. That's all. What did they say?"

"They feel badly." Debra hesitated. "They wished it was possible to join us tonight."

"We're only a plane ride away," I said. "And what did they say about the future? Would they let a similar thing happen again?"

"My parents like you a lot," Mordechai said. "And they love Debra to death."

I noted the diplomacy of his answer. "And if you had an opportunity to make it right for me, would you take it?"

They responded together, "Of course!"

"No question," Mordechai added.

"Good," I said. "How about tonight?"

Rebecca turned sharply. "I don't like the sound of that."

"Think of tonight as Daddy's Sheva Brachot dinner." I tapped the brake pedal as we approached the next street corner, where the synagogue would become visible. "I missed the wedding, so we'll celebrate this event my way, okay?"

Grateful for a stop sign and no traffic behind me, I waited for a response.

"Sure," Debra said. "But what are we supposed to do?"

"Accept my gift of a very special night. Go with the flow, so to speak."

"What have you done?" My wife pulled her phone from her purse. "I'm calling the caterer!"

"All I'm asking is that you enjoy the evening as it is, without passing judgment. Eat, drink, and sing along with my music."

"I love your piano playing," Debra said. "Did you write a song for us?"

"You could say that."

The car made the turn, and the front windshield filled with the glow of a thousand lights. I honked the horn and sang, "*Our finest gifts we bring, pa rum pum pum pum!*"

"Oh, my God!" Rebecca dropped her phone. "What the hell is this?"

"Welcome," I announced, "to the first-ever Christmas Nosh!"

From an objective standpoint, it was just a building dressed up with all the familiar Christmas lights, an explosion of red, green, blue, and gold. The giant tree up front looked surprisingly natural, filled with blinking stars and hundreds of trinkets. Even the real plants—the tall Saguaro cacti, lush oleanders, and red bougainvillea—were fitted with a chain link of fiber optic flames that gave the illusion of a burning bush that wasn't consumed. In the midst of this very American holiday season, when every shopping center could be seen from outer space on a clear night, no one would have paid any particular attention to what *Lights4U* had done for me here. Except that this was a synagogue, which explained why cars slowed down as they passed before it, and why Rebecca was about to turn violent.

"Calm down," I said in my most casual tone. "It's just a bunch of lights. There's no crosses or nativity scenes. It's strictly kosher fun."

"Daddy is right," Debra said from the back seat. "It's beautiful!"

She was correct, of course. It was beautiful. Better than I had imagined.

We were a few minutes early, which allowed us to park close to the entrance. I came around the car and helped Rebecca out. Between her long dress, her clenched teeth, and her vision, which was jarred by the flashing rainbows, she needed my arm to steady herself.

Debra and Mordechai joined us, and we approached the mound of snow, where a couple of neighborhood kids were sledding on plastic garbage bags.

I let go of Rebecca and put my arms on their shoulders, Debra on my right and Mordechai on my left. "When I left Pillars of Joy on Sunday night," I said, "it felt like I was leaving behind everything that was me—that I was losing the person whom I had perceived to be me until that moment, when old *Mean-Tseh-Berg* ruled that I was a gentile, a shaygetz, undeserving of a

Jew's rights and privileges, undeserving of the honor of standing with the two of you under your chuppah as your father. Do you understand?"

They nodded.

"So on the cab ride into Manhattan, the songs on the radio, the holiday decorations everywhere, the millions of happy people in that huge city, made me remember my own feelings as a boy, how I used to wait all year for Christmas to arrive." I pulled Mordechai closer. "It might be a gentile holiday, especially for you, I know, but please understand that my feelings, my longings, were stimulated by the holiday, not by faith in Jesus, in his birth and crucifixion and all that. Maybe I once did believe in him, as a kid, when I still believed in Santa Claus."

Mordechai nodded, smiling. Debra also smiled. But Rebecca didn't.

"So that's what I'm trying to do," I said, "build a bridge between my current life, you, and my childhood's happiest holiday. I'm trying to have a real Christmas, just like the ones I used to know, happy and warm, shared with the people I love. Does it make sense to you?"

Cars began to arrive, and Jose ran to direct them.

"I understand, Daddy." My daughter reached up and gave me a kiss on the cheek.

"What the heck," Mordechai said, "I'm fine with it, Dr. Dinwall."

"And I'm going to kill you," Rebecca said. "But not right now."

"Too many witnesses?" I let go of the kids and hugged Rebecca even though she tried to push me away. "Come on," I said, "humor me."

"You're asking too much!"

"Then think of all this as another one of old Rusty's jokes, will you?"

"Come on, Mom, look at this stuff." Debra gestured. "It's only decorations."

"Very festive," Mordechai said.

Rebecca glared at me, and while a group of friends was approaching us, I leaned closer and whispered in her ear, "Chill out. We can always move to New York, right?"

"After this—we'll have to move!" She slipped away from me and stepped forward. "Hello! Welcome!"

———

Part Seven
The Christmas Nosh

O Come, All Ye Faithful

The Gathering Hall was lit with old-fashioned recess fluorescent rods. A string of windows along the top of the exterior walls gave the impression that the ceiling floated without support. Normally dark at night, the windows let in the colorful glow of the Christmas lights along the roof overhang.

A sliding sectional wall separated the space from the Prayer Hall. During the high holidays it was pushed aside on tracked wheels to allow setting up rows of additional chairs. A series of Judy Levy's oversized canvas oils covered the walls with scenes of southwestern wildlife. The only human Judy allowed into the series was a feathered Native American riding a buffalo at the foothills of the Superstition Mountains. She titled it: EXTINCT TOGETHER.

Tonight, the partitioning wall was closed. The caterer had set the tables for two hundred guests. The dominant color was red, somewhere between Rebecca's dress and Debra's cap. Two tables were reserved for Father Donne and his group.

Jose had rolled the piano over from the Prayer Hall before closing up the partition, placing it near the podium. The sight of the piano jolted me with nervous excitement. My plans for tonight relied heavily on music as the primary vehicle for delivering a message that should be inoffensive yet explicit—a tough balancing act.

Following my instructions, Pinky had propped up my Christmas tree near the piano. The tree seemed small compared with its former dominance of our living room. She must have spent time grooming it, for it did not look like a tree that had been toppled over, expelled from its first home, and lain for half a day in the back seat of my Volvo under the Phoenix sun. Its broken branches had been pruned nicely, its bearded superheroes, menorahs, and Jewish stars had been repositioned in a proportional spread over the conical shape of its boughs, and the blue-and-white lights had been rearranged to appear more subtle, as if the tree itself was budding with lights. Several spotlights had been placed strategically to illuminate my tree from below, endowing it with graceful radiance near the speaker's podium and the piano.

I could not detect a shred of irritation in Rebecca, who stood at the door with me, Debra, and Mordechai to receive our guests. A few of them made bemused comments about the extravagant decorations that had welcomed them outside, but none showed anger or expressed criticism.

Judy Levy, however, was upset. "I'm the chair of the building committee," she berated me. "Why didn't you call me? I have this piece of a farm combine that I've turned into a cactus with huge, natural-color fruits that glow like Chernobyl. I've been waiting for a chance to display it!"

"Next year," I said and moved away just as Rebecca tried to elbow me.

And Aaron, as soon as he entered, pointed at me and crooned, "*We wish you a Merry Christmas, we wish you a Merry Christmas, we wish you a Merry Christmaaaaaaaaaaaaas...and a Happy New Year!*"

"Brutsky!" His wife hit him with her purse. "Shush!"

He hugged me. "You're a maniac," he said, "but I love you anyway."

"Same here."

His expression changed as he looked up at me. "You don't look well. What's wrong?"

"Playing doctor again?" I nudged him. "Go. Go. You're holding up the line."

He tried to say something, but Miriam pulled him away.

Many guests congratulated me on winning Jonathan Warnick's donation. Larry Emanuel hugged me and declared,

"Finally, you won't hit me for donations anymore! I can start saving for retirement!"

When the stream of guests dwindled down to the last few, the four of us went to our table up front. Two chairs were waiting for Rabbi Rachel and Cantor Bentov. I had not mentioned to anyone what had happened to the rabbi. Under the circumstances, it would be better if she didn't make it tonight. But where was the cantor?

We honored Mordechai with the recital of the blessing on the bread, which he did in a clear and sonorous voice.

Aaron followed him with a toast. "Little Debra," he said, "is a married woman. The world has gone crazy!"

Everyone clapped.

"I'm supposed to tell a funny story," he continued, turning to Debra, "that puts you in a ridiculous light."

"It's a toast," I said, "not a roast."

"Don't worry," Aaron said, "because unlike her father, Debra has never done anything dumb for me to recall here. You were the cutest baby, with red cheeks and chubby *pulkehs*. You then became a perfect little girl, polite and curious, and, might I add, viciously smart. And as a teenager, you gave your parents a balanced mix of exciting rebelliousness with excellent report cards. And now?" He uttered an exaggerated sigh. "You make us all so proud! Our very own representative to Columbia University in New York!"

More clapping.

I smiled at Miriam. Their two children were attending Arizona State University, which had disappointed Aaron. But rather than show jealousy, he had been bragging about Debra's achievements as if she were his own daughter.

"All I can say is," he concluded, lifting his glass, "Uncle Aaron is looking forward to many years of pleasure from you and Mordechai. So, to the new Mrs. Levinson, Mazal Tov!"

The buffet meal was served on counters that lined both side walls. According to Rebecca's specifications, there were twelve different salads, six types of hot sides, three choices each of fish and chicken, and a beef brisket that attracted the longest queue. An open bar served cold drinks and wine, but no heavy alcohol, which usually had few takers anyhow.

Roaming the hall, I shook hands and patted shoulders like a politician after a surprise win. People had a lot of questions about the Warnick donation, which I couldn't answer with much detail. No one asked about the rabbi. Perhaps they assumed she wasn't here due to embarrassment over the e-mail mishap. For me, her absence was a relief, but the cantor's no-show was a problem. I knew Debra was looking forward to his rendition of the seven blessings. It occurred to me that the cantor might have called me on my dead Blackberry, leaving a message I couldn't retrieve.

Stopping at Aaron's table, I asked him discreetly if he knew where Cantor Bentov was.

"He sent me a text message," Aaron said, "that Rabbi Rachel needed his help at the hospital. I think she does grief counseling once a week, but why would she need him there?"

Before I could enlighten Aaron, Mat Warnick saved me, bringing over his mother-in-law to shake my hand. Meanwhile I saw the servers clear up the buffet and begin to bring out desserts. The vacant tables were still awaiting Father Donne and his group. Had he decided not to join my attempt at interfaith bridge-building?

Rebecca beckoned me from the front. It was time for my speech.

Approaching the podium, my mind was racing. The evening had gone peacefully so far. The Christmas decorations made for a thunderous statement, an assertion of my right to have it my way. Wasn't it enough? Should I leave it at that, limit my comments to a few benign sentences, and invite seven friends to recite the blessings? The night would come to an amiable conclusion, and we would go home to help Debra and Mordechai pack for their morning flight back to New York. It was a tempting prospect, but when I reached the podium and turned to face the hall, Jose walked in with Father Donne, his black gown buttoned tightly at his neck, and ten or so parishioners following behind.

Jose led the group to the reserved tables. He gestured at the dessert trays along the wall.

I waved at Father Donne from the podium, and he nodded. With the microphone clipped to my shirt, and all those faces watching me in silence, I cleared my throat. "Welcome, everyone," I said, "to our special event, which doubles as a Sheva Brachot dinner for Debra and Mordechai, and a Christmas Nosh for our larger community."

A tide of murmurs swept the hall.

"I want to extend a special welcome to Father Donne and those who came with him. And to paraphrase a famous Christmas song," I cleared my throat and sang, "*Although it's been said many times, many ways—but not in a synagogue—Merry Christmas to you!*"

In the total silence of the hall, Father Donne responded, "The same to you."

"Thank you." I took a deep breath, calming myself. "You might guess why I chose this line. Anyone?"

No one had an answer.

"Did I quote it because it has become the most popular of all Christmas carols? Or because the line was so fitting for this occasion?" Turning to Debra and Mordechai, I said, "Yes on both counts, but the third reason is that 'Chestnuts Roasting on an Open Fire' was written by Mel Tormé and Bob Wells, whose real names were Melvin Torma and Robert Levinson, and whose respective parents were kosher Jews."

I waited for the various expressions of surprise to quiet down.

"And now, let me say something that might shock you. As few of you know, Debra's wedding wasn't an altogether happy occasion for me. Rather, it was one of the most devastating experiences of my life."

This statement incited wild chattering as everyone turned to ask their neighbors if they knew what I was talking about.

"Let me explain," I said, tapping on the mike to silence them. "Our daughter made a stunning bride, the magnificent wedding hall and abundant kosher gourmet were as breathtaking as the underlying costs, and the affair started beautifully. But when the officiating rabbi discovered my first name and learned of my non-Orthodox conversion, he banished me from the chuppah, from the ceremony, and from speaking with the bride—my own daughter."

Many in the hall uttered a loud "No!" Some of the women pulled out handkerchiefs. Rebecca stood, came over to my side, and held my arm.

I leaned forward on the podium, struggling to maintain my composure. At his table, Father Donne was speaking to his parishioners, his forefinger raised in emphasis.

When the hall quieted down, I continued. "What happened in New York broke my heart. It did. But it didn't shake my resolve to continue to be a good Jew."

Everyone clapped, which surprised me. What did they expect?

"It also made me realize that becoming a Jew shouldn't require a total rejection of who I used to be, of what I cherished before my conversion, or of the world around us, which is predominantly Christian. And so, here we are."

I stepped over to the piano while Rebecca returned to her seat.

"Why music?" I tapped a few keys. "Because it connects us, especially at Christmas time, when most of the popular songs were written and composed by Jews. I'm thinking of 'Silver Bells,' for example."

I played the beginning notes and sang, "*City sidewalks, busy sidewalks, dressed in holiday style, in the air there's a feeling of Christmas.* Do you know who wrote it?"

No one volunteered.

"Jay Livingston and Ray Evans, Jewish kids from Pittsburg and Buffalo who started a band at the University of Pennsylvania and wrote hits together, including 'Silver Bells.' And how about this one?"

I played while singing, "*…he sings a love song, as we go along, walking in the…*"

"'Winter Wonderland!'" someone yelled.

"Good guess," I chuckled. "The composer was Felix Bernard, born in Brooklyn as Felix Bernhardt to Russian-German Jewish immigrants."

They clapped.

My fingers tapped the notes on the piano, and I sang, "*Let it Snow, let it snow, let it snow.* This one we owe to Sammy Cahn-Cohen and Jule Styne, who also wrote 'The Christmas Waltz.'"

I played the rest of the song, letting a few brave voices sing the lyrics.

"And how about this one: *I'll be Home for Christmas...*" The slower, almost melancholy tune filled the hall, and I saw Aaron pantomiming the use of a microphone as he sang to Miriam, "*You can count on me...*" She rolled her eyes, laughing.

"The promise to be home for Christmas, which millions of listeners have identified with, was created by Walter Kent, born to a Yiddish-speaking Kauffman family in New York. Kent wrote with Samuel Buck Ram, a Jewish partnership that gave us other great songs, including one that's perfect for a marriage celebration." My fingers ran on the keys, I looked at Rebecca, and sang, "*Only you...can make this world...seem right...*"

She smiled. I winked, and she winked back.

"And now, the ultimate 'Sleigh Ride.'" I played the familiar tune. "*Giddy up, giddy up, giddy up, let's go, let's look at the snow...*"

They clapped with the rhythm, and I kept playing to the end of the song.

"That's by Mitchell Parrish, a good Christian name if there ever was one, only that he was born Michael Hyman Pashelinsky in Lithuania and ended up also writing lyrics for the all-American Jazz immortal 'Stardust' with Hoagy Carmichael."

Spontaneous applause came up from my audience, and I breathed in relief. They were not bored with my pitch!

"Now, I know that everyone would agree with these words." I played the first line and sang: "*There's no place like home for the holidays...*"

Many voices kept singing in the crowd while I played the rest of the song.

"That was Al Stillman," I said, "another Jewish lyricist, just like Joan Ellen Javits, who co-wrote 'Santa Baby.'"

Someone said out loud, "Really?"

"Yes," I said. "Really. But the longest list of hits came from the man who wrote everyone's all time Christmas favorites." I played rapidly each first line as I named the songs:

"*Rudolph the red-nosed reindeer…*"
"*I heard the bells on Christmas Day…*"
"*Rockin' around the Christmas tree…*"
"*A holly jolly Christmas…*"
"*Run, Rudolph, run…*"
More clapping.

"All five songs were written by the same Jewish virtuoso, Johnny Marks, who also served America in the Second World War, earning the Bronze Star!"

This time I joined the applause myself.

"But no one," I continued, "not a single composer did for American songwriting and for Christmas as much as the Jewish man who gave us 'God Bless America' as well as 'I've Got My Love to Keep Me Warm…'" The piano keys danced under my fingers with each line. "The same song writer who wrote the perennial, pulling at the heartstrings, *I'm dreaming of a white Christmas…*" I stopped playing and declared, "The great Irving Berlin!"

The clapping was deafening, many standing up to honor that most prolific composer of the twentieth century.

"And I wonder about this genius, this tireless fountain of immortal songs, this Irving Berlin who was born as Israel Baline to a destitute immigrant cantor from Belarus, I wonder, what did he know about Christmas? What gave him the inspiration to write: *I'm dreaming of a white Christmas, just like the ones I used to know…*"

I let the last piano note echo through the hall.

"How did Irving Berlin, who grew up as a poor Yid on the lower east side of New York City, know to describe so aptly the longing that every gentile feels for a white Christmas? How did he know the aching homesickness that was felt by every GI, every prairie farmer's son, and small-town boy from Middle America when Christmas came and they were stuck in the balmy trenches of the South Pacific, the swampy rivers of Vietnam, or the scorching sand dunes of the Arabian Gulf? How did Irving Berlin know how they felt?"

There was complete silence, their faces looking at me expectantly.

"Because we all experience Christmas," I said, "all of us, no matter what our faith or what language our parents spoke, we all experience Christmas. And we do it through music, because music is the common language that we share, Jews and Christians alike."

The first notes of "O Come all Ye Faithful" generated humming around the hall. It was a very old Church hymn, but its fame had grown after Pavarotti sang it, his rendition now replayed by every radio station multiple times during the holiday season.

"We're all faithful," I said, "Jews and Christians, praying to the same God on this birthday of a Jew named Joshua, or Jesus, who was a righteous man—whoever fathered him. So let us all join in a song for God. You know the tune, but the lyrics I wrote especially for tonight. You'll find a folded piece of paper under your plates."

My fingers repeated the first notes while the noise of unfolding papers told me they were complying. I hit the keys hard and started singing:

> "*O come, all ye faithful,*
> *Joined in love and kindness,*
> *O come ye, O come ye to brotherhood,*
> *Come and behold God, who made us in His image;*
> *O come, let us be brothers,*
> *O come, let us be brothers,*
> *O come, let us be brothers,*
> *Christians and Jews.*"

To my great relief, many in the audience joined me, at first hesitantly, but in growing numbers. I made the transition on the piano, running up and down the scale of notes, and continued with the next verse:

> "*O come, friends and neighbors,*
> *Sing in gracious chorus,*
> *Sing all that heard in heaven, God is Shalom,*
> *Give up thy fury, grace is all the mightiest;*
> *O come, let us be brothers,*

O come, let us be brothers,
O come, let us be brothers,
Christians and Jews."

Singing left me out of breath, so I played the tune from the beginning while the majority of the guests sang with full voices from the lyrics I had prepared for them. I shivered, my eyes on my fingers, tapping the keys, afraid to look up and break the magic that only music could create.

But eventually the song came to its natural end, and I joined everyone for the last words of my lyrics, "*O come, let us be brothers… Christians and Jews!*"

The hall erupted with cheers. They kept it up, and eventually I had no choice but to stand and bow. "Thank you," I said, "thank you so much!"

As the applause gradually quieted down, singing could be heard. It was Father Donne and his parishioners, who resumed the same tune, but sang the common lyrics, a literal translation of the original Latin words of '*Adeste Fideles.*'

"*O come, all you faithful,*
Joyful and triumphant,
O come ye, O come ye to Bethlehem.
Come and behold Him, born the King of Angels,
O come, let us adore Him,
O come, let us adore Him,
O come, let us adore Him…"

Here, Father Donne and his parishioners paused, looked around at the stunned hall full of Jews, and at the top of their voices, chorused the last line:

"*Christ the Lord!*"

A collective groan came from the guests, amplified through the loudspeakers with my own sigh. So much for my hoped-for interfaith camaraderie.

I stood, intending to calm the gathering storm.

Before I could speak, Father Donne raised his hand. "We would have liked to heed your call for brotherhood," he declared. "We would have liked to make the effort for peace. But not on this most sacred day of the year. Because Christ is the Lord! And today He was born to Mary and the Holy Father!"

"Please, Father Donne." I took a few steps forward. "Why can't we concentrate on what's common to all of us, the faith in one God?"

"Because this is a Christian holy day!" His voice was rising, his thin face tight with righteous indignation. "For too long we have watched cheap commercialism and gaudy ornaments dilute the spirit of a true Christmas!" He pointed toward the exit door. "Right outside this Jewish temple you've constructed a glaring example of the abomination that's been visited upon our most sacred day with growing frequency and aggression! Flickering lights, hewn trees, caricatured saints, and imported snow!"

Only now it occurred to me that his own church bore no decorations whatsoever. The man was a prude, and I had invited him to a dance. "I'm sorry, Father, that you feel that way, but—"

"What would you feel," he interrupted me, "if we invited you to a pig roast on Rosh Hashanah? Or decorated our church with a thousand glowing crosses on Yom Kippur?"

"It's not the same," I said meekly.

"Isn't it? Why? Is your Jewish star less sectarian than our cross? Is your Rosh Hashanah holier than our Christmas? Don't you know that tonight we celebrate the birth of our Lord Jesus Christ?"

"Yes, but why—"

"Tonight we celebrate the beginning of His mission on earth, His coming, which you rejected!" With his arm stretched, his finger pointing, he turned slowly, covering the whole room. "You rejected the true Messiah! You caused His suffering! You turned your backs on Him and have continued to defy Him for two thousand years! And now you dare to be squatters in His domain? To usurp His day of Christmas?"

"We do not!" Rabbi Rachel entered the Gathering Hall in a wheelchair, pushed by Cantor Bentov. Her left leg was in a cast. She pointed at me. "This man does not represent the King Solomon Synagogue!"

Her entrance shocked everyone, especially me.

"Dr. Dinwall had no right to besmirch our sanctuary with pagan symbols and insult you in the process!" The rabbi swiveled her chair to face the priest. "Please accept our apology."

Father Donne responded with a cryptic, one-shoulder shrug.

"It is true," she continued, "that we do not share your faith and therefore have no right to partake in your Christmas. We'll turn off all the Christmas lights immediately and have the place cleaned up by tomorrow morning."

"So be it." Father Donne beckoned his companions, and they headed to the door. But before exiting, he stopped and turned to us. "Do you think I've gotten so upset because of a foolish party in this little…*shtetl?*" He uttered the last word in derision, clearly aware of American Jews' pride in their professional and financial achievements barely a generation or two removed from that pitiful Eastern European Jewish existence, so aptly depicted in *Fiddler on the Roof.* "Do you think I would bother to come here because of one man's futile attempt to alleviate his guilt for betraying his Savior?"

"I resent that statement!" My voice was louder than I intended, the mike still attached to my shirt. "That was uncalled for!"

He looked at me, shaking his head. "I came here to give you a message on behalf of all good Christians: We're sick of Jews composing stupid songs that cheapen our holiest of days! We're tired of Jews fluffing up their department stores to lure the faithful away from God's true worship or dressing up fat men in red coats and cotton beards to seduce our children with toys they don't need! I came here to tell you that we're tired of Jews concocting devious ways to carve off pounds of flesh from our Holy Christmas!"

His words affected me like a punch to the chest, delivered while I was expecting an embrace. I wanted to yell at Father Donne that the only flesh I carved was that of my patients, most of them good Christians whom I brought back from the dead. I wanted to tell him how wrong he was, but I couldn't speak, all my energy and willpower directed to fight off a sudden tide of nausea while thinking furiously: *A chair! I need a chair!*

I started toward my seat and would have collapsed halfway there, but Mordechai must have noticed the look on my face and rushed forward to help me. Debra held up a glass of water for me, and I gulped it down.

The hall was dead silent. Everyone was looking at me.

"I'm fine." My voice sounded odd even to me. "Really, I'm fine."

"But I'm not fine!" Rabbi Rachel shifted in the wheelchair. "I must say, Father Donne, that your words are very painful. How can you blame the Jewish people for commercializing Christmas? Are we the inventors of free markets?"

"Yes, you are," he said with a passing grin, "the instigators of commercialism and capitalism, as well as communism, socialism, liberalism, globalism—"

"And monotheism," I said.

"Yes," Father Donne conceded, "our faith is the divine evolution of yours. Which is why I would not have come here tonight to protest your greed alone."

"There's more?"

"The ultimate insult is that, while you profit from twisting the true spirit of our Christmas by converting the faithful into obsessive consumers, you simultaneously work to destroy the very holiday that enriches you."

"That's a blood libel," Rabbi Rachel said. "What facts do you have to support such a vile accusation?"

"Facts are hard to come by when an evil deed is accomplished so insidiously." He paused, looking around with a knowing expression. "You chip away at the Christian character of this great country until little is left. You, a tiny heretical minority in this United States of America—*One Nation Under God!*—have been manipulating the Congress and the courts to cleanse Christianity from our soil."

"With all due respect!" Larry Emanuel stood up, his deep voice full of the authority that had helped him rise to top management. "The legal concept of separation of Church and

State comes from the Constitution. You can't blame us for it! There wasn't a single Jew among the founding fathers!"

"I have read the Constitution." The priest pulled a little booklet from his pocket and waved it. "It doesn't say anything about erasing the Ten Commandments from our public institutions! About forbidding prayer to His grace in our public schools! About scrubbing off any mention of His name from our public life!" Father Donne was yelling now, his voice growing hoarse. "This was a Christian country until our courts succumbed to evil *misinterpretations* of the Constitution, cooked up by clever Jewish lawyers!"

"That's complete nonsense!" Larry yelled. "You're twisting history for the sake of bigotry!"

"And even now," Father Donne continued, "our own elected officials fearfully send out cards that say: *Happy Holidays!* What holiday is it, whose name may not be mentioned? What holiday is it, that its very mention would be offensive? What holiday is it, that a coalition of enemies have concerted an attack on its very spirit?"

His rhetorical questions earned no response from the stunned hall.

Supporting myself on Mordechai's arm, I rose to my feet. "Your accusations, Father, are yet another sad example in a long Christian tradition of blaming the Jews for every plague, natural disaster, and economic crisis. Just like the Romans did to a Jew named Joshua, you crucify us again and again for crimes we didn't commit."

He waved his hand in dismissal and exited through the double doors ahead of his parishioners. But a moment later, while everyone was still hushed, the priest poked his head back in and yelled, "*Merry Christmas!*"

God Rest You Merry Gentlemen

"See what you've done?" Rabbi Rachel glared at me while Cantor Bentov wheeled her all the way to the podium and turned her to face the hall. "I'm not angry at Father Donne," she continued. "He has the right to feel resentful over this. How in the world could anyone expect this to end well?"

The "anyone" in her question was me, so I answered. "Why shouldn't we expect our Christian neighbors to join us in prayer? Don't we believe in the same God?"

"You want them to join us after you insulted them?"

"I did not!"

"Christmas Nosh?" The rabbi sneered. "Do you realize how demeaning it sounds to a devout Christian to be invited to a tongue-in-cheek *Nosh* only hours before their solemn Midnight Mass?"

"It wasn't meant as mockery."

"Then as what? A poke in the eye?"

"An opportunity to bring us together, Jews and Christians."

"Dr. Christian Dinwall, what's gotten into you? *Satan?*"

Rebecca tensed up, and I thought she would lash out at the rabbi, but she didn't.

"You're playing Scrooge without even knowing it!" Rabbi Rachel shook her head in dismay. "Let me illuminate it for you: How would you feel if they invited us to celebrate Debra's wedding with a cozy Swingers Night?"

A few people chuckled, but most only sat in silent discomfort. They were members of the synagogue who respected the rabbi as spiritual leader and me as lay leader. The two of us doing battle in front of them was inappropriate, I knew, and no one would have the guts to take sides.

Except maybe Aaron Brutsky, who stood up and said, "First of all, Rabbi, we're sorry to see that you've been injured. On behalf of the congregation, we wish you a quick and full recovery."

She reclined her head. "Thank you, Aaron."

"In the meantime," he continued, "we should return to the main purpose of this evening, which is to celebrate Debra's marriage and take joy and comfort in God's blessings."

Cantor Bentov looked at her. "May I?"

"Of course," Rabbi Rachel said. "Go ahead, gentlemen."

"Hold on," I said, "about our Christian guests."

Rebecca hissed, "Rusty!"

"I want to remind you of the Prophet Isaiah," I continued, "who quoted God: '*My house shall be a prayer house for all the gentiles.*' God wants us to invite non-Jews to pray with us, because His house, this synagogue, is for people of all nations and faiths. We shouldn't give up on Shalom."

"You're taking the quote out of context," the rabbi said. "The paragraph, at Isaiah fifty-six, verses six to eight, starts by referring to those gentiles who have joined Judaism to serve God, observe His laws, and be bound by His covenant. Only they are invited to pray at our temple. You're taking undue liberties!"

Her animosity was shocking, as if our long friendship had been shattered by an offense she could not forgive. Was she still upset over the Warnick vote at Judy's house? Did she really believe the congregation was better off living hand-to-mouth in a contiguous state of pleading for small donations and overdue membership fees?

"It's pathetic," the rabbi continued, "trying to bridge over two thousand years of hate with an invitation for a kosher dessert."

"And how else," I asked, "could we end the hate, if not by reaching out to them? Isn't it better to get together and break bread than to break bones?"

"Clever wordplay won't change deep-rooted reality. Didn't you hear what Father Donne said? Any day but Christmas!"

"Why?"

"Because their infant lord was born on this day! Their *faith* was born—"

"We can share their celebration without sharing their faith."

"You want us to celebrate this terrible day in a synagogue? Have you forgotten the terror which Christmas Day has brought on Jews in the past two millennia? The wholesale expulsions of Jews from their homes, the Inquisition cellars, the burnings at the stake? Have you forgotten the pogroms that priests instigated every Christmas, sending mobs to kill Jews nonstop until the New Year? Have you forgotten the Christmas revelers who screamed *Jesus killers!* as they barred the doors on whole congregations and burnt down the synagogues over their heads?" Rabbi Rachel pointed in the general direction of Father Donne's church and cried, "Their Christmas is our Memorial Day!"

With her last words hanging in the air, she turned her wheelchair and rolled to the side door, which led to the foyer and the synagogue offices.

Rabbi Rachel's exit left a deep silence. Had she departed for the evening or was she coming back? I wasn't sure, but it didn't matter. In my heart, I knew she was wrong. History didn't have to control the future of Jewish-Christian relationships. What had happened in the past, painful as it had been, must not be allowed to perpetuate hate. And wasn't my life, like many other successful interfaith marriages, the best proof that the acrimonious past could be set aside?

But it was unfair for me to put all our guests through any more of this. I turned to Debra and Mordechai, who seemed paralyzed with discomfort. "I'm sorry," I said quietly, "it was supposed to be a special night. I screwed up."

"Yes, you did," Rebecca said.

But Debra smiled, leaned over, and kissed my cheek. "It's okay, Daddy. Good intentions count more than anything else, remember?"

"It's pretty weird," Mordechai said, "but this night will make a great story back in Brooklyn." He grinned and pressed my hand, and I felt optimistic for the first time since Father Donne had finished singing "O Come, All Ye Faithful" with the punch line "*Christ the Lord!*" My efforts had not been in vain.

Aaron came over and took the microphone. "Let us fill our wine glasses and begin with the first blessing."

Everyone was a bit dazed, but the clinking of bottles on glasses indicated that they were going along with Aaron's invitation. He beckoned Cantor Bentov, who came over to our table, filled a glass and cleared his throat while waiting for silence. Our eyes met, and the cantor stepped closer and whispered in my ear, "I tried to convince her to go home from the hospital. They gave her a lot of pain medications, but she insisted on coming here."

"Is it the Warnick donation?"

He hesitated.

"Why is she so angry? It can't be the name change."

The cantor started to move away from me, but changed his mind and put his lips back near my ear. "She thinks you'll fire her. And me also."

In the midst of all the chatting around us, I thought I didn't hear him well. "What?"

"She's afraid you'll hire a better clergy team." He gestured at himself. "We're not exactly multi-million-dollar material, right?"

Now that I had heard clearly what he said, I couldn't believe it. "Where's this nonsense coming from?"

"It makes sense," Cantor Bentov said. "The rabbi is convinced people already blame her for the synagogue's decline, so when all this money comes in, what's the next logical step? She's desperate."

"But even if someone pushed for that, your contracts run for another two years. You're safe!"

He nodded, but I could tell he wasn't convinced, that he genuinely believed that Rabbi Rachel was right, that once the King Solomon Synagogue became the very wealthy Golda and Leo Warnick Synagogue, we would get rid of the rabbi and the cantor in order to hire a more glitzy duo.

"I'm deeply hurt," I said, "that you think it's something I would do. But I understand the concern, and it's your livelihood. We'll discuss it after the Sheva Brachot, okay?"

"Of course." Cantor Bentov returned to the podium and waited.

The guests were busy chatting, probably about the dramatic argument that had taken place before them. I sat with my family and we had a few minutes of peace. Rebecca brought me a plate of food, and I nibbled, feeling deflated. The whole evening had taken a wrong turn, gone in a direction I hadn't expected and didn't like. I was ready for it to be over.

Aaron again stood and asked for silence. Cantor Bentov filled his lungs, and bellowed, "*Blessed be He, Master of the Universe, creator of the fruit of the vine.*"

Everyone chanted, "Amen."

He turned to Debra and Mordechai and continued, "*May God rejoice this beloved pair as He once rejoiced the first couple who lived in Eden; blessed be He, Hashem, who rejoices bride and groom.*"

Again everyone responded, "Amen."

Cantor Bentov opened his mouth to begin the third blessing, but a loud pop sounded, a window high near the ceiling exploded, and a white object flew across the hall, hit our table, and bounced into Debra's chest. She flipped backward with her chair, falling to the floor, and we all screamed.

———

Run, Rudolph, Run!

Hell could sometimes appear in an instant, a concentrated dose of fierce torture, achieved not by immersion in boiling tar, but by the sight of a terrible accident involving the person you love most. My hellish moment lasted for eternity, between watching the object fly like an evil shooting star across the hall, the unreal splash of the impact, and the unknown extent of her injury. When Debra fell backward, out of my sight, and the Gathering Hall filled with the deafening noise that terrified people make, all my wishes and desires in this world instantly narrowed down to a single, all-consuming plea: *Let her live!*

I tried to look over Rebecca's shoulder, but Debra's chair had fallen on its side, hiding her from me. Dropping out of my seat to the floor, I reached and grabbed the fallen chair, and there she was, my daughter, lying on her back, her eyes closed. The red cap had come off, and dark hair spread around her white face.

Bending over Debra, I checked the small of her neck for a pulse, praying for that fluttering sensation at the tips of my fingers.

It was there.

Aaron was next to me. He didn't hesitate. With both hands he clasped the dress under her chin and pulled in opposite directions, tearing the cloth downward almost to her navel. Just above her bra, on the right side, a bruise was forming, about the size of a fist.

I murmured my habitual prayer instinctively, "*Blessed be Adonai, Master of the Universe, healer of the sick and infirm,*" and put my ear to her chest, but the noise in the hall was too great. "Can't hear a thing!"

Cupping his mouth between his hands, Aaron yelled, "Quiet! Quiet! Quiet!"

Many others began shushing, and soon the hall approached a nervous silence.

My stethoscope was in the car, but there was no time. I pressed my ear to her chest and held my breath.

The heartbeat was normal, a healthy beat that I rarely had a chance to hear in a patient's chest. I moved to the side, then the other side, searching for the telltale crackling of a collapsed lung, but her breathing was slow and clear.

"Nothing," I reported to Aaron. "All normal." With open hands I felt around the bruise, pressing lightly on the skin, searching for broken bones or irregular tissue formation. Again I said, "All normal."

Only now I noticed that Rebecca was kneeling next to me, her clenched hands pressed to her chest as she rocked back and forth, murmuring the same few words as a mantra, "Please, God! Please, God! Please, God!"

"She's okay," I said, just as Debra's head moved from side to side, her eyelids trembling.

"Debra?" Aaron shook her shoulder. "Can you hear me?"

She opened her eyes and slowly looked around, searching. Her gaze met mine and continued to Rebecca and beyond, until it stopped, and her lips curled in a faint smile. "Mordechai," she said and reached for him.

Rebecca cried in my arms while I fought off tears, both for Debra's survival and for her seeking Mordechai for the comfort she had used to seek from us. But that was the way of the world, and we watched him help Debra up from the floor, wrap her in his suit jacket, and hold her as they sat down at the table, her head on his shoulder.

One of the servers brought a bag of ice. Rebecca packed a few cubes in a cloth napkin, and Debra pressed it to the bruise.

I caressed her head, and she looked up, making a brave attempt at smiling to reassure me that she really was fine.

Mordechai said something to her. She nodded, and they began praying together. I could not hear the whispered words they were reciting, but I could read my daughter's expression, her complete and utter devoutness, her sincere conviction that the words of the prayer were true, and her wholesome faith that God was listening to her and would extend His grace to her and to Mordechai. I saw in my daughter's face the truth that I had tried to deny since the moment I had seen Mordechai's black yarmulke on Skype on the eve of Rosh Hashanah. I had been wrong all along. Debra wasn't playing Orthodox because she was in love with Mordechai. Rather, she chose him because she had become Orthodox and wanted to share her life with a *ba'al* who belonged in that tradition, a husband who shared her faith in the God of strict Halacha, the God of Brooklyn and Rabbi Mintzberg and Rabbi Doctor Yosef Schlumacher, the God of Sabbath observance and kosher food, the God of Orthodox conversions as the only path for a shaygetz like me to become a real Jew.

Pulling myself up from the dark hole of sadness and resignation, I looked around at my guests, who stood in clusters, conversing quietly. The last thing I wanted to do was to take charge, but I had no choice. As the leader of the congregation and the host of this virtuous event, which had turned ugly, people expected me to act. Should I ignore what had just happened and continue with the seven blessings? Our synagogue had suffered infrequent hostilities in the past, an occasional anti-Semitic graffiti or minor vandalism, but always during the night, when the place was empty. This was the first attack aimed not only at the building, but also at us, the Jews who worshipped the God of Israel. It was my responsibility to calm everyone down and communicate with the police, which must have received a dozen calls already from guests, several of whom were speaking urgently on their phones.

Rebecca gripped my arm and pulled me down so she could speak directly into my ear. "Fix what you broke!"

"It's only a window." My attempted humor earned eye rolling. I scanned the hall for Cantor Bentov, intending to ask him to pick up where we had stopped, but I was too late.

God have mercy on us!" Rabbi Rachel held up the flying object, which turned out to be a rock wrapped in paper. She tore off the sheet and showed it to us.

A swastika!

A woman behind me uttered a frightened yelp.

The rabbi turned the paper over. On the back, a message was scrawled crudely:

THE JEWS ARE STEALING CHRISTMAS!

"That's what you get," Rabbi Rachel announced, "when you cross civilized boundaries, when you insult other people's faith, and when you violate their sacred traditions!"

What could I say? She was right. The evidence was irrefutable—the paper in her hand, the rock, the broken glass. Whoever threw it at the window had also exposed me for what I really was: A fool.

"Señor Doctor!" Jose pushed his way through to me. "Me sorry!"

"Don't worry." I patted his shoulder. "Everything is okay."

"No. No okay." He pointed at Debra. "Your girl hurt! Me no—"

"What are you doing here?" Rabbi Rachel rolled over on her wheelchair. "Don't you have work to do? Go! Out! Do your job!"

Jose stepped back, his hip hitting a table.

The rabbi kept rolling the wheelchair at Jose and uttered a quick sentence in Spanish.

He ran off.

With the mike near my lips, I announced, "Please be seated. There's no reason for alarm. Let's continue with the blessings for Debra and Mordechai."

People stopped talking, but they didn't sit down, only looked at me in indecision.

"We have gathered here to honor them," I said, "and to ask God to bestow upon them the seven blessings for a happy and fruitful life together. Let us complete the remaining five blessings and prove that hate never wins."

With slowness that told of mixed feelings, our guests returned to their seats. I saw Aaron speak into his phone, his hand covering his mouth. The rabbi was talking with Judy Levy and Cantor Bentov, their heads close together. They stopped abruptly when I approached.

"Thank you." The cantor accepted the microphone from me.

When everyone was seated, he held up the glass of wine and recited the next blessing. And the next, and the one after that, making a commendable effort to sing the traditional tune with adequate celebratory spirit. As he finished the last words of the sixth blessing, "... *rejoice the groom and bride*," we heard a pop, and another window exploded—at the far corner, all the way in the rear where no one was sitting.

The hall filled with shouts of panic. Guests dropped to the floor and crawled under the tables. And then, finally, we heard police sirens approaching.

I began to circle the tables and help people up. Keeping my voice even and free of anxiety, I asked again and again, "Is anyone hurt?" Aaron was doing the same down the opposite side of the hall. Soon everyone was accounted for, and not a single injury.

A group gathered around Judy Levy, who was examining one of her paintings. I went over. She traced a long line with her finger, where the rock had given Extinct Together a glancing blow, ripping the canvas and separating the Native American warrior from the buffalo he was riding. Suddenly the whole painting fell off the wall, causing the group to scatter out of the way. The fall broke the wooden frame, and the painting crumpled in a heap. Judy tried to hold it up, but the wood sections had splintered in the fall, and the dry oil paint cracked along the creases. Judy let it go. I recalled her telling me once that her art pieces were as dear to her as her children. The devastation on her face confirmed it.

A group of officers in blue trotted into the Gathering Hall. I walked over, introduced myself, and asked, "Did you arrest them?"

"Must have been some kids," one of the officers said. "There's no one outside. Area is secure."

"We'll be done in a few minutes." I said. "We still have one more blessing to complete."

"God has punished us!" The rabbi had gotten hold of the microphone and was yelling into it. "As the leader of this congregation, I plead with the Almighty: Forgive us, Adonai, for the sin of arrogance!"

Groaning, I headed in her direction.

"The police," she yelled, "are here to escort you out!"

"Rabbi Rachel," I protested, "what are you doing?"

"Leave before the next attack! In the name of God, run out to your cars immediately! Run! Run!"

"Stop it!" My voice was lost in the noise as people ran for the doors. I tried to stop them. "Please! Don't leave yet!"

It was no use. The bottleneck at the doors slowed them down only briefly, and within moments the Gathering Hall was almost empty.

I looked around in disbelief. It was over, and we hadn't finished the seven blessings. Would God still bestow a happy and fruitful life upon my daughter and her husband? They had remained seated with Rebecca, all three looking dazed. I assumed that the God I believed in didn't count blessings the way some humans counted pennies. But still, it was a bad omen, which I knew would fester in me forever. Debra deserved all seven blessings, even if her father had screwed up so royally. Could we still do it?

Other than Rabbi Rachel and Cantor Bentov, only Aaron, Judy, and Mat stayed behind. I gestured at the empty hall. "At least my board of trustees didn't run away. Except for Larry. Where is he?"

No one responded.

"Maybe he'll call in," Aaron said.

Outside, car engines revved and tires screeched as the guests sped away.

The hall began to spin like a merry-go-round, the air too thick to breathe even as I tried to expand my lungs, to force it in. I grasped the side of the podium, shut my eyes, and forced my mind to focus on inhaling.

"What's wrong?" It was Rebecca, her arm around me, guiding me into a chair. "Are you feeling sick?"

I took shallow, slow, methodical breaths. "It'll pass…in a moment."

She wiped my moist forehead with a napkin.

Gradually the awful feeling passed. I straightened up carefully, flexing my aching shoulders and arms.

Bringing a glass of ice water to my lips, Rebecca helped me take a few sips. "Are you in pain? Tell me what's wrong!"

"It's nothing." I drank a little more. "Didn't sleep…last night. Probably a bit dehydrated also."

"Let's go home," she said, helping me stand up.

"Not yet." I was lightheaded, my knees were weak and my balance tenuous, but this wasn't the time to give up. I knew what I had to do. Rather than asking Cantor Bentov, I went back to the podium. With the full glass of wine in one hand and the open prayer book in the other, I recited the seventh blessing, which I especially liked because it concluded with a reference to "…*boys celebrating with their music.*"

"Amen," Aaron declared, and the others mumbled after him, "Amen."

Mordechai helped Debra up, and they headed for the door. I put my arm around Rebecca's shoulder and leaned close to her ear. "I have to stay here and deal with this catastrophe."

She looked at me, clearly preferring that I went home with them.

"It's my responsibility." I dropped my car keys into her hand and gestured at Debra. "Watch her closely. If she exhibits dizziness or shortness of breath, take her to the ER right away and call me."

Rebecca nodded and hugged me, not in a perfunctory way, but tightly, with her ear pressed to my chest and her arms locked around me, saying without words that she still loved me and was determined to do what it took for us to climb together out of the emotional and social hole we had found ourselves in and find a way to save our relationship with Debra and Mordechai. I kissed her forehead.

As they reached the door, Jose appeared with a broom and a plastic trash can. He bowed politely and stepped aside to let them pass. His respectfulness was so exaggerated that it seemed to proximate fear.

When my family was gone, Jose hurried to the corner, where the floor was covered with broken glass.

"Go back out," the rabbi told him, "and turn off those damn Christmas lights!" She was still using the mike, and her voice echoed from the walls. "Shut them down, every last one of them!"

"No," I said. "Leave the lights on."

"Turn them off!" The loudspeakers amplified her angry tone. "Now!"

Jose started for the door.

"We shouldn't give in to violence." I walked over and plucked the mike from her hand. "And stop yelling. This is still a house of worship."

She glared up at me, then turned the wheelchair toward Jose. "I told you—"

"He works for me tonight!" I pointed at the glass shards. "Please clean it up before someone gets hurt."

"I am asking you for the last time," Rabbi Rachel said, "to turn those lights off. This situation has already caused injury and damage. Isn't it enough already?"

"As president of the synagogue," I said, "it's my decision whether to turn lights on or off, because I'm the one who has to beg people for money to pay the electrical bills. And your salary!"

"This is too painful." The rabbi's shoulders slumped. "I've tried my best to serve God in this community for two and a half decades. I've been through all your happy and sad days, doing my best to give comfort and share the gift of Torah to each and every member of this congregation. After all these years, do I really deserve this treatment?"

"Nice show," I said.

"A show?" She pressed a fist to her chest. "All the years I've given to this congregation were a show? All my work, a show? All the holidays, the sermons, the funerals and celebrations, a show? This is my synagogue! This is my life! I have nothing else but this!"

Shaking my head, I said, "You should be on Broadway."

"Rusty, please!" Aaron took my arm. "Let me take you home. It's not worth it."

"It's not?"

He shook his head.

"Then what would be worth it?" I turned to the rabbi. "Your behavior has been unacceptable tonight. An embarrassment to the God you're supposed to serve. I expect you to apologize to the congregation again, as you've already had to do today over that vicious e-mail. Otherwise the board of trustees will have to place you under probation."

"Actually," the rabbi said, "I would like to call an emergency board meeting right now to discuss the president's behavior, especially his turning this synagogue into a Christmas parody, insulting our neighbors, and causing a violent attack on the congregation."

"You need two members to call a special meeting," I said.

"I join the call," Cantor Bentov said. "We should sit and talk about all the issues."

This was unexpected. It had been my initiative to invite both of them into the board as equal trustees after I had read an article a couple of years ago about improving synergy between the clergy staff and the lay leadership. And this was my reward!

"You can meet," I said, "and talk all you want. But I will not attend."

"So be it." The rabbi signaled the cantor to wheel her to the meeting room. Judy and Mat followed, but Aaron hesitated.

"Go," I said. "You can speak for me in there."

"Then come in and speak for yourself. They might push for your resignation."

"A favor, if there ever was one."

"Then resign now," he said. "Go home and patch things up with Rebecca."

"And cause the synagogue to lose ten million dollars?" I dropped into a chair by a table with half-eaten desserts. "I've had enough arguing for one day. You know what has to be done."

Their meeting dragged on, as did my physical discomfort. Everything hurt, my body protesting the abuse I had put it through. I got up and paced up and down the Gathering Hall, rotating my left arm, trying to relieve the pain. Had I torn a ligament? It could be a real problem. There was a long list of patients waiting for surgeries after the New Year.

I noticed the rock that had hit Debra. It rested on a table next to the note with the Swastika. I turned over the paper and looked at the words: THE JEWS ARE STEALING CHRISTMAS!

The police officer had dismissed the incident as the handiwork of kids. But the writing was too orderly, the cursive letters too mature, and the grammar too accurate to be the scribble of a hostile kid. It was even a bit...familiar.

I walked over to the foyer. The rabbi's office was down the hallway. The door wasn't locked, and the lights were on. I searched the pile of papers on her desk, finding a condolence card she had written but hadn't yet mailed. Placing the paper from the rock next to the card, I groaned. There was no mistake. The same hand had written both!

Refusing to believe my eyes, I rummaged through her papers, finding a half-written letter. Again, the writing was identical to the sheet in my shaking hand. THE JEWS ARE STEALING CHRISTMAS!

With the three pieces of writing in my clenched fist, I left the rabbi's office.

Jose was dragging the trash bin across the foyer. I held up the creased paper, the Swastika facing him. He recognized it, stepped back, and started to shake his head in denial of the accusation I was yet to utter.

I stepped forward, took the broom from him, and held it next to the paper. "Do you know," I said, pronouncing each word with care, "what are finger prints?"

He glanced over his shoulder at the glass doors of the synagogue, which let in the rolling lights of a police car that had remained to guard us. His reaction was as good as an explicit confession.

"Did she make you do it?" I controlled my voice for fear that he would bolt. "Did the rabbi threaten you?"

He nodded, and in his moist brown eyes was all the sorrow of Arizona's Latino laborers, making hourly pay, feeding large families, living in fear of Sheriff Arpaio's raids and his parched tent cities. Jose didn't need to explain why he had taken the rock from Rabbi Rachel, why he had agreed to throw it at the window, or why he had thrown a second one, albeit more carefully, after she sent him back outside, yelling, *"Don't you have work to do? Go! Out! Do your job!"* And he didn't need to explain to me why he was now trembling uncontrollably.

"Don't do it again." I handed him the broom and went back to the Gathering Hall, my legs heavy as logs, my mind fogged up from an overload of conflicting emotions.

———

I'm Dreaming of a White Christmas

Raised voices came through the door. Their meeting should end soon, and the outcome would not be a happy one for Rabbi Rachel. Should I have realized the depth of her fears about her job? How could I, when it had seemed impossible to feel anything but excitement at the huge donation and relief at solving the synagogue's chronic deficit?

I had to admit that the rabbi's fears were not completely irrational, but her behavior was selfish and damaging to the congregation. She should have understood this and expressed her personal concerns openly to the board, perhaps even ask us for a written commitment to keep her as our rabbi even after the money came in. But now it was too late. Her actions today could not be justified even by the deepest desperation. She had sabotaged her standing in the congregation, possibly also her ability to ever serve as a rabbi anywhere else. Even under the influence of powerful painkillers, the dread of losing her job could not justify sending Jose to throw rocks at the synagogue!

And what about Cantor Bentov? Had he been present when she had told Jose to do it? Hard to believe. The cantor would not go along with such an extreme action, which I would not believe about the rabbi either, if not for the irrefutable evidence. But when had she found a moment to write the note and instruct Jose? I recalled that she had left the hall at one point, before my discussion with the cantor and the recital of the first two blessings. Surely she hadn't intended for anyone to get hurt, only to discredit me by demonstrating how my Christmas Nosh was achieving the opposite result, rather than the peace and brotherhood I had so naively hoped for. But her deed had crossed the line from legitimate to criminal.

I was determined to protect Jose, whom she had coerced into it, but I had to share the information with the other trustees. Considering her long and loyal service, we should offer Rabbi Rachel psychological counseling and the opportunity to resume her career somewhere else, assuming she expressed regret and demonstrated a full recovery. With the Warnick donation coming in, we had too much work ahead and no time to waste on bickering.

I looked around the Gathering Hall. Even this formerly grand room was showing the poor state of our congregation. The walls had not been painted in years, the crooked ceiling tiles were discolored, and the bulky loudspeakers were outdated, having gone up in the corners during an era when music had been played on cassette tapes. The tip of my shoe dug into the fraying carpet. Properly refurbished, we could rent out the Gathering Hall for substantial fees, turning it into a profit center for the synagogue. Same with the Sunday school facilities, which needed modern teaching aids, audio and video equipment, and competent administrators and teachers. And the building's appearance, from its dated exterior to the dark foyer and the outmoded Prayer Hall, could use a facelift. A facility that projected modernity and sophistication would attract new members and higher dues. And, come to think about it, a new rabbi would be the best draw for young families as well as those who had left the congregation in the past few years. It would be a fresh start! There was so much we could do once the money arrived!

But not tonight. I should call a taxi and go home. My hand patted my hip in search of my Blackberry, and I remembered what had happened to it. Aaron would give me a ride.

Sitting at the piano, I let my fingers find their own way on the keys, hitting random notes, until they picked up "White Christmas." I went along with it, and soon my lips started moving with a quiet humming and words emerged, almost by themselves. *"...where the treetops glisten and children listen..."*

The white streets of Tarrytown came to my mind.

"I'm dreaming of a white Christmas..."

I kept playing, but only with my right hand. The left arm was hurting too much, and I let it dangle by my side. My orthopedic knowledge was rudimentary, having had no involvement with the field since medical school, but my mind still tried to diagnose the condition. Had I pinched a nerve? Compressed the cartilage? Or was it my shoulder, perhaps a rotator cuff?

Playing with one hand, I whispered, *"May your days be merry and bright..."*

The door opened and Aaron emerged, followed by Judy Levy, Mat Warnick, and Cantor Bentov pushing Rabbi Rachel's wheelchair, who handed me a piece of paper. I read it.

BY A SPECIAL MEETING OF THE BOARD OF TRUSTEES OF THE KING SOLOMON SYNAGOGUE, IT IS RESOLVED THAT DR. CHRISTIAN DINWALL IS HEREBY REMOVED FROM THE POSITION OF PRESIDENT. THE BOARD THANKS THE OUTGOING PRESIDENT FOR HIS LONG AND DEVOTED SERVICE. JUDY LEVY SHALL SERVE AS INTERIM PRESIDENT UNTIL THE NEXT ANNUAL MEETING. SO VOTED UNANIMOUSLY.

I stood, leaning on the table for support. "Unanimously?"

"Yes," Rabbi Rachel said. "Unanimously!"

My gaze went to Cantor Bentov, who looked away. Judy's eyes locked with mine, pained but not ashamed, and then she glanced at the crumpled canvas of EXTINCT TOGETHER. Mat continued to the exit, keeping his back to me, and I realized he was more resentful of Jonathan's financial swagger than I had suspected. His vote had not been against me or for the rabbi, but in defiance of his nouveau riche brother.

That left Aaron.

I faced him and asked, *"Et tu,* Brutsky?"

"It's better," he said very quietly, like someone offering condolences to the bereaved. "Better for everyone, especially for you and Rebecca."

"Shouldn't that be my decision?"

He lowered his eyes. "We had no choice. She's the rabbi."

"And what am I? Chopped liver?"

Aaron smiled sadly. "You are who you are, which is why you can never *really* understand."

"Understand what?"

"This." He gestured at my Christmas tree. "Only a born Jew, the son and grandson and great-grandson of Jews, could understand why this is so terribly wrong."

I turned away from him, the searing pain making me grimace.

On the table before me were the three pieces of Rabbi Rachel's writing. On top was the note: THE JEWS ARE STEALING CHRISTMAS! I wanted to reach out and pick up the papers, but my hand didn't move. She deserved to be unmasked, but did Jose deserve jail and deportation, being torn away from his wife and kids? The board's decision was a clear message to me. DR. CHRISTIAN DINWALL IS HEREBY REMOVED FROM THE POSITION OF PRESIDENT. What would I gain from destroying her? Did I even want to recover the position of president? What for? These people were not the friends I had believed them to be, and this building had just ceased to be my place of worship. I was a stranger amongst them.

The sound of commotion made me turn. Jose came in with a wheelbarrow. The cantor went over and helped him load up my Christmas tree. They pushed it out the door while a few of my decorations fell to the floor.

I followed them.

They dumped my tree at the curb near the pile of snow.

I came closer.

In the glowing Christmas lights from the synagogue, I noticed a man and a woman standing on the sidewalk, a young couple, both of them tall and trim, she in a short dress, he in uniform. Even from a distance I could see the cross hanging from her neck. She pointed at me and said something to the man, and he waved. I held up my hand in a hesitant greeting, took another step, and another. I ignored Jose and the cantor, who passed by me with the empty wheelbarrow on their way back inside. Now the couple's faces emerged more clearly, and I heard my own voice, full of wonder. "Mom? Is that you?"

She nodded.

The man beside her waved again, and I recognized him from the photo at her bedside.

He was my father.

Joachim Dinwall.

"Dad!" A great swell of joy broke over me. I leaped forward, my arms open to take them both into an embrace, into a family hug, into a realization of an old dream—the dream I had shared with every other fatherless child, the dream I had summoned often to comfort a terrible longing, the dream I had used during childhood to suspend disbelief in the adults' insistence that my father was gone and was never coming back. It was an old dream, one that I had seldom visited in recent years, but it came back roaring, as real and tangible as the ground under my feet. *My father was back!*

I ran toward them, breathless with happiness, but the pain in my left arm suddenly spiked into my chest in a sharp, stabbing jolt. My legs folded under me, and my view twisted sideways as I fell onto the side of my face, then rolled onto my back.

In detached observation, like a physician reaching an unexpected yet logical diagnosis, I observed that the aches I had experienced on and off over the past few weeks had not been the benign manifestations of stress, lack of sleep, muscle cramps, or an orthopedic injury, but the warning signs of very real and deadly heart disease. Just like my mother, I was physically active and not overweight, and yet my genetic disposition and overwrought, dutiful way of life had brought me down to an end very similar to hers—and at about the same age.

The sky above me was dark. Aaron's face appeared, his forehead creased. He was probably feeling my wrist for a pulse, but I could not feel his fingers, nor could he feel any pulse. I wanted to see my parents again and tried to look for them, but whiteness descended around me, resembling a thick, glowing fog that materialized in the dead of night, blocking off all sounds, bringing peace.

His mouth opened, his lips moved, but I could not hear Aaron's voice.

He grabbed my arms and dragged me over to the pile of snow. Judy and Cantor Bentov appeared. He spoke to them, and they began to dig up snow and cover me. I understood. I would have done the same—lower the stricken patient's body temperature to minimize the damage to the heart until CPR could bring back a steady beat, followed by surgical intervention. But did I want to stick around for that, or would I rather join my parents?

I wasn't sure.

Aaron placed his hands on my chest and pressed down rhythmically. He paused and leaned over to give me mouth-to-mouth, and our eyes met.

His face contorted in anguish, his eyes wide behind his glasses, filled not only with horror and disbelief, but also with terrible guilt.

With the last bit of air in my lungs I managed to say, "I... forgive...you."

Part Eight
One year later – Christmas Day

Noel, Noel, Born is the King of Israel

At 2:18 a.m. on Christmas morning, at the maternity ward at Mount Sinai Hospital in New York City, Debra gave birth to a baby boy. He had wisps of his mother's dark hair and a wide mouth with pink gums that seemed ready to accommodate his father's healthy teeth.

Bundled up in a white-and-blue blanket, the baby suckled fervently on his mother's breast.

Mordechai sat on the side of the bed, and they watched the creased face of their newborn son, marveling at his natural instinct, a miracle that enabled him to feed without prior experience or a printed manual.

Soon the baby was full.

Mordechai draped his shoulder with a towel and burped the baby gently.

Standing by the window with his newborn son, the dimly lit room behind him, Mordechai could see a section of the dark sky between the tall buildings of Manhattan. It was the first clear night after almost a week of rain and snow, and the stars burned brightly.

A nurse came in with a writing pad. "Sorry to bother you with this, but we have to fill out an application for a birth certificate as soon as possible after the delivery."

"Sure." Debora beckoned her to a chair by the bedside. "Go ahead."

"Mother's name?"

"Debra Dinwall-Levinson."

"Father's name?"

"Mordechai Dinwall-Levinson."

The nurse looked at Debra and asked, "How did you manage to make him agree to that?"

"Actually, it was my idea," he said.

"It's true," Debra said. "We're equal partners. Neither of us wanted to give up our own last name, but we wanted to share the same one. So we combined the two."

"We put Dinwall first," he explained while placing the baby back in her arms, "because alphabetically it comes first."

"I should have kept my last name," the nurse said. "Would have made the divorce a lot less irritating." She filled in the address of their studio apartment on the upper west side and asked if they had decided on the baby's name.

"We have," Mordechai said, "but we're not supposed to reveal it until the circumcision ceremony in eight days."

"You're safe with me." The nurse made like she was locking her lips.

"Joachim," Debra said. "Joachim Dinwall-Levinson."

As if responding to his name, the baby opened his gummy mouth and whimpered, his tiny hands moving up and down while his mother rocked him gently.

"After his great-grandfather," Mordechai added. "He was a Marine in Vietnam."

"A beautiful name," the nurse said. "It sounds…biblical."

"That's correct. Joachim was one of the greatest kings of Israel."

"And he's born on Christmas!" She touched baby Joachim's cheek with a light finger and began to sing softly:

"The first Noel, the angels say,
To Bethlehem's shepherds as they lay,
At midnight's watch, when keeping sheep,
The winter wild, the light snow deep,

Noel, Noel, Noel, Noel,
Born is the King of Israel…"

Little Joachim's eyes were closed when the nurse's voice faded away.

"Thank you," Debra said. "It makes me think of the birthday parties we'll have for him every year, on Christmas. Too bad we can't sing this one. It's so pretty. *Born is the King of Israel…*"

"We could," Mordechai said, "with different lyrics."

"A Jewish theme?"

"Yeah! Maybe…praise for the biblical King Joachim. Should I ask your dad?"

"You won't have to ask him twice."

The nurse paused at the door. "Is he a song writer?"

"A physician…but he's very creative."

"What's his specialty?"

Debra looked at Mordechai, who answered for her. "My father-in-law is a heart surgeon, but now he does everything. He's with Doctors Without Borders. In Vietnam."

"My mom is teaching English there." Debra sighed. "It's so far."

"Don't worry, sweetheart." The nurse pointed at the baby. "That's a grandma magnet. She'll be back in no time."

When the nurse left, they sat quietly, watching Joachim's face under the knitted cap, listening to the subtle purr of his breathing. After a while, when they were certain that he was sound asleep, Mordechai picked him up carefully, held him for Debra to kiss each tiny cheek, and placed him in the bassinet.

Then, for the first time, Mordechai recited the traditional Jewish father's blessing over his child: "*May God bless you and guard you; May God shine His face upon you and judge you kindly; May God watch over you and keep you in peace.*"

"Amen," Debra said.

"It's time to share the good news." He took out his iPad and tapped on the Skype icon. "Who should I call first? Your parents or mine?"

"Try Rabbi Mintzberg," she said, and they laughed.

THE END

Acknowledgements

I am grateful to all the composers and lyricists of Christmas songs, who inspired me to write this novel, and to my friends, both Jews and Christians, who shared with me their thoughts and feelings about Christmas. Their input lent this story its richness and humanity.

As with my previous novels, editor Renee Johnson and the helpful staff at CreateSpace made the book a great deal better. And to my friends and family members who read the manuscript in its various iterations and provided insightful comments, thank you!

Lastly, this novel owes its spirit to all 'mixed' couples, whose bond is a bridge suspended over deep gullies of faiths, ethnicities, and cultures. Their love is tested more often than the rest of us by the blasting winds of society's prejudices and bigotry, yet they serve as a fountainhead of tolerance, openness, and human progress.

The songs and lyrics mentioned or quoted in the novel are acknowledged with a deep sense of gratitude and respect, including:

"Adon Olam" by Solomon Ibn Gavirol (1021-1058);

"All I Want for Christmas Is You" by Mariah Carey and Walter Afanasieff (1994);

"The Christmas Blues" by Sammy Cahn and David Jack Holt (1946);

"The Christmas Song," commonly subtitled "Chestnuts Roasting on an Open Fire" or "Merry Christmas to You" by Mel Tormé and Bob Wells (1944)

"The Christmas Waltz" by Sammy Cahn and Jule Styne (1945);

"Deck the Halls" by unknown lyricists, first composition by John Parry Ddall (c. 1710–1782)

"Do You Hear What I Hear?" by Noel Regney and Gloria Shayne (1962);

"The First Nowell" ("The First Noël"), published by William B. Sandys in *Carols Ancient and Modern* (1823) and *Gilbert and Sandys Carols* (1833), later arrangement by John Stainer in *Carols, New and Old* (1871) and *The New English Hymnal* (1986);

"Frosty the Snowman" by Walter "Jack" Rollins and Steve Nelson (1950)

"Go Tell It on the Mountain" by African-American spiritualists, later compiled by John Wesley Work, Jr. (1865), later adapted by Peter Yarrow, Noel "Paul" Stookey, Mary Travers and Milt Okun as "Tell It on the Mountain" (1963);

"God Bless America" by Irving Berlin (1918);

"God Rest You Merry, Gentlemen" ("God Rest Ye Merry, Gentlemen"), published by William B. Sandys (1833) (authorship unknown);

"Hark! The Herald Angels Sing" by Charles Wesley, altered by George Whitefield (1739);

"Have Yourself a Merry Little Christmas" by Hugh Martin (with Ralph Blane) (1944);

"Hine (or Hinay) Ma Tov" (Jewish hymn based on Book of Psalms, verse 133) by King David.

"A Holly Jolly Christmas" by Johnny Marks (1965);

"(There's No Place Like) Home for the Holidays" Al Stillman and Robert Allen (1954);

"I Heard the Bells on Christmas Day" by Henry Wadsworth Longfellow (1864), adapted by Johnny Marks (1950);

"I'll Be Home for Christmas" by Kim Gannon, Walter Kent and Buck Ram (1943);

"I've Got My Love to Keep Me Warm" by Irving Berlin (1937);

"It's the Most Wonderful Time of the Year" by Eddie Pola and George Wyle (1963)

"Jingle Bells" by James Lord Pierpont (1822–1893);

"Let It Snow! Let It Snow! Let It Snow!" by Sammy Cahn and Jule Styne (1945);

"The Little Drummer Boy," (based on Czech carol "Carol of the Drum,") by Katherine K. Davis (1941);

"The Lumberjack Song" by Terry Jones, Michael Palin, and Fred Tomlinson (1969);

"O Come All Ye Faithful" ("Adeste Fideles"), John Francis Wade (1751) (original authorship unknown and disputed, possibly 13th century by John of Reading);

"Only You" by Buck Ram (1955);

"Put One Foot In Front Of The Other" by Jules Bass and Maury Laws (1969);

"Rockin' Around the Christmas Tree" by Johnny Marks (1958);

"Rudolph the Red-nosed Reindeer" by Johnny Marks (1948);

"Run, Rudolph, Run" ("Run, Run, Rudolph") by Johnny Marks and Marvin Brodie (1958);

"Santa Claus is Coming to Town" by John Frederick Coots and Haven Gillespie (1934);

"Sheva Berachot" ("Seven Blessings"), unknown attribution, appears in the Talmud, tractate of Ketubot, pages 7b-8a (c. 500 C.E.);

"Silent Night" (German: "Stille Nacht, heilige Nacht"), Father Joseph Mohr, English translation by John Freeman Young (1959);

"Silver Bells" by Jay Livingston and Ray Evans (1950);

"Sleigh Ride" by Mitchell Parish and Leroy Anderson (1950);

"We Wish You a Merry Christmas" (Sixteenth-century English carol);

"White Christmas" by Irving Berlin (1940);

"Winter Wonderland" by Felix Bernard and Richard B. Smith (1934);

Also by Avraham Azrieli

Fiction:

The Masada Complex – A Novel

The Jerusalem Inception – A Novel

The Jerusalem Assassin – A Novel

Non-Fiction:

Your Lawyer on a Short Leash

One Step Ahead – A Mother of Seven Escaping Hitler

Author's website:

www.AzrieliBooks.com